# SCORPION BAY

## *A Novel*

## *Pat Steele*

# CONTENTS

# PREFACE

I was married with children at a young age, my 1st child was born when I was 21 and my wife was 19.

We pursued the American dream by accumulating valuable resources. I was working 6 days a week as a roofing contractor and after hours building and remodeling houses with my wife.

By the time our youngest child was 21 we were ready for a re-evaluation of our priorities. One of my clients, a General Contractor, offered a house sitting opportunity in Mainland Mexico. My wife and I are avid surfers and the Mexican house was an isolated location with great surfing.

We rented our house, put our jobs on hold and waved good-bye to our shocked adult children.

The area we lived in had no T.V., radio or phone reception. The only contact with the U.S. was a fax machine in a village 45 minutes away. Once we decompressed, our lives became extremely simple. Eat, surf, sleep and explore. After a couple of months of exploring, we had seen everything interesting in the vicinity.

With an enormous amount of free time for the 1st time in my life, I started writing. Creative writing had been my only successful endeavor in school. After 6 months of pecking away, I had a rough draft.

After I got back to the States, I showed my book to my friend Tom. He inspired me to clean up the grammar and pursue publishing.

My wife and I have returned to the American dream of over work and no free time. Aloha.

# CHAPTER 1
# THE PURSUIT OF HAPPINESS

I don't trust being happy. Every time I get a whiff of happiness, it is crushed out of me like a car tire running over an aluminum can. In fact, I think happy people are either naive, sheltered, or imbeciles. Maybe it's because I was raised by a single alcoholic parent that has me so cynical. Quite frankly, he was capable of ruining any happy event. There was the time he passed out right before my birthday party when I was nine years old. I had to meet my friends and their parents at the door to tell them the party was canceled. One time he tripped on the stairs and took out the Christmas tree and smashed half the presents.

Sometimes he would show up at parent teacher meetings or some other event smelling of booze. I would see the looks they would give each other behind his back. I heard a psychologist say "a parent passing out in front of a child is equivalent to a soldier seeing a comrade die." If that's the case, my sister and I have seen whole battalions massacred.

We tucked him into bed every night, instead of vice versa. Sometimes, we just threw a blanket over him. Don't get me wrong. He wasn't violent, instead he would get mushy. He would want to hug and kiss you with his vodka and cigarette breath.

Occasionally I would wish he was violent, so I could hate him. He never mistreated us; we always had food, clothing, and adequate shelter. Granted he had an excuse, he missed our mother. Now that I'm an adult, I think that's a cop out. Get over it. Life's not fair. You can't live in the past. Of course those are my mottos, not his. He's stuck. So I refuse to use him as an excuse. I will succeed. What I didn't know was I was about to have the happiest day of my life.

I'm a supervisor for a crew of framing carpenters. Framers build the skeleton of the building out of lumber. Like most construction jobs it's mostly physical labor, technique and some brain work. The money's good and it keeps me in shape.

On this particular day Jackie and I were hanging 2" x 12" fascia two stories off the ground. To hang fascia you have to stand on rafter tails which are 1.5" wide, bend over past your feet and nail it into the rafters. The 2 x 12s are 16 feet long and when wet, are very heavy. You are dependent on your partner not to make a mistake; otherwise, you'll be hurtling through space and have a guaranteed ride to the hospital, at the very least.

I looked down at Jackie. This guy had a pierced nose, ear and tongue and more tattoos than a drunken sailor, but I knew he wouldn't screw things up. It's funny. Although I wouldn't trust him five minutes alone with my sister, I would trust him with my life.

Just as I got my miter cut into place, I heard Jackie drive his nail home. He was a good carpenter; in fact, my whole crew was made up of good carpenters. They were also psychopaths, dopers, sexists, racists and God knows what else. I made it a point to make it none of my business. Show up on time without a hangover, do your work without whining, don't ask to borrow money or tools, and I couldn't care less what you did after work.

As Jackie and I were nailing the fascia, Jose, the job gofer, yelled up to me, "Will! Mr. Joseph wants to see you in his trailer."

I yelled back, "What for?"

Jackie started throwing nails at Jose, who deftly dodged the nails without making eye contact.

"Will! Mr. Joseph wants to see you in his trailer," Jose repeated, then turned and ran as a nail whizzed by his ear.

I stared at Jackie. "Why do you have to be such a dick?"

Jackie stared back. "You mean to Jose?"

I didn't answer.

"Will, don't you see they're taking our jobs? Pretty soon we won't have work, you know what they did to the dry-wallers."

"Jackie, I told you I didn't want to hear that crap. I want you to put in some fire block while I talk to Mr. Joseph."

Nailing in fire block was usually reserved for apprentice carpenters, so Jackie knew he was being punished. To his credit, he took it without complaining. I had told every one of my crew, "No racism, politics, or religious bullshit on the job. If you want to hate, do it on your own time. Work is hard enough."

I threw my nail bags in the back of my truck, put on a clean T-shirt and ran my fingers through my hair. I kept my hair short because that made the suits, the money people, feel more comfortable. It's not like Mr. Joseph was like a real suit. He was in fact one of the best builders in San Diego and a straight shooter who knew every facet of building from digging the foundations to installing the roofing. His father had come from Canada with the clothes on his back and nothing else and within ten years had his own business. Mr. Joseph took over where his dad left off.

America is the most democratic country in the world because we're capitalist. Green, black, brown, stupid, fat, ugly; if you've got money, people respect you. All you have to do to succeed is make your boss money. Period. Bosses will put up with practically anything as long as you bring in the dough and Mr. Joseph loved me because my jobs came in on time and under budget.

Mr. J. was sitting at his desk inside his custom job trailer with a cigar in his mouth, I had never seen him smoke a cigar, but he always had a chewed up butt in his mouth. It was odd for him to be here because this was Wednesday and he usually checked on this job on Fridays. It was also unusual that he asked for me; he usually talked to the job superintendent, some kiss ass named Steve Lloyd.

"Have a seat, Red." He called me Red even though my hair was mostly brown. "It's Will, sir."

"How do you like your job, Red?"

Not knowing where we were going with this, I became evasive. "It's okay."

"How much do you make a year, Red?"

"$50,000," I said, adding about $10,000.00. I was starting to pay real close attention.

"How would you like to make $60,000.00?" He studied my face.

"What do I have to do, Mr. Joseph?" He stood up and walked to the window. "I want you to take Steve's job."

Mr. Joseph reminded me of my first boxing coach, not a lot of people skills, but his word was his bond.

"What happened to Steve?" I asked the back of his head. He turned and looked at me. Let's just say we came to a crossroads and he chose a different road.

The real reason was Steve was skimming off the sub contractors. He would let his pet contractors know what to bid and maximize their profits, at a percentage of course. I was glad the weasel got caught. I hate thieves. "Make it $70,000 and a new pickup."

Mr. J countered with $65,000 and no pickup. He said he'd pay for gas and service on mine.

I held out my hand. Deal."

He firmly shook my hand. "Deal."

" I need one last thing," I said. " I need the rest of the day off. I want to propose to my girl. Until now, I really didn't think I had enough money."

For the first time, Mr. Joseph smiled. He knew married employees were more reliable.

"By all means. Congratulations."

I was floating as I headed for the door. "Callahan!"

I turned and looked at Mr. Joseph.

"Don't mess with me."

I smiled. "That's not my style, sir."

I picked up some flowers and Danielle's favorite champagne. I personally don't drink. After watching my father stumble through life, I have no desire. Danni is the first girl that Mr. Happy and I have agreed on. Mr. Happy is my penis. He got that name because he is naive, sheltered, and an imbecile. When I was younger Mr. Happy talked me into a whole bunch of stupid escapades. His little head is filled with three things: boobs, butt, and bush. I'm able to ignore him most of the time now, but he loves Danni. Just thinking about her causes him to wake up.

Today is Danni's day off. She works part time and goes to school full time. So, today, I'm going to surprise her and propose. Then she can play with Mr. Happy the rest of the day. Tonight we can go pick out a ring. It's possible she's still sleeping, so I quietly tip toe across the living room. Halfway to the bedroom, I hear her moan sexually. Damn! She must have heard my truck pull up. I moan back; she moans even louder. I can't help laughing to myself. She's got such a great sense of humor.

I froze in the door to the bedroom. She is having intercourse.

Specifically, she is sitting on some stranger and moaning that special moan that is my moan. I dropped the champagne and the top snapped off with a big pop. Champagne sprayed across the room. Danni let out a startled yelp and jumped off her lover.

I've seen enough and go back to the living room. I sat down numbly. I can hear Danni starting to cry and some low mumblings coming from the guy.

I am in such shock that my bowels are calling to me just like before a big bout in the Golden Gloves boxing tournaments. After ten minutes, he comes out of the bedroom half dressed, stands before me, and with an apologetic look says, "Sorry man."

I look up at him, "Sorry man ain't gonna' make it. You think you're gonna' come into my house, screw my woman in my bed and walk out the door with 'Sorry man?' To get through that door, you gotta' go through me, man!"

"Listen. I'm sorry. I don't want any trouble."

"Listen, asshole! You've got trouble!"

I got out of the chair and started to bounce on the balls of my feet, just like I would before the first round of a boxing match.

"Who are you calling asshole, asshole?" He was getting pissed.

I took off my shirt. I didn't want him to be able to grab it. He looked at me with a very impatient look.

"I have to warn you. I'm a black belt in Tae Kwon

Do." I responded with "I'm a red belt in DO RE MI."

Sometimes I say the stupidest things. For the first time, I really looked at this guy. He had at least 20 pounds on me. He had martial arts skills.

Damn! Why couldn't she have boned some wimp? That would be the topper, he screws my girl then kicks my ass.

I forced myself to focus. Fighting is not all about strength, it's about speed. If I was quicker, I had a chance. My problem is I hadn't boxed in three years. We started out slow, a few jabs from me, a few kicks and jabs from him. Not only was he stronger, he was quicker. I was screwed. I had one last hope. If I could pick up a tendency, I could set a trap. The bad part of this strategy meant I was going to take a beating.

He pounded on me hard. I know he broke my ribs on my left side because I had broken them once before. I think he also tore some ligaments in my knee with one of his kicks, which were viscious. I had a cut on my eyebrow that was blinding my right eye. I was mostly defense trying to read his patterns. I had gotten in some good licks on his abdomen. I could see the welts.

Truthfully, I was just about ready to throw in the towel, when I saw him push back with his front foot putting all of his weight on his back foot. Finally my chance had come. He was going for a head kick. I decoyed him and left him an opening. At the last moment, I ducked it. I threw a hard jab into his thigh, which was still extended. This spun him into an open position. I threw a hard right into his throat.

By the look on his face, I could tell he was reeling. I always was a strong finisher. I gave him a hard shot under the rib cage. This brought his head down. I took my time and nailed an uppercut right on his nose, which crunched when it broke. He was out cold on his feet and fell in what seemed like slow motion. Just before his head hit the carpet, his temple caught the corner of the coffee table. There was a loud crack. His head lay at a 90-degree angle. There is no way anyone could have their head going sideways like that and still be alive.

Just to make sure he was dead, I kicked him hard in the balls. He didn't flinch, so I did it again. To this day, I'm concerned about my behavior. I had just killed a man, then I kicked him in the balls. Granted, he had just screwed my girl and beat the tar out of me. Maybe one kick woulda' been okay, but the second kick that concerns me. That was downright sick.

I remembered now why I had quit boxing. It hurts. After the adrenaline wears off, the pain sets in. This guy had done some real damage. Every breath I took sent a sharp stab into my rib cage. I was limping badly on my left leg. I probably needed stitches on my eyebrow. I knew how to tape it to stop the bleeding.

I didn't want Danni to see that I had killed him. I needed to talk to her before she got hysterical. I dragged him into the guest room. Besides his head rolling back and forth, he didn't even look hurt. I could hear Danni's snorting from the hall. When she really cried hard her nose stopped up and she had trouble breathing. She ends up snorting and sobbing. She had her head on her forearms and she was sitting up against the wall. I stood in front of her.

She slowly looked up at me with swollen red eyes, if she was acting it was pretty good. I mouthed the word "why." She choked on the words, "Because I love you so much, William."

"Let me get this straight. You love me so much, you have an affair?" I was so tired that I could barely get angry. It felt like my life force had drained out of me.

"William, I have never loved anybody like I love you. It scares me. The other day when we got in that argument, I realized how much I need you. You don't seem to care as much as me. I needed to do something to make me feel some distance. Can you please try and understand? I love you more than anything. I'm sorry if I hurt you."

"Did you know why I was here early, Danni? I came here to propose."

She dropped her head on to her arms again and she started sobbing, "No. no. no. no."

I went into the bathroom and cleaned up my eyebrow. Right where the eyebrow is, the skull stops and the eye socket begins. This ridge is susceptible to being cut. The scar tissue that was there from previous fights tears easily. I put some super glue on both sides and taped the cut shut. I learned that trick from one of my trainers. Half the time it works great.

When I went back in the bedroom, Danni was standing up. She was still naked. Damn, she had a great body. Beautiful round breasts, olive skin contrasting her dark hair and blue eyes that were almost green. She was still crying. She flopped on to the bed. Mr. Happy wanted to talk to me, but I ignored him.

"Can you forgive me, Will?" she asked without looking at me.

"Baby, I don't know. I just don't know. I'm so tired. I feel completely exhausted."

"Will, lie with me please, I feel so bad. Please just hold me."

I looked at her. She had crawled under the sheet. "I'll lie down, but I need to sleep. I feel like I'm going to pass out."

My head was spinning. I lay down on the bed. I could feel Danni taking off my shoes and my pants, and then I was asleep. I might have had a concussion. Sometime in the night, Mr. Happy had sex with Danielle. I'll never forgive him for that, he has no pride and it reflects on me.

The next morning I woke up to the smell of coffee, Danielle was cooking in the kitchen. It took me a few minutes to get out of bed,I was stiff and sore all over. Danielle handed me a cup coffee and kissed me on the cheek. She had her hair up the way I like it. She was cooking waffles with bacon and eggs. She was humming to the radio; I could tell she thought everything was going to be all right. Just because she had made up with Mr. Happy, didn't mean that I was over it. That was a typical Mr. Happy maneuver. Now things would be complicated.

"Danielle we need to talk."

She turned and looked over her shoulder, her spatula resting under an egg. "There's a lot about me, you don't know. I'm a loner. You're the first person I've been close to except my sister, which of course was different. I really have issues with closeness. All I ever desired as a kid was to be self- sufficient. I hated the fact that my sister and I would have to eat cereal for dinner because my old man couldn't get off his bar stool. I hated the fact our electricity got turned off because of lack of payment. He had the money, but he would lose the bill. I hated running out of gas in the car every other month. I promised myself I wouldn't depend on anybody, ever. I didn't anticipate falling in love."

"Will, listen. I was insecure, I'm sorry. It was no big deal. It was meaningless. I promise it will never ever happen again. You are the best thing that has ever happened to me." She slid the eggs next to the bacon on a plate. She grabbed some butter and salsa out

9

of the refrigerator and handed me the plate. Save some room for your waffles."

"All that moaning sounded pretty serious to me."

She frowned. "Don't be crude."

"One of the reasons I boxed was so I could defend myself, so I could take care of myself. Getting involved with you was going against my instincts, but I made myself get over it. I let down some walls. Now I'm back where I started. The walls are back in place."

The egg was undercooked. I started doing figure eights with a slimy part that had the texture of snot. Cooking was definitely not her forte.

Danielle was looking out the kitchen window. "Where are you going with this, Will?" Her voice had taken on a detached resignation.

"I'm going to go away."

The words hung in the air for a long time. She turned and looked at me. I could tell her teapot was about to whistle. "Why wouldn't you tell me you had issues? How was I supposed to know? If you had talked to me, it would never have happened. Did you ever think of that, Mr. Callahan!? I loved you so much it scared me, but you couldn't reassure me, could you, macho man? Well, you are the one responsible for this. You screwed everything up!" A thin trail of smoke came out of the waffle maker.

"Oh, I screwed things up. And what were you doing yesterday with Mr. Taekwondo? You know, Danielle, you and your father and your mother and your brother all sleep around and then blame it on some one else. Take some God Damn responsibility! It's simple. You don't have an affair, we don't have a problem. Do the math! Is it my fault you were scared, insecure, or whatever?! Bottom line, you blew it! "

I was starting to get a twitch in my eye as my blood pressure rose. Danielle pulled the plug on the waffle machine, which now had black smoke coming out of it. She opened the window, then played her ace in the hole.

When she looked at me tears were coming down her cheeks. "You're right, Will. I don't deserve you. You are the best, most honest, handsomest man I have ever met. I understand if you hate me, but I truly love you with all my heart." She put her hands over face and sunk to the floor.

Damn it. Tears always ruined me. "Danni," I said softly, "even if I wanted to stay I couldn't."

"Why Will?" she asked through sobs.

"Because he's dead."

She looked up quickly. "What did you say?"

"His head hit the table."

Danni wiped her eyes with the backs of her hands. "Where is he?"

"In the guest room."

"What are we going to do?"

Danni and I stood at the door of the guest room looking at our dead guest. He had taken on a pale hue. I pushed his foot with my toe and could feel the rigor mortis. I had mixed feelings. One side of me relished the fact that I didn't allow some guy to come in my house and lay the wood to my girl with no regard for my presence. Did that justify killing him? I would have to say "no." Or was it manslaughter? This was going to take some time to sort out. I had always pictured myself as a moral man, now I was confused. "What's his name?"

Danni squeezed my biceps and said," Mitch."

"Was he any good?"

"Dammit, Will, he's dead for God's sake!"

She squeezed my arm again. I wondered if she was feeling some primal pride in her conqueror. She couldn't stop looking at him.

"You know, what you did was despicable."

What I know about women you could put on the head of a pin and still have room left over.

"We need a sheet."

Danni handed me a sheet. I covered him and closed the door. I took Danni out to the living room and sat with her on the couch.

"This is what I need from you. Number one: do not call the cops for five hours. Number two: I am going to take half of the money in our savings account. Number three: I need to leave some tools in the garage, Okay?"

"No, it's not okay. I think you are being ridiculous. You said he hit his head on the table. Tell the police that. They'll understand. Don't run away from this Will, it will just make it worse. Please stay with me and work it out." She grabbed both my hands and looked lovingly into my eyes. "Will, I blew it, forgive me. I love you."

"Let's get something straight, I am not staying. There are some things about me you don't know. I can't stay. I also feel like I have had a lobotomy. I have no idea what my feelings are for you. Part of the intimacy was feeling exclusive. That's gone. Permanently? Who knows? I have to get grounded again. I need time to sort things out and I'm not doing it in a jail cell. Can you for once stop thinking of yourself? I came here to propose, remember?"

"Will I am so sorry. I will do what ever you want. Please just re- member I will be waiting for you and I love you with all my heart."

It took me about an hour to get my gear together. I stored the rest of my stuff in the garage rafters, loaded a few essential tools in my toolbox, put the rest in the back corner of the garage and threw a tarp over it. Danielle stood on the porch as I pulled out the driveway and gave me a sad wave goodbye. I looked at her in the rear view. Jeezus! Twenty four hours ago was the best day of my life.

My blood boiled over just thinking how screwed up my life was now. I pounded on the dashboard with my fist and yanked on the steering wheel until I was panting. Thankfully, I felt better. It takes about twenty minutes to get across town and I kept my mind totally blank. My watch said 8:30, so I had an hour and a half to kill before the bank opened.

I pulled my truck into the parking lot behind The Malarkey Bar and Grill and parked next to an old Ford Van. The Ford van is where my Dad lives, or more like sleeps. All of his waking hours are spent in the tavern; either getting a buzz, thinking about getting a buzz, coming down off a buzz, or buzzed. I rapped gently on the side of the van. I could hear him stirring inside. "Who's there? Johnny said it was alright to park here."

"Sorry, Mr. Callahan, this is officer AI Coholic. We have a warrant for unlawful trespassing and we need you to come downtown."

The van shook as he put on his pants and shoes. "With all due respect, Officer Coholic, Johnny Rumba said I could stay here and he's the owner. Well his real name isn't Rumba. Its Blane, but he had a way with the women and he knew how to rumba and Mike Kenney started calling him Johnny Rumba and it stuck."

The side panel door swung open and Thomas William Callahan jumped out.

"Anyway Officer...Will! What are you doing? You scared the hell outa' me."

He hugged me and I smelled booze, cigarettes, B.O and urine.

"What happened to your eye? Did you take a fall?"

"Yeah."

He had a two-day-old stubble that was almost all white. His red and gray hair, what was left after male pattern baldness, was pulled back into a ponytail. He looked thin except for his gut, which pushed hard against his T-shirt like a ripe melon. He patted me on the back and said, "Let's go see Johnny."

The Malarkey already had four customers. They sat silently at the bar with their drinks, money and cigarettes in front of them. There were no cars in the parking lot so they all probably had D.U.I.'s. Why they would come here to drink was a mystery to me. Nobody talked. They all stared blankly into space. They could get drunk at home for a quarter the price. Johnny Rumba was a different story, he was always upbeat. He looked like Sean Connery in his James Bond days.

"Bless me lucky stars! If it isn't William Michael Callahan!" He shouted in a perfect Irish brogue, even though there wasn't a drop of Irish blood in him.

"I'm going to go drop the kids at the pool," Tom said to me. This was Tom's way of saying he was going to the bathroom and also getting out of dealing with his tab.

Johnny Rumba had on at-shirt that said "REHAB IS FOR QUITTERS."

He shook my hand firmly and raised his eyebrows at my bandaged eye. I ignored his inquiry. "How much is Dad's bill?"

Johnny reached under the bar and pulled out his notebook. "Let's see... last month $157.00 and this month counting yesterday $84.00." I pulled out my checkbook and wrote a check for $600.00 and handed it to Johnny. "I'm going to be gone for a while. Can you watch over him, Johnny?"

Johnny folded the check and put it in his top pocket, "You can count on it, Will."

"Now, can you give me a bottle of Jack Daniels, two coffees, a pack of Marlboros and a Budweiser?"

Johnny put everything on a tray, "I'll only put a 20% mark up on the Jack Daniels."

"You're like family, Johnny Rumba."

"I know that," he mumbled as he wrote down the numbers in his notebook.

I headed to the booth in the back corner, this is where Tom liked to sit. When I put the tray down, Tom reached immediately for the cigarettes. I watched my dad's hands tremble as he lit his cigarette. Tom took a large draw off the cigarette and closed his eyes and blew the smoke out slowly. "When's the last time you brushed your teeth, dad?"

Tom opened his eyes and focused on the Budweiser. I pushed it over to him. Tom tilted his head back and let the beer pour down his throat. When he put it down, it was half gone. "Whew! That hits the spot. I must have been dehydrated."

"Alcohol causes dehydration. It doesn't cure it," I said as I opened the bottle of Jack Daniels and poured some in both coffees. "Will, I don't need two coffees."

"One's mine."

"When did you start drinking?"

"Today."

"Are you sure you want to do this?"

"Hell, yes. Look what it has done for you."

"Will, that's not like you to be mean."

"Sorry, Dad. I'm sorta' confused right now.

Tom drained his beer and lit another cigarette. I noticed that Tom's hands weren't shaking as much. "Will, I know I've talked to you about this before, but it's very important."

I thought to myself it's either about Grandpa or Mom. I guess he doesn't care what I'm confused about.

"You know, your grandfather was one in a million. He lost his father when he was 11 years old. He had three younger brothers and two younger sisters, which would be my Uncle George, Uncle John, Uncle Robert, Aunt Mary Alice and Aunt Eleanor."

"I know who your aunts and uncles are. Did I tell you I was confused?"

Tom drank a third of his coffee and filled it back up with whiskey. He then took a big sip and smacked his lips as if he was a wine taster with a defined palette.

"You know, Will, I've switched over to Marlboro lights. Gatta' watch out for your health, you know." I poured some sugar and cream into my coffee to try and kill the awful alcohol taste.

"Anyway, your Grandfather was always working even as a kid to help the family. He finally dropped out of school to work full time.

The whole time he was being dad to those brothers and sisters. The reason it's important you know is because he is part of you. He was a leader. Its just like if you take two black dogs and mate them you're probably going to get a black dog. That's why it's important. You're like him, Will. You're a leader."

I was starting to feel the booze, which helped considerably.

"Anyway, you know the brothers and sisters didn't appreciate their big brother bossing them around. In fact, they hated it. So, this is what makes your grandfather different. He didn't care he had a job to do and he was going to do it. Like the time Aunt Mary Alice said she was going out on a date when she was fifteen. Well, your grandfather said, 'No, you're not.' Well, she said, 'Try and stop me!' So, he ripped her new dress right off her. She screamed at him, 'I hate you,' and ran upstairs crying even though she knew he was right. Or the time he heard there was a bully taking money from Uncle John and Uncle George. Well, he went right down there and beat that bully up; but that doesn't mean he wouldn't lay into them if they caused problems or didn't put their bicycles up. To this day, you ask any one of your aunts or uncles, the ones that are still alive, and they will tell you he did a good job. And Will, they appreciate it." Tom stood up. "I gotta drain a vein. Be right back. Could you get me another Budweiser?"

Will went up to the bar. The four customers were still there.

Occasionally, one would sip his drink or light a cigarette. "Johnny, could you give me a Budweiser and a 7UP in a glass?"

Will poured the Jack Daniels into his seven up. Tom filled up his empty coffee cup with whiskey and chased it with the Budweiser.

"So, dad, I'm going to be leaving town for a while."

"That's fine, Will. So, anyway, your grandfather works his way up from a box boy at a market all the way to manager in seven years. One day he meets your grandmother in the store; the problem is she comes from money and he's blue collar. Your grandfather had a couple of things going for him. One, he was good looking; some people think he should have been in the movies. And two, he was determined.

"Anyway, they dated for a while until your grandfather got a job in California. Now this is the amazing part, they didn't see each other for seven years. They wrote back and forth and that was it. What are the odds that neither one would find someone? Anyway, your grandfather took the train back to see if there was still a spark and sure enough, their love was still alive. Ain't that a hoot! So, anyway, they have a big wedding and she moves to California. Well, in two years, they have their first child, your Aunt Sue.

This is about the time of Pearl Harbor and your grandfather is twenty- seven years old. The Army and Navy take all the young men first and eventually they start drafting the older guys with families. So when your grandfather goes to the draft board, they tell him to go over to the Navy line. He tells them he doesn't want to be on a ship. They finally let him go in the Army, but they're not happy.

Since he was a manager of a store and had employees, they sent him to officer training school after boot camp. He lands in France with his platoon and they fight their way all the way to Germany on the front lines. He doesn't see his wife and family for three years. Imagine that! Three years away from home fighting every day.

He said that they were supposed to get the best food because they were on the front lines. Instead the supply officers would sell all the good food to the black market and some of those sons of bitches got rich. Once his platoon lived on cheese and crackers for two weeks, pass me that bottle, will you? "

"Dad, I have to go the bank. What do you want for lunch?"

"Get me one of those pastrami sandwiches from Jimmie's. Extra cheese and chili fries with onions."

I withdrew half of the money in my joint account with Danielle, which came to $1,256.00. I also closed my personal account, which came to $4,432.00, for a total of $5,688.00. I put $300 cash in my wallet. Then I unscrewed part of my dashboard and found a nice stash spot for the rest of the money.

Back at the Malarkey, Dad was standing at the bar talking to Johnny Rumba. When he saw me, he came over with two cold Budweisers. We ate in silence, the fat from the sandwiches dripping onto the paper plates. The bag that holds the fries was spotted with grease. It was delicious. Dad still chewing his last bite of food takes a swig of whiskey right from the bottle, which he chases with his beer.

"Man, that hit the spot. Hey thanks for taking care of my tab. I have a job interview tomorrow. Johnny pays me to sweep up and empty the trash." When I don't respond, he adds, "You've always been a good son."

I nod my head.

"Anyway, about your grandfather this is why it is important. If you don't know the story, who's going to tell your children? This man cannot just be forgotten. He is your blood. You know the Indians they would write songs about their heroes. For us, it's out of sight and it's out of mind. So him and his platoon fight their way across Europe. They become real savvy veterans because they're almost in constant contact with the enemy. You know what? That ain't nothing compared to the night he got his Purple Heart and Silver Star.

His platoon was on a scout mission right before dark when they ran into a Nazi tank with about 50 Nazi foot soldiers, the fighting was fierce with heavy casualties on both sides. Luckily, your grandfather's sergeant, a man named David Greenlee, took out the tank with a bazooka, or they would have been mowed over. The bad part was, after he shot the bazooka, he was shot in the stomach. Another bullet hit the bazooka sending a piece of shrapnel the size of a quarter through your grandfather's thigh.

Your grandfather and David take cover in a ditch behind a log. Your grandfather yells for the radioman to call in their position and ask for medical assistance. By now, it's dark. One of the men yells back that the radioman is dead about 100 yards west of your grandfather. David is in bad shape. He is also your grandfather's best friend, they have been together since boot camp. He asks your grandfather, 'How bad is it?' When he looks inside the shirt, he can see intestines bulging out. He folds his jacket and tells David to press it against the wound.

He takes part of his handkerchief and stuffs it into the hole in his leg, then ties the rest of the handkerchief around his leg. Then your grandfather crawls out of the ditch and starts looking for the radioman. Before he finds the radioman he crawls right by three enemy soldiers dug into a foxhole and mortally wounds all three.

It takes him almost an hour to find the radioman, Paul Gomez, who has the back of his head blown off. Your grandfather calls in the coordinates and then heads back to David. David is dying. He asks your grandfather to hold his hand. Another soldier somewhere in the darkness has become conscious and starts yelling out, 'Lieutenant Callahan! Help Me!' David tells your grandfather to tell his girlfriend and his mother that he loves them and that it was an honor to serve with such a fair and honest man. It takes David another hour to die. When the sunrises the next morning, the Nazi's are gone. They had retreated some time in the night. The medics show up around noon. Out of 1 6 men, only three are still alive and they all are wounded. Your grandfather received a Silver Star and a Purple Heart, as well as a letter from the President. He told me this story after I found his medals in the bottom drawer of an old dresser. He never talked about it. He never owned a gun after he was discharged. He went back to the market and worked his way up the ladder until he was in the main office of corporate headquarters. He was a great father and husband, and you should be proud. "

Tom reached into his pocket and threw the two medals on the table.

"I want you to have them, Will."

I picked them up and looked at them. Many men had received these medals at a horrible cost. I felt honored and slipped them into my top pocket. "Anyway, Will, I want you to know you're lucky to have me as a father and not your grandfather."

"Because?"

"I'm a fuck up. It doesn't take much to be better than me. I'm a loser. I couldn't come close to being the man my father was. I'm a drunk. You have no pressure."

I had no response.

"You know I didn't drink when I was with your mom. She was a saint. God, I loved her. I would do anything for her. She brought the best out in me. What do you remember about her, Will?"

I thought about it for a while.

"I remember when she would bring my pajamas out of the clothes dryer and they would still be warm. I had just taken a bath and those pajamas would feel so good. Then, she would tuck me into my bed and lie with me until I fell asleep. I remember being proud, she was so pretty when she took me to school."

Dad took a long pull off the bottle, he was beyond chasing it with beer.

This was a bad topic for us and I knew where it was going.

"Tell me more, Will.

"Dad, let's not do this."

I knew we were past the point of no return. I really hated this. "Will, my life was over the day she died. If it weren't for you and your sister, I would have killed myself."

"Dad, let me ask you. Do you think a healthy relationship has one of the partners totally dependent upon the other?"

He took another long pull on the bottle. "What do you know about love?" After yesterday, obviously nothing.

"Tell me about the time in the hospital." He was starting to slump into his seat. It wouldn't be long now.

"Which time?"

"The last time. Will." He was starting to slur.

"Well, Van and I went into her room because the nurse said Mom was going to see God real soon. It was important we see her because she probably wouldn't wake up. The nurse told us not to touch anything and left us standing by the side of the bed. Mom opened her eyes and smiled so we climbed onto the bed with her and put our cheeks on her cheeks just like we used to do. We were careful that we did not pull the tubes. Mom smelled real different.

The nurse came in and made us get down. Mom squeezed our hands one at a time. When she let go of mine, she whispered, 'Take care of your father.' The nurse made us go. Van cried, but I didn't."

Dad had tears running down his face and dripping off his chin. I have told him this story over and over since I was a little boy. It always makes him cry. He rested his head on the table with his eyes closed.

Johnny Rumba came over. "Let's take him out to his van."

As we picked him up, he reached back and grabbed the bottle and shoved it into his coat pocket. Johnny and I got him comfortable on his cot. Before I had the door closed, he was snoring. I went back in and phoned my sister.

"Evangeline?" I was the only one who called her by that name. I only did it because she hated it. She usually went by Evan or Van, but I liked to rattle her cage. I could hear my two nieces playing in the background.

"What do you want, Zit?"

At one time I had a minor acne problem, so this was her retaliation for calling her Evangeline.

"I'm leaving town for a little bit. Can you check in on Dad?"

There was a silence. She and Dad had some unresolved issues.

"Van?"

"I really don't want to. He scares the girls."

"You don't even have to talk to him. Johnny Rumba will keep you updated."

"If I have to. Where are you going and why?"

"Danielle and I broke up."

She immediately turned sympathetic. " Oh, Will, I'm so sorry. What happened? You were doing so well."

"Let's just say something came up, literally."

"Come and stay with us, please. Dan and the girls would love it."

Dan, her husband, was as solid as a rock and didn't drink, the exact opposite of our dad.

"Thanks anyway. I'm going to do a little traveling." We were close. We would always be close.

"Will, if you need anything call please?"

"I will. Remember to check on Dad."

"Bye, be careful."

# CHAPTER 2

# MY SISTER'S KEEPER

Talking to Van, made me think of our childhood. A little girl is standing by a young boy's bed. It's night out and the room is mostly dark except for a street light that shines through the window. The light distorts the shadows into surreal shapes. The little girl is holding on tightly to her stuffed chimpanzee, Joe Bananas. She taps the boy gently on the shoulder and whispers, "Will? Are you awake?"

The boy moans sleepily. "Will?"

The boy whispers impatiently, "Van, I'm sleeping. Go talk to Dad."

"Will, Dad's not here. I'm scared."

"So?" the boy answers curtly.

"Let me sleep with you, Will. Please. I'll make you breakfast."

"All you can fix is cereal and we don't have any milk."

"I'm scared, Will. There's something in my room."

"There's nothing in your room. Go back to your bed."

"I'm not going to my room. I'll sleep here on the floor."

She lays down on the floor with Joe Bananas. The boy looks down at her and lets out a sigh.

"Okay, Van. You can sleep here, but as soon as Dad gets home you're leaving. No talking and you have to sleep on the wall side."

The little girl scrambles over the top of the boy and burrows under the blanket. "Thanks, Will. I'm so glad you're my brother," she says contentedly.

"Shhhhhh! I'm trying to sleep."

The little girl feels happy and safe. She tucks Joe Bananas in, turns and looks at Will. "Why doesn't Dad come home?"

"That's it. Go to your own room, Van!"

"I'm sorry. I won't say another word promise."

They both look up at the ceiling. The shadows of the front yard tree are swaying in the evening breeze. The boy would never admit it, but he gets scared too. He knows that it would not help his sister if she knew. He slides half his pillow over to her. She turns on to her side, hugs Joe Bananas and is soon fast asleep. Will is awake now. He plays his favorite game, 'What If?' What if Mom was alive? What if I had an older brother? What if Dad doesn't come home? What if I was rich and could have anything I wanted? The boy plays the game until he falls into a restless sleep.

Will and Van are sitting on the floor in front of a television that is turned up loud. Their father is passed out on the couch behind them snoring almost as loud as the TV.

"Will, I'm hungry."

Will is entranced with the show and ignores his sister. Van waits for a commercial.

"I'm hungry."

"Wake dad up, Van."

"Will, I'm hungry."

Will gets up grumbling, "I'll make some peanut butter sandwiches."

"We had that last night and for lunch. Can we have something different?"

"I watched dad make macaroni and cheese. I think I can make that."

Van gets a big smile. "I'll help you, Will."

Van is standing on a chair watching the water boil. Will is trying to read the directions. "I don't know some of these words but the pictures say we pour the noodles in boiling water."

Van watches intently as Will pours the noodles into the boiling water. "What now?"

"We wait for the noodles to get soft. Get the strainer out of the cabinet and put it in the sink. Once the noodles are soft, I need to dump them in the strainer."

Van jumps down and gets the strainer. "Will, you are so smart. I wish you were my dad."

"Don't be ridiculous, I'm only eight."

Will pours the water and noodles into the strainer. He then puts the noodles back in the pan and adds the package of cheese with some butter. "Get us two glasses of milk, Van. I want to watch TV while we eat."

They eat right out of the pan taking turns with their spoons. Van licks her spoon clean after every bite. "Don't you just love macaroni?"

Will doesn't answer, his attention is on the TV. With a full stomach, Van falls asleep on the floor. Once his show is over, Will makes Van go to bed. He follows her into her bedroom. He pulls off her shoes. She climbs into bed with her clothes on. He pulls the blankets up for her and turns on her night light.

"Good-night, Will."

"Good-night, Van."

I was unlocking my bike at the bike rack after school. Van was blabbering on about some school assignment. Two boys from my fourth grade class came up to me.

One of them asked, "Will, we need another player for a basketball game. Do you want to play?"

"Sure I'd like that. I'll give my sister a ride home and then I'll be right back."

"Can't she walk home? We want to play now."

"It will only take twenty minutes and I'll be right back."

One of the boys pointed to another boy. "Let's get Larry."

"Sorry, Will. We can"t wait." They ran over to Larry.

"I can walk home, Will." Van was sad for me.

"I didn't want to play anyway. Get on."

Van climbed on to the seat. I pedaled standing up and she would sit on the seat and hold on to my waist.

"Do you think dad will ever get married again?' Van asked.

"Who would marry him? He can't keep a job."

We rode in silence while Van digested this information. Our house was at the top of a hill, the street was too steep for me to pedal the two of us up. I got off and walked my bike. Van walked beside me. She was in one of her moods I could tell.

"What do you think you'll be when you grow up, Will?"

"I don't know. Maybe a fireman. That would be a cool job. I know one thing. I'm going to be the best father to my kids. I'll have a big dinner table and we'll all eat dinner at the same time. I'll say grace before the meals. After dinner I'll throw the football around on the front lawn, just like Mr. McGregor does with his kids. I might have a beer now and then, but I'll never get drunk."

We went around the back of the house. I opened the back door with a key that was hidden in a planter on the back porch.

"I'm going to the store. I found where Dad hides his money."

"Can I go Will, please?"

"Okay, but we can only spend ten dollars, otherwise he'll know we found it."

We rode down the hill to the neighborhood grocery. Mr. Johnson was sweeping by the front door. He held out his broom and blocked our entrance to the store.

"Sorry Will, I can't give you any more credit."

I held up the ten. "I've got cash, Mr. Johnson."

He smiled and lowered his broom. With a bow, he said, "In that case, please enter. I see you brought the lovely Evangeline with you."

"Call me Van, Mr. Johnson."

"I'll be glad to, princess."

I put milk, cereal, soup, bread, and crackers on the counter. Mr. Johnson totaled it up; it came to eleven dollars and eighteen cents. I tried to figure out what to put back. Mr. Johnson winked at Van. "Oh, I forgot there was a sale on crackers. Let's see, with a discount that comes to ten dollars even."

"Thank you, Mr. Johnson," Van and I said at the same time, which made all three of us laugh. Mrs. Johnson came out of the back room.

"You're not giving those kids any more credit, are you?"

"No dear. They have cash."

Mrs. Johnson came up to us. "When is your father going to pay his bill? Is he working?"

"Yes ma'am. He got a job down at the paint factory. I'm sure he'll pay on Friday when he gets paid." She looked at me with disgust. "He better."

I picked up our bag. Mr. Johnson faced Mrs. Johnson and held two suckers behind his back so that she couldn't see them. Van grabbed them and put them in her pocket. We ate the suckers as we climbed the hill. Van said, "Mrs. Johnson reminds me of the witch in The Wizard of Oz." This made us laugh so hard we had to stop walking and sit for a while.

I realized I was different on the first day of school. It wasn't just the clothes. My clothes were clean, but wrinkled. Everyone else had new clothes. It wasn't the lunch pails and thermoses. I had a brown bag. It was the mothers. They were like an extension of the child's being, a support system. They straightened hair, tucked in shirts, cooed and coddled. The other children didn't even notice their mothers, but I noticed. Not only did I not have a mother, the other mothers were staring at my father in an odd way.

They were on alert. He sent out some odd message that made them stare at him.

The first few days were fine, as none of the children knew each other. After a few weeks a definite pecking order was established. Groups were formed with various common denominators. I was left out. Nobody knew where I fit. Once it was established that I was different, it was impossible for any group to accept me without jeopardizing the group's credibility. I accepted my fate and learned to entertain myself. One other girl had the same problem as me; she of course wanted to form a partnership. I refused. At least I was above her.

This alienation continued until fifth grade when a remarkable thing happened, a new boy joined our class. His name was Mark Stottlemeyer. He was an outcast like me, but he didn't accept it. He made people miserable. He would punch, shove, kick, steal and intimidate whenever he could get away with it. I had a new role model. All of those early years had built up an enormous resentment. We terrorized our classmates, always with the threat of retaliation if they told. I had a new respect when I walked the halls. People moved out of my way. Mark and I made a pact. We would never rat, steal, or lie to each other. If one of us was losing a fight, the other would jump in. He watched my back and I covered his.

Mark had four older brothers that were meaner than him. If we saw any of his brothers on the street, we would run. They would always shake us down for our money, or beat us up. I was afraid of them. Mark hated them. The only person Mark was afraid of was his father, an ex-Marine who didn't put up with any guff.

Mark and I had the store owners wired. He would go in, blatantly rip off an expensive item and run out the front door. The owner would give chase. After a while Mark would drop the item. The owner would stop to recover the item. Mark would get away. In the meantime, I would be left in the store alone. I would either hit the cash register, or take what we wanted. We always had money. In school we passed by cheating on tests and copying homework. Most of the teachers would pass us with the minimum grades so they wouldn't have to teach us for another year.

I hardly ever went home except to sleep, wash and check on Van. Van was a straight A student. School was her refuge and the teachers were like parents. Van and I were opposite but we had our own understanding. Her friends were afraid of me. She hung out with the nerds and the jocks.

Mark and I started smoking cigarettes in the eighth grade. In the ninth grade we started smoking pot. Mark also started drinking but I refused. I didn't want to do anything similar to my old man. By eleventh grade we were ditching school more than we were going. In what would have been my senior year, I stopped going to school altogether. I got a job in a car wash and partied whenever I was off.

Mark and I were at his girlfriend's house smoking some dope when a guy came by and told us he had seen Van holding hands with one of the football players. Van was in the tenth grade and mature for her age. Mark and I crashed the party and sure enough we found Van with a football player. I jumped the guy and Mark double-teamed him from the back. If it wasn't for Van pulling us off, we might have killed him. When his buddies surrounded us, Mark pulled a knife. When the cops came, we were still surrounded by the jocks. Both of us were holding weed. The aggravated assault with the weed got us both a year in Juvenile Hall. Two more fights in Juvy got me put in California Youth Authority. It took Van a long time to forgive me. I never saw Mark again.

Juvenile Hall was like going to a school with all the worst students. There was a dormitory atmosphere with two boys to a room. The room had a bunk bed and a desk. There was a day room with TV and ping- pong. Everybody went to class during the day. That was all gone after my second fight. California Youth Authority was run like a prison. I was in a cell with a Hispanic gangbanger, who barely could speak English. That was fine with me. I didn't feel like talking. I had one goal and that was to make everyone I came in contact with as miserable as me.

One day, I was sent down to the Warden, that's what everybody called the head honcho. He looked like any other adult in a power position. He had on a suit and his hair was gelled into a wave. Next to him sat a white- haired older man in good shape. His nose was crooked and his complexion was ruddy. He was dressed in sweats. "Mr. Callahan, I'd like you to meet Walter Debranski."

Mr. Debranski stuck out his hand. I ignored it and gave them both the stink eye. "Mr. Callahan, please go with Walter."

Walter led me across the yard into the gymnasium. He handed me some boxing gloves and I followed him over to a boxing ring. The gym was empty except for the two of us. He helped me put on the gloves, then put on some gloves himself. He left the laces loose.

"Okay Mr. Callahan, for our first lesson, I am going to teach you some defense," he said in a slight East European accent.

"How are you going to do that, Walter?"

"Try and hit me, son."

"I don't hit senior citizens."

This made him laugh.

"Mr. Callahan, I heard you were a fighter. Try and hit me. Don't worry. I'll be alright."

I threw a couple of punches at half speed, he blocked them. I threw a couple of more punches at full speed, he blocked them .easily. I bore down and attacked him, he blocked everything. It was as though he knew what I was going to do.

"Okay, Mr. Callahan. Now, you block my punches."

He started bobbing his head and weaving with his shoulders. Almost all of his punches were getting through, sometimes two and three at a time. One punch hit me directly on the nose, this sent me into a rage. I charged him, wildly swinging my arms like a windmill. Boom! One of his punches knocked me one my butt. I jumped up again and charged. Boom! I was on my butt again. I cursed and screamed at him and then tried to tackle him. Boom, boom and boom! I was flat on my back. I had nothing left to charge with. He pulled me to a sitting position.

"What you lack in skill, you make up for in desire," he said.

I shook my head. I was fuzzy.

"Can you teach me? I would like to learn."

"I can teach you but before I teach you, I need you to listen to me. If you want to throw your life away, there is nobody that can stop you. If you are determined to punish everybody for some perceived injustice, this will be your life. This is the only life you have. Is this the way you want to live it? You cannot beat the system. You will be locked up for the rest of your life with a bunch of people as angry as you, or you will be killed. I will not waste my time with someone who doesn't care. When you are ready, I will be here. Do not come unless you are sure."

He took off my gloves and left. A guard came and took me back to my cell. I thought about what Walter had said. What a crock of shit. I wanted to learn to box so I could kick ass. I figured I could play his stupid game. "I'll just tell him what he wants to hear."

I met with Walter the next day.

Walter's life made mine look like a picnic. His family came from Czechoslovakia. They had suffered through persecutions, executions, torture and abysmal poverty. His father had made it to the United States after World War Two. He worked two jobs seven days a week. One by one, he brought over his family. He made the ultimate sacrifice for them. He gave his life so that they could have a better one. Walter had no patience for excuses; as far as he was concerned the United States was heaven on earth. A poor man could become rich. An uneducated man could go to college. This truly was the land of opportunity. He decided to make me one of his projects.

All of Walter's time was donated, it was his way of giving back. He was vice-president of a major retailer. He had a wife, two grown daughters and four grandchildren. Walter had learned to box in the Army where he was welterweight champion for three straight years. Walter used the G.I. bill to go to college. He graduated with a business degree. At college, he met his wife, Gloria, a grammar school teacher who also had roots in Eastern Europe.

I met with Walter at the gym. He was jumping rope. The rope was humming as he whipped it around. He was jumping foot to foot, like skipping while his hands crossed back and forth. I had to admit it was impressive, especially if you were into jump ropes. I'm not. He stopped and threw me the rope.

"First lesson, you need to be able to jump rope like that."

I tossed the rope back. "No, thanks. I want to box, not play jump rope." Walter threw the rope back to me. "Son, we need to get something straight right away. I tell you what to do. You do it. That is the relationship. Take it, or leave it."

"Really, Walter, what could jumping rope have to do with boxing?"

Walter was getting peeved. "I need you to have confidence in my judgments. I am not going to explain every step to you. This once I will explain. Boxing is the coordination of the hands and the feet. The feet are as important as the hands. All the power in the hands comes from the legs and hips, which means you have to move the feet. Next time just do what I say."

"Fine, Walter," I said as sarcastically as possible.

Walter came over and grabbed the rope out of my hand, "You're done for today smart aleck."

"What's the matter? What did I do?"

Walter came up close to me. "I will not be your whipping boy. You do not talk down to me, ever. You will treat me with respect, or no lessons. You are forgetting I have something you want. Now leave. Come back tomorrow, but only if you have the right attitude. From now on you call me, 'Coach,' or 'Sir.' Do you understand?"

He had a point. "Yes, sir."

I jumped rope for a week. I still wasn't as good as Walter, but he let me move on. I then ran laps around the gym, carrying hand weights for a week.

"When do I box, coach?" Walter was working with another boy on the speed bag. He glared at me.

" Sorry, coach."

I kept running. Walter gave me a sheet of calisthenics to be combined with my running and jumping. Boring. I was dying to hit some one. Walter let me hit the heavy bag for a while each day just to appease me; other than that, it was all training to get in shape.

"Boxing is in the legs and lungs, son."

Personally, I felt that was bullshit but what could I do? The old fart could deck me, so he must know something. I did the calisthenics. I did the running. I worked on the speed bag and the heavy bag. Finally, he called me into the ring.

He tied my hands to my sides. "You need to know where to position your feet. I will simulate situations. You get into position." He danced around the ring, throwing punches and calling out where I should be. Boring.

"This has to be reflexive because once you are in a match, you need to act on instinct."

We worked on my positioning for days. Walter wasn't satisfied but I begged him to let me box. He then tied just my right arm. He had two giant pads on his hands that I was to hit as he moved around the ring.

"Son, you don't understand if you are not prepared, you will fall back into your old techniques. A good boxer will cut you to ribbons. You need to have an arsenal in both hands. In your left, you need a jab, a hook and an uppercut. In your right, you need a cross, uppercut and a straight punch. You need to learn each punch and when to throw it. You need to know when to combine punches, and you need to know this without thinking."

We worked on my left and then my right. We worked on the combinations. I ran laps throwing combinations, jabs and hooks. I was feeling it. I was in the best shape of my life. I was ready to kick some ass. Walter sat me down one day.

"I know you are anxious to box, but we have to deal with your mental state. You must want to destroy your opponent. You must channel all of your energy into every punch. Make your opponent be surprised at your speed and power. When he throws a punch, he is most vulnerable. Punish him with counter punches. Rotate your hips into every punch. Use your legs for power. You must be invincible. You can feel no pain. The hero and the coward feel the same thing, except the hero uses his fear. He projects it into his opponent. It's what you do with that fear that counts. I am going to let you spar with one of the heavier boys for a workout. When I blow the whistle you break."

I put on my head gear, mouth guard and gloves, Walter tied them for me. My opponent was an overweight gang banger. I felt no fear. I could hardly wait. Walter was referee. He made us touch gloves.

"I'm going to chop you down like a big tree," I thought to myself.

He circled me, throwing jabs. I blocked them and waited for an opening. I jumped under his reach then threw a left, right, left combination. "Good," Walter said.

The big tree kept jabbing me, which was getting annoying. I jumped in to throw another combo and was met with a straight right that knocked me on my butt. I jumped to my feet and rushed in swinging wildly. The tree ducked my blows and hit me with a combo. I went crazy and tackled him. I got him down and was pummeling with punches.

Walter angrily pulled me off. "Couldn't you hear the whistle? Unacceptable behavior. Take off your gear and meet me outside."

He went and talked to the other boy. I walked outside and leaned against the wall. I was breathing hard from the exertion.

Walter came out and stood in front of me. "Son, you have no discipline. Boxing is about discipline, self denial, will, integrity, independence and character. You must learn these things to be successful in boxing and in life. You are going to have to start over from the beginning."

"You mean jumping rope?!"

"Exactly."

"That's bullshit! I refuse, Debranski, you stupid Polish asshole! I quit!" Walter looked hurt. He said patiently, "I'm not Polish. That's why your here, son. You're a quitter."

'Whatever. Fuck you and the boat that brought you."

I left Walter staring at me. Who cares? I went back to my cell. I passed my free time staring into space. I soon realized that the boxing had been something to look forward to. Deep down inside I knew Walter was right. I had quit on myself. I had an overwhelming feeling that this was a crossroads.

After a week, I went back to Walter. I couldn't look at him. I looked at my feet.

"I'm sorry, coach. Can you give me another a chance?" Walter threw me a jump rope. "Coach...about the Polish thing..."

"Will, I am not Polish. If I was I would not be ashamed of it. You are of Irish heritage. Just a hundred years ago, the Irish were at the bottom of the barrel. You should know we are all just people. All races have good and bad. Judge a person by their heart, not their race. What you said to me is already forgotten. We are starting over. I do not hold a grudge."

I had to wipe my eyes with the back of my hand. Tears were starting to form.

"I got something in my eye, sir."

"Go ahead. Get to work."

My life went through a transformation; granted, nothing earth shattering, but different. I did what Walter told me. I didn't argue. I didn't analyze. One of Walter's quotes made sense: "Over analysis leads to paralysis." I thought about boxing, day and night. I put my soul into it. I was starting to react without thinking. When I did spar, I became adept at counter punching. Walter seemed pleased. I started to even enjoy the training; it gave me some relief from the bitterness that had permeated my being. After a few months, Walter took me and three other boys to an amateur tournament.

We had a guard or chaperone go with us in the van. I was excited or nervous. I couldn't tell which. I boxed in the second match. Walter was in my corner. The match was for three rounds.

"Son, you will lose the butterflies after he hits you the first time. Watch for his tendencies. Pick up his patterns. Set traps for him. Work hard."

When the bell rang for the first round, I was really nervous. My opponent came right out and walloped me on the side of my headgear. Walter was right. That cleared out the jitters. I was surprised at how hard his punches were.

I was faster. When he would set up, I could beat him to the punch. I threw a couple of combinations, he hit me with some fierce body shots. The first round seemed like it lasted an hour instead of three minutes. After the round I sat on a stool in my corner. Walter talked to me.

"You're doing great. Side step his jab and step in with your uppercut. Throw your combinations after he throws his right. Stick and move. Rotate your hips. Punish him."

The bell rang for the second round. I started to feel more comfortable. My combinations were landing. I was setting my feet up and I heard him wince on one of my uppercuts. Out of nowhere, he knocked me down. I jumped back to my feet, more embarrassed than hurt. The referee gave a mandatory standing eight count. I was tentative for the rest of the round. Walter poured water into my mouth.

"You only have three minutes left. Give me everything you have. Don't hold back."

"What about the knockdown?" I asked.

"Forget it. Everybody gets knocked down. It's what you do when you get back up. Remember all the work you have done? Make him pay for all that sweat. Be somebody!"

I charged out of my corner. What I lacked in accuracy, I made up for in intensity. I hit him with a barrage and I never stopped. He retreated into the corner. I felt one of my combinations snap back his head, he went down. I jumped in the air in celebration. The referee led me to a neutral corner. My opponent was back on his feet. The referee gave him a standing eight count. We traded punches to the final bell. My opponent embraced me, I hugged him back. The referee made us stand on either side of him. He held our wrists in his hands down by the sides of his legs. He waited for the judges' decision. It was a draw. The referee held both of our hands up. I was disappointed.

I watched the other bouts. I was completely drained. On the ride back, Walter came and talked to me. "You have a fighter's heart. You showed me something today."

"But I didn't win."

"You need more work. That is all. The main thing is you have it here." He pointed to my chest.

"I am proud of you, Will."

That was the first time he called me by name. I felt good inside, really good. It was an unusual feeling. For the first time in a long time I had a purpose. I loved training. I would get a natural high from the workouts. I respected Walter and I would walk through fire for him. I added about ten pounds of muscle on my frame, which put me in the light heavy weight category. I found the bigger the opponent, the slower the speed of their punches. On the down side, they were stronger. I was developing my own style and strategy. I could slug it out with anyone. The boxers who would jab and then tie me up in a clinch gave me the most problems.

After my first bout, which was a draw, I had three straight victories. I wanted to fight more accomplished opponents. Walter told me to have patience. One day when I was working out on the heavy bag, Walter called me over.

"Will, I've put in a request for an early release for you. We have a meeting with a judge this Thursday." I was in shock. "How will this affect my boxing?"

Walter smiled. "There are other gyms."

"Will you still be my coach?"

"Yes, Will. You're stuck with me."

He put his arm around me. "I need you to get a haircut and wear some nice clothes. Leave the rest to me."

Going to court made me more nervous than any of my boxing matches. The judge looked too serious for my liking. When my name was called, Walter and I went and stood before the judge.

"William Callahan?"

"Yes, your honor."

"Walter Debranski has told me some good things about you. Walter and I go way back. Do you see my name on that name plate?"

The nameplate read 'Judge Alan Sworski.'

"Walter's word," the judge continued, "is better than any contract. He promises me that there will be no more trouble with you. Is that correct?"

"Yes, your honor."

"The reason you are in here is for fighting. Now, Walter has taught you some boxing skills. Is this going to be a problem?"

"No, your honor."

"Well, I'm going to make sure it is not a problem. If you get in any trouble with your fists, I will make sure you serve a minimum of two years in a correctional institution. When is your eighteenth birthday?"

"Next month, your honor."

"After your eighteenth birthday, all time will be served in a penitentiary. Do you know what a penitentiary's like, Mr. Callahan?"

"No, your honor."

"It is a very unpleasant experience. Are we clear on this subject?"

I nodded my head.

"I can't hear you, Mr. Callahan."

"Yes, your honor."

"Good day, Mr. Callahan."

Walter knew I was getting out. He had all my belongings from the CYA in his trunk. He gave me a ride home. I stood by the open door.

"Thanks, Walter."

"You're welcome. The Mrs. and I would like you to have you over for dinner this Sunday night."

"Can I bring my sister?"

"Of course. Get settled in and we'll start working out again next Monday.

Here's my address. See you Sunday around six o'clock."

Walter drove off. I walked around the back of the house. It was weird. I didn't feel like I belonged here anymore. My relationship with Van had deteriorated the day I assaulted her boyfriend. I knew she loved me, but she didn't understand me. I had been her protector, her big brother. Now, she just needed a friend, a confidant. This was a role I wasn't prepared for. The thought of somebody putting their hands on my little sister drove me nuts. She had broken up with the football player, or he had broken up with her. Now, she was dating some freshman in college. The guy seemed nice enough, but it still bugged me. I chose to not think about it. I wanted a relationship with my sister. She was my only real family.

We took the bus to Walter's. Walter's house was in a nice neighborhood. There were kids out in the yards playing, parents doing yard work, you know, normal things. I felt a little out of place. I couldn't tell how Van felt. Walter was watering his lawn when we walked up. I introduced Van and he took us in the house.

The house was warm and friendly but most noticeable were the smells coming from the kitchen. Van had become a decent cook, but I had a real weakness for home cooked meals. Maybe never getting them had something to do with it. Mrs. Debranski was in the kitchen. She hugged us warmly. She reminded me of Mrs. Santa Claus. Van started helping without being asked, which was her way. Walter showed me around their house. On one of the walls were pictures of his family. Some of the older pictures had some weird characters in weird clothes, obviously remnants of the old country. He showed me his scrapbook of his boxing career. Just by the pictures, I could tell he had been gnarly.

Mrs. Debranski called us to the dinner table. Walter said grace. We had pot roast with potatoes, asparagus, salad, dinner rolls, and homemade pie with ice cream. I promised myself when I got married, my wife would cook just like this. Walter and I went to the living room to watch a ball game while the women cleaned up. I was used to cleaning up at home and volunteered, but Walter insisted I come with him. Walter lit a cigar.

"This is my weakness. I smoke one cigar a night."

He savored the smoke, rolling it around in his mouth.

"So, where are you working, Will?"

"At the local convenience store."

"What do they pay?"

"Minimum wage."

"Would you like a job in construction?"

"Sure. Doing what?"

"Apprentice carpenter."

"That would be great. When could I start?"

"My friend needs someone right away. You could start tomorrow. Here's the construction site address. I'll call him tonight and tell him you're coming. His name is Ray Bartkowski."

"Thanks, Walter."

We played cards for an hour. Walter drove us home. Van and I walked around to the back of the house.

"Van, are you ever going to get past it?"

You mean, what you did to Bert?"

Yeah, the football player."

"I can, if you're done beating people up."

"I'm done."

She stopped me and then hugged me tight.

"I love you, big brother."

"Thanks, little sister."

I told the convenience store owner that I was quitting and that I'd be in later for my check. The construction site was going full speed when I got there. I asked where Ray was. A plumber pointed up on one of the walls. Ray was setting trusses with another carpenter. I yelled up to him. He came down. He shook my hand. His hand was weathered, so was his face. He could pass for one of Walter's brothers.

"Your name?" he asked.

"Will Callahanski."

He looked at me with a quizzical look.

"Just kidding. Will Callahan."

"So... you're a comedian."

I should have known better. I immediately did the backstroke.

"No, sir. I'm here to work."

"Okay. We need that lumber piled there stacked on that slab. Call me when you're done."

I hauled lumber all day. It was like a workout in the gym, except I was outside. I loved it. This was better than the convenience store. I was a gofer for the first month. Ray showed me how to run a skill saw without cutting myself. Ray was very safety conscious, especially since he had cut his thumb really bad. He told me his thumb was hanging off when he went to the hospital. They sewed it back on. The thumb never worked right. The doctors told him there was ligament damage and they could fix it with another operation. Ray never went back. When Ray wanted to hammer, he would bend his thumb in place and it would stay like that. When he wanted to hold a soda, he would straighten it out. We all knew when break was over because Ray would bend his thumb.

I watched Ray and the other carpenters and I learned. Whenever I could, I would frame something on my own. Ray wouldn't say anything unless it was wrong, then he would show me how to fix it. After six months Ray hired another gofer. He told me to buy myself some tools. I was still boxing.

Luckily Ray was a fight fan. Sometimes after a bout, I'd be so sore that I was worthless. Ray would give me something easy to do. Ray was building an addition on his own home. He worked on it on weekends. I volunteered my labor. Ray explained the 'why' of carpentry as we framed. He patiently answered all my questions. It was like going to school. Ray was well known for his craftsmanship. I looked forward to work everyday. I loved being able to look at something I had built. I even loved the smell of the wood. I had become a carpenter. I had a title. I was somebody.

As my carpenter skills grew, my need for boxing diminished. I wasn't angry anymore. I didn't feel like hurting people. I didn't know how to tell Walter. I owed him everything. I was undefeated and he was talking about me going professional. He seemed so excited. I didn't want to let him down. Weeks passed and I kept working with Ray and working out with Walter. Whenever I got the nerve to tell Walter, something would come up.

Walter signed my first professional fight; five hundred to the winner and two hundred to the loser. I was going to tell Walter after the fight that I was done, but he was so pumped on my career that I dreaded telling him. My carpenter job had given me something I had never felt before, an identity. I was done with the tough guy routine. On the job, Ray would actually confer with me on decisions. I can't tell you how good that made me feel. I figured I'd give Walter one more fight, my best fight.

Ray gave me the day off the night of the fight. I would rather have worked. Sitting around made me jumpy. Walter was as nervous as an expectant father. He kept going over the same strategies until I couldn't take it anymore.

I went home and took a nap. With my carpentry money, I had bought an old Ford pick-up. I drove it to the arena. Walter was waiting for me. We went inside and I got dressed. Walter taped my hands.

"You know, Will, I never had a son. I never told the Mrs. but I really wanted one. I always wanted a boy, someone who could understand boxing. The women just don't know how men feel about it. It's in my blood. The Mrs. just doesn't understand."

I would have to wait until after the fight to tell him. I forced myself to block everything out but the fight. My bout was the first of five fights. The main event didn't start for three hours. The knowledgeable fans wouldn't show up for another two hours. That was fine with me. I was sketchy just knowing Van and Ray would be watching. One of the attendants came to the door and told us it was time. Walter pulled out a gift box.

"This is for you, Will."

I opened it. Inside was a green boxing robe with 'Kid Callahan' embroidered in white on the back. On the front was 'Irish Pride'.

"Damn it, Walter. What did you do that for?"

"You don't like it?"

"Are you kidding? I love it."

I hugged him.

Walter and I walked out to the ring.

The arena was almost completely vacant. I could see Ray and Van clapping and whistling. My opponent was a Hispanic kid from the barrio. He had a pretty big turnout; they let out a cheer that echoed throughout the empty arena. I wondered what his background was. Now that I had my carpenter job, I didn't need this. I bet he did. Walter yelled in my ear. "Start moving. Get loose kid. This guy's going to kick your ass if you don't snap out of it. No mercy. It's dog eat dog."

It was almost like Walter was reading my mind. For Walter's sake I was going to give it everything I had. The referee came out and gave us the same old instructions, "Break when I say break. No hitting below the belt. Go to the neutral corner on all knockdowns."

My opponent was trying to intimidate me with a glare. One good uppercut is worth a thousand glares.

The bell sounded for round one of six rounds. I went out and landed my first jab. I could feel it. My timing was there. I had one of those rare experiences in sports when the action slows down and everything comes together. He couldn't touch me. I was throwing multiple combinations and everything was landing. The rounds seemed to fly by. Walter was telling me that I had won the first three rounds; one more and I could cruise. I looked out at Van. She was beaming. I was thinking maybe I wouldn't give it up.

I went out for round four and got rocked. My opponent had dug deep for something extra. His corner must have told him it was now or never. I even had to tie him up a couple of times, or he might have knocked me down. After the round Walter was freaking.

"Will, get it back! He's taking the fight to you! You're all defense! Back him up. Throw some punches!"

The fifth round was even worse. I had to hand it to him. He wanted it bad. After one of his onslaughts, the referee gave me a standing eight count. I welcomed the break. My face was getting puffy on the right side. My rib cage hurt after every breath. Thankfully, the bell rang ending the round. Walter knew I was taking a beating. He laid off the rah-rah.

"It's the last round. Now, we will see what you are made of," he said with resignation.

I actually felt nauseated, but decided to go out swinging. I met my opponent in the middle of the ring and we started slugging. I knew I was getting tagged. I also knew I was landing some major shots. I couldn't see out of my right eye, so some of his punches would hit me without warning. I really couldn't feel the pain anymore. I just kept swinging. I didn't even pretend to have a defense as I focused on his head and threw every punch I had ever learned.

They had to ring the bell three times because neither one of us could hear it. Walter came out and got me. He lifted me up and carried me around the ring. I asked him to put me down. The referee came and took me out to the middle of the ring. My opponent was on the other side.

The ring announcer yelled into the microphone, "In a split decision in his first professional fight, the winner is Kid Callahan!"

Walter picked me up again. After he put me down, I went and shook hands with my opponent. They had two Q-tips stuck up his nose to stop the bleeding. He also had a cut on his eye. I put my robe on, high fived Ray and Van, then went back to the dressing room. Thank God this was over. I never wanted to fight again. Walter took off my gloves and then cut off the tape with a scissors.

"Walter, I'm sorry, but I don't want to fight anymore."

"Listen, Will. You're sore right now. Every fighter feels that way right after a fight. In a week you'll be back at the gym ready to go. That last round was magnificent. You stood toe to toe and let him have it!"

Walter jumped out to the middle of the room, pantomiming the last round, throwing punches into the air as fast as he could.

"It was almost like I was in the ring myself! I loved it. You were great, son."

He put his arm around me. "You make me proud."

"Walter, seriously, I'm through. I don't want to hit anybody anymore. I feel sorry for that kid that lost."

"Okay, Will. I hear you, but don't give me your final decision now. Enjoy the victory. Shower and I'll take you out to dinner."

I don't know how you can enjoy a victory when it feels like you've been in a head on collision. I went to the rest room. I had blood in my urine. Walter told me not to worry about it, unless I still had blood tomorrow. The right side of my face was swelling up. My right eye was closed shut. I had taken so many body shots I couldn't identify a specific pain. My body was throbbing everywhere. Walter gave me some ibuprofen and aspirin. I held an ice bag to my face all the way to the restaurant.

Walter ordered champagne and prime rib for everyone. Ray and Van were almost excited as Walter. I tried to be social, but with my face all puffed up, I felt like a mutant. I don't drink, so I shined the champagne. My jaw was so sore I couldn't chew, so I had to sip soup. Those guys looked like they were going to stay for a while rehashing the fight. I told them I was going home. Ray told me to take the day off. Van kissed me on the cheek. I looked at Walter.

"Walter, will you walk me to my truck?"

"Sure, Kid. Kid Callahan, undefeated professional!"

They let out a hoot and high fived each other. I waited until we were outside before I told Walter.

"Coach, I was serious. I'm through."

He listened.

"The only reason I fought that last fight was for you. I owe you. I will always owe you. I will do anything for you. You have taken a worthless, bitter individual and given him a life. I am a carpenter. I can build things. I am productive. I am somebody. I owe you. If you say to keep fighting, I will. I'll do anything you say."

Walter hesitated before he spoke.

"I would never ask anyone to fight if their heart wasn't into it. I just got caught up in the moment. It was like I was back in the ring. Like I told you in the beginning, it's your life and you have to live it for you, not for me, not for Van, but for you. I am happy you have made the next step. You know I have been helping out at the CYA for years. I've helped a lot of boys, but you are my favorite. You have the heart of a lion."

"Thanks, coach."

We hugged gently on account of my ribs.

"So son, does this mean I won't see you any more?"

"If you don't mind, I'd like to come over for Sunday dinners."

"The Mrs. would like that and so would I."

"Can I bring Van?"

He laughed. "Of course."

Van and I never missed a Sunday at the Debranski's. The Debranskis became our surrogate parents. We met their children and their grandchildren. We spent Easter, Christmas and Thanksgiving at their house. They even made Dad welcome.

Things changed fast in the next few years. I moved out of the house.

Van got a full scholarship to college. She moved into a dorm. I sent her spending money. I was making more than I could spend with Ray. Dad got evicted. After we left the house, it wasn't a priority for him. He lived out of his van. I gave him spending money. Van was dating a mechanic named Dan, a good guy who didn't drink. Van liked that. During Van's sophomore year she got pregnant. Dan and Van got married. I was the best man. I thought that was a classy thing by Dan.

Dad stayed sober until the reception where he made a complete ass of himself. Luckily, Dan and Van had already left when dad was at his worst.

I gave him a ride back to his van.

"You know, Will, you are the best son a man could have. I love you so much."

He tried to kiss me while I was driving. I straight-armed him.

"Dad, sit still."

"I just love you and Van."

"Dad, that's your booze talking." I was starting to get indignant.

"Do you think leaving young kids to fend for themselves is a display of love?"

"Who did that?"

"You did."

"I never did. I was always there for you kids. You guys are the most important thing to me."

"That's bullshit. The most important thing to you is sucking on that bottle. Anyway, passed out on the couch does not count for being there."

"I don't know what you're talking about. Sure after a hard day I might have had a nip or two, but I always waited until you kids were asleep."

He pulled a flask from his jacket pocket. He offered it to me, then took a swig. "I don't drink, Dad."

"You don't? How come?"

I should have let it go like usual, but I was pissed that he had gotten drunk at the reception.

"Because I don't want to be like you."

He took another swig.

"That's a helluva' thing to say to your old man," he slurred.

"That's not all I have to say. You embarrass me. Everything that is good in my life came in spite of you, not because of you. I almost threw my life away because I was so pissed at you and mom."

"Mom?! What did she ever do to you? You wouldn't be here without her?"

"Did you ever think that maybe a kid needs a mom? Hell no! You were too busy thinking about your own pain. You're selfish. Van and I suffered. And yeah, I am mad that she died. I needed her!"

"I can't believe you're saying this. She didn't choose to die. I miss her too. ya' know. I can see her face like it was yesterday. It shoulda' been me. She coulda' raised you kids. She woulda' known what to do. I tried. Ya' gotta' believe I tried."

He slumped against the window and started to cry. I knew better than to get into this discussion because now I felt sorry for him. He had his eyes closed as he finished off his flask. By the time I got to his van, he was passed out. I put him to bed in his cot. I whispered that I was sorry. He wouldn't remember anything the next morning. He was right. He had tried. Life can be a bitch. I already knew that.

I eat breakfast every morning at "Helen's Home Cooking." Helen has long since died or retired and an old Navy cook owns it. The food is edible and it's close to home. It was at Helen's where I met Danielle. Normally, I read my paper and drink my coffee while I'm waiting for bacon and eggs. Danielle was going to school when she got a job working part time at Helen's. Her very first day, she came up to me and smiled like I knew her. I'm not very good with women. My relationships last for about six months, then they start a slow deterioration until they have a total meltdown. I have never remained friends with any of the girls I've dated. In fact, I would be safe in saying they wish bad things would happen to me. I have never been mean to them, but I have been honest. Sometimes I wonder if it would be better to lie.

I do not want a complicated life. After all the trouble I had growing up, I want things simple. I get up every morning early, eat breakfast, go to work, come home, read the paper, shower, eat dinner, watch the tube and go to sleep. Saturdays, I work a half-day in my office at home. I go over architect plans, lumber lists and organize the following week's work. The rest of Saturday is spent cleaning house, doing laundry, basically domestic stuff. Saturday night I might go to a movie, or go out to eat. Sunday morning is for sleeping in and reading the newspaper in bed with coffee. I am in an athletic club and we play ball on Sunday afternoon. It's basketball, touch football, or softball, whichever is in season.

My teammates take these games seriously. They will talk for hours about the games at the local pizza parlor. I enjoy the camaraderie more than anything. It's also a good workout. Every woman I've dated loves the fact I'm not a party animal and that I don't drink. After a few ·months, they tire of my routine and need some changes. They want me to make adjustments. I don't want to. They take it out on Mr. Happy. They withhold sex. It's all down hill from there. What surprises me is how much anger some women carry around. Breaking up can get viscous. Bottom line I don't need the grief.

I ignored Danielle's smile and ordered my breakfast. I had my face in the paper when she brought my food. She put her hand on my arm and said, "Here's your eggs."

I personally feel that I have a two foot radius around me that is my space. I don't like strangers to break that plane. By touching me, she had violated my space. I put my paper down and studied her as she walked away. I have to admit that was quite a caboose. I had learned the hard way that it takes more than a great caboose to have a relationship. Mr. Happy was trying to get my attention, but I was sick of listening to his advice. The guy is an idiot.

Every morning Danielle would give me a big hello. After a while, I looked forward to seeing her. Sometimes, she would sit with me and chat while I ate my breakfast. I wanted to ask her out, but I couldn't handle it if I was denied. Finally, one morning she sat down and asked, "So, Will, are you ever going to ask me out?"

"I thought someone as pretty as you must have a steady."

"Well, I don't."

"Would you like to go to dinner and the movies?"

She put her chin on her hands and nodded yes.

"Friday?"

She nodded again.

I picked her up at her apartment. She looked outstanding. We laughed all through dinner. She had a great sense of humor. The movie was a bore. We left early and since it was a nice evening we walked home. She gave me a good night kiss and made it clear that that's all there would be. I liked that. I hate playing games, probably because I'm no good at them.

Danielle was busy with work and school, so it was difficult to get together. We had Saturday afternoons until Sunday afternoons to spend time together. She insisted on no sex. She only had sex in a relationship. She wanted me to sleep over because she enjoyed my company, but no intercourse. We did some heavy petting and I saw her almost all the way naked, but I never got past second base. If it was a psychological ploy, it was working. I would think about her all day. To tell you the truth, I never felt this way about any woman and it was intimidating.

One Sunday I called in sick to my basketball game. That was a first. I wanted to go to the beach with her. We threw the Frisbee around, swam, beachcombed, barbecued and watched the sun go down. I didn't want the day to end. After I dropped her off, I realized I was in love. I had to smile to myself. So this is what it feels like. Man, this is powerful. I wanted to be with her all the time.

I tried to stay nonchalant, but she could tell. We were dating exclusively, but we still did not spend enough time together. One night she called me.

"I have some bad news."

"What is it?"

"I'm moving back in with my parents."

My jaw hit the floor.

"Where do they live?"

"San Francisco."

"Why?"

"I can't keep up with my finances. All I have is one more year, then I can graduate. My next year will be my hardest and I can't study and work, too."

I was devastated.

"When will you be leaving?"

"I need to enroll in school up there. So, I have to go next week."

"When will I be able to see you?"

"There will be breaks and I will be out of school in a year. Do you want to come over tonight?"

"Sure, " I mumbled.

I felt like someone had hit me with a sledgehammer. I couldn't concentrate. I was worthless at work. I drove to her house in a fog. After a quiet dinner, which I pouted through, Danielle announced she had a going away gift. She insisted I close my eyes.

"Danni, I don't have anything for you."

"That's all right," she yelled from the other room.

"Open your eyes."

She was standing before me totally nude. I tried to be cool, but my eyes were bugging out.

"I don't see a present."

"I'm your present."

I picked her up and carried her into the bedroom. We made love. It was the best feeling I have ever felt. We lay side-by-side holding hands.

"I think I love you, Danni."

"You think?"

"Cut me some slack. I never have felt this before .and it sure as hell is a scary thing to admit."

She lay on top of me.

"Well, do you think, or do you know?"

"I haven't heard you admit to anything yet."

"I'm waiting for you."

"Yes, I love you. I don't want you to go."

She got teary eyed and kissed me tenderly.

"Yes, she whispered, "I love you, too."

"What are we going to do?"

She didn't answer.

"Would you move in with me? I'll pay for the rent."

She looked at me for a while.

"I promised myself I would not live with some one until I was married."

That made me hesitate and in my heart I knew there was no turning back.

"Marriage is a possibility, but I'm not ready yet. I have to get used to this love thing first."

"My dad always used to say, 'why buy it, when you can rent it?'".

"Listen. I'm telling you I have to go slow. Trust me. I have never been to this stage before. You make me feel complete. I can't imagine living without you. Give me some time, please."

"Okay. I'll do it."

I was ecstatic. She moved in the next weekend. Life had new meaning. For the first time, something was more important than work. I couldn't wait to go home. Danielle would be studying and I would be reading the paper. It felt like a family.

With other women my feelings would decline, but with Danni it just got better and better. I wanted to spend all my free time with her. I never knew I was capable of feeling this strong an emotion. My life had become good. It seemed like a different person who had stood at the crossroads years ago with nothing to live for. Thank you, Walter.

Days turned to weeks, weeks to months. Danni and I had a lot in common. We had the same quirky humor. We had our own careers. We were comfortable just being together. I could always be myself, which was important. I never brought up my past. There was no use bringing up a dark side that I had gotten over.

If I were making more money, I would propose. I didn't want to have financial problems, money can mess up a relationship. I could picture Danni and me with kids. That was one of my lifetime goals. I wanted to be a real father for my kids, a role model. Danni would be a great mother. She loved children and animals. We were a great team. I felt contented. I didn't even look at other women. I had what I wanted. As far as I was concerned, she was the most beautiful woman in the world. I didn't feel stupid bringing her flowers, or slow dancing in the living room. When she was happy, I was happy. Life's a lot easier when you're not thinking about yourself.

# CHAPTER 3
# COMFORTABLY NUMB

I headed east for no particular reason and drove all day. The next morning, I got a job at a housing tract under construction somewhere in the suburbs of Tucson. I was on a framing crew and our supervisor was a real asshole. The guy was a wanna' be cowboy named Marion Thompson. He wore a big cowboy hat. I don't know whether it was his name that gave him an attitude, or his ugly face. We hated each other from the first handshake when he pulled some weird power play and squeezed my hand extra hard. I stared at him and squeezed back until I saw a slight doubt flicker in his eyes. I knew right then I could kick his ass.

Tract workers are the lowest form of construction labor. The quality is terrible and guys will do anything they can get away with. We were getting paid piecework, instead of by the hour. Marion was pushing everybody way too hard, it was just a matter of time until somebody got hurt. Marion was getting an extra percentage that he wouldn't talk about, so he probably was scrapping some money off of our footage. When you work by the foot, you can make good money if you hustle. You can also make next to nothing if you have a bad crew.

Marion had put together a decent crew. A couple of them were tweakers, speed freaks. You could tell. Tweakers, when they're jacked up, either chain-smoke or eat sunflower seeds. They don't eat lunch, but drink beer instead and then never shut up. I wasn't tweaking, but I was drinking beer with my lunch. After my first drink at the Malarkey, I took to alcohol like a teenage boy takes to cleavage. I would drink beer all afternoon, then hang out at a dive called The Office. I would drink until I was drunk enough to go back to my motel room and pass out without thinking of Danni's supple body. The reason the bar was named The Office is so guys could tell their wives they were still at the office. The irony was the place was filled with blue collars, cowboys and bikers, not a white collar in sight.

Marion and I were getting closer and closer to our inevitable showdown. The other carpenters were coming to me for advice because I knew more than Marion. This drove him crazy because his shallow little ego couldn't handle it. He would purposely by-pass my advice even if it was faster and more efficient. This was causing some real friction because we were all trying to make the most money. I was building an interior wall when I heard Marion getting into it with Dennis, one of the tweakers.

"I don't give a fuck how Will would do it" Marion was screaming.

Dennis was screaming back, "It's faster, you jackassl"

"Go into the office and pick up your check. You're done here."

Dennis raised his hands up. "You're firing me?"

Marion got right in Dennis's face and said, "You got a problem with that, jackass?"

Dennis backed down. He rolled up his cords and picked up his tools and drove off. Jimbo asked Marion who was going to take Dennis' place. Marion pointed to the woodpile where his brother-in-law, an apprentice, was cutting 2x4's on the cut off saw.

Jimbo laughed. "You mean Ted? He doesn't know his ass from a hole in the ground."

"You can go to the office and pick up your check, too, if you want." Marion was losing it. "Ted get some nail bags out of my truck. Today you are a journeyman." Ted got a big grin on his face and almost ran to the truck.

Later that afternoon we were standing a wall on the second floor. In framing, you build the wall flat, then tilt it up in place and secure it with wood braces. Normally, this is not a problem; but if the wall is extraordinary long and has a lot of windows with headers in it, then it can be top heavy. The danger is the bottom kicking out and landing on the carpenters, or actually getting it over too far and having it fall over. With a wall like this, we each were going to be lifting at least 150 pounds and pressing it over our heads and then pushing it up straight as we walked it into position. I didn't like the set up, especially with Ted taking Dennis' place.

"Why don't we use the Pettibone?" I asked Marion. The Pettibone was a forklift that also extended out. We could tie the top of the wall to the forks off the lift and it would take all the danger out of standing the wall. The problem was that the Pettibone was at the other end of the tract and would mean a half hour delay.

"I don't want to wait. What? You afraid you can't carry your share, pussy?"

"Whatever. I'm ready." I shook my head.

Marion purposely put Ted next to me so I would have to lift part of his share. Ted probably weighed one hundred forty five pounds even with his nail bags full of nails. Ted was a year out of high school, but looked like he belonged in junior high.

Marion looked at everybody and said, "Listen. Under no circumstances do you drop the wall. This will start a chain reaction that will get us all hurt." He obviously was saying this for Ted's benefit because the rest of us had stood a thousand walls. Everybody got in position. The key is momentum so it helps to be synchronized.

Marion was on the far corner, we were all looking at him. "Okay! On the count of three. One! Two! Three!" With a mighty grunt, the wall slowly went up. I don't know about everybody else, but I was maxed out. My testicles lifted up on my initial lunge. I could feel my arms shaking and my thighs burning as I struggled to press it over my head. It was too long and too heavy for us. Marion miscalculated. We were committed now that we were halfway underneath it, no man's land. We couldn't put it down and we were losing momentum. Marion yelled out," 1..2..3..Go!"

We all strained at once and it was moving again. "1..2..3..Go!" and again it moved and kept moving. We were going to get it up.

I took a quick glance at Ted; the strain had his face beet red with veins bulging in his neck. Right when we had it perpendicular, Ted, out of ignorance, gave one last push. This caused the wall to lean too far. Marion had let go to grab a brace. Someone yelled, "Hang On!"

We were now all pulling when just a second ago we were pushing. Marion dropped the brace and grabbed on, but it was too late. It had gone too far.

Everyone knew it was going. Everyone, that is, except Ted. "Let Go!" I yelled. "Let it go!" Jimbo yelled almost at the same time.

Ted froze. We all watched him go with the wall over the side, falling ten feet with a big crash. We scrambled down the side of the house. I was the first one to get to him. He was holding his wrist, which was already starting to swell. The bone in his lower leg was fractured and you could see it bulging against the skin. I positioned myself so he couldn't see his leg. I could hear Marion on the cell phone calling an ambulance. Ted was in shock. I wiped the dirt off his face and kept telling him, "You're going to be alright."

It took the ambulance 20 minutes to get there and another 1 5 minutes to load him up. As the siren faded down the street, I told Marion, "I'm done for the day."

I walked towards my truck. Marion yelled after me, "Who's going to clean up this mess?"

"Not Ted." I yelled over my shoulder.

His reply was, "See you tomorrow, candy ass." And he laughed his disgusting evil laugh.

The next day we had a new carpenter on the crew named Bob. After work, I went and saw Ted at the hospital. He looked drugged.

He smiled at me, "Pretty stupid, huh?"

"It happens to all of us, Ted."

"What's the stupidest thing you've done, Will?"

"Well, once I cut the cord on my saw when I was ripping plywood. I was so pissed off, I started fixing it right away. I needed to get the plastic off the copper wires in the cord. So, I stuck the wire in my mouth to rip it off with my teeth, but I had forgot to unplug it. Bang! The electricity knocks my head back, luckily pulling the cord out of my mouth at the same time. My two front teeth were black. For the rest of the job every one called me 'Sparky.'"

Ted laughed.

"Did I ever tell you about the time I was working on a shopping center and OSHA showed up?"

Ted shook his head "no."

"Well, it was a big project and there were eight of us carpenters sheeting in the roof. All of a sudden, someone yelled, 'OSHA inspector is climbing the ladder!' OSHA are the people who inspect job sites to make sure they're safe. If they find infractions, they fine you. All of the carpenters had their saw blade guards tied back, which is a $1000 fine. So we had to throw our saws off the roof rather then get caught. So, eight $150.00 worm drive skill saws flew off a two-story roof and broke to bits. Luckily, no one was working down below."

He told me about the surgery he had on his leg last night and about the surgery they were going to do on his wrist tomorrow. I hung out for a while, then went to The Office and got buzzed.

I was getting real tired of Marion. The first coffee wagon rolls into the tract around 9:30, signaling the first break. Marion would steal from the coffee wagon everyday. He would wear his nail bags up there and when the girl wasn't watching he would throw candy bars and cigarettes into his bags.

On this particular morning, I still had my hang over. When Marion went to pay in the back of the truck, I followed him. She looked at the items in his hand and gave him a total. "What about the stuff in your bags, Marion? Are you paying for that, or is it a five finger discount?"

Marion slowly turned and looked at me. "Be careful, you may get more than you bargained for."

The coffee wagon girl, Angel, was looking in Marion's bags. She gave Marion the new total and told him not to come back. During the break we were sitting on the lumber pile eating. Marion was giving me the stink eye. "You think you're a badass Callahan, but you ain't shit. Your nothing but a punk. For two bits, I'd beat the crap outa you."

I reached into my pocket and grabbed a quarter. I threw it over to Marion. It bounced off his leg.

"Let's see what you got, *Miriam.*"

With a yell he charged me. I sidestepped him and hit him with a cross. His hat flew off and he went down. Like most bullies, he didn't have much. I ducked a wild headshot, then gave him two jabs and a straight right. He threw a looping left hook. I took it on the forearm and counter punched with a quick right-left-right combo. He went down again. He was done.

"You're fired, asshole!" he yelled from his knees. There was blood on his teeth and his eye was puffy.

"Bye, Marion." I took my time rolling my cords then picked up all my tools. At the office, they cut me a check. I was at The Office by lunch and was shitfaced in an hour.

I have been getting drunk everyday for two weeks. I have no motivation. Sometimes, I look for work. My heart isn't into it. A couple of times, I've gone over to The Office when it opens at 7:00 A.M. and have my breakfast: a Bloody Mary and a microwave burrito.

Sometimes, I think of going back to Danni and then I get pissed and say to myself, 'Screw that'. I smoke cigarettes and sit at the bar staring at nothing. My goal is to get totally wasted while still remaining coherent and not getting sick. I know that some days I am not coherent. Oh, well. Thoughts come into my mind that seem important and sometimes I even jot them down. The next day, when I read them, they don't make sense. I feel this is my destiny. You know, you can inherit the alcoholic gene. I think. Whatever.

I had just finished my lunch: a double tequila shooter, two Buds and microwave nachos,when a bunch of bikers came in. I hate bikers. They're loud, rude, tattooed, and worst of all, they think they're tough. I mean, seriously, some of them are tough. The majority are overweight, out of shape morons that ride overgrown bicycles. All they ever talk about is their bikes, drugs and sex. I listened to the biggest and loudest moron go on and on about his sexual prowess until I couldn't take it.

"Big Fucking Deal," came out of my lips unintentionally. They all turned and looked at me, including the cowboys. I put my bottle of beer to my lips and chugged. The giant moron slowly got off his stool and walked over to me. He looked to be about seven feet tall with these big black boots and tattooed biceps that had to be thirty inches around. One of the tattoos was a skeleton with a scepter and one of those weird hats the pope wears. Underneath the skeleton, 'Born to Lose' was written in script. He had a shaggy black beard and hair. His nose had been broken a couple of times and he had a nasty scar on his forehead.

"Did you say something, piss ant?"

"I've heard that people that talk about sex all the time are usually dysfunctional. Are you sure you can still get it up?"

I was having an out of body experience. He started to size me up, trying to figure out if I was crazy or suicidal.

"Let me guess. They call you Bear, right?" I asked.

"That's right."

"I bet even a bear wouldn't have sex with a guy as ugly as you." I heard a few chuckles from his buddies. The rest of the bar cracked up.

"Stand up" he growled.

I got to my feet. I stomped on his toes as hard as I could and hit him with a haymaker right to the chin.

He bellowed, "Now you've pissed me off!" Bear swatted me with his giant paw and the force spun me around. I moved inside and hit him with a few body shots. He made a giant fist and conked me on the top of the head, which buckled my knees. I started to sober up. Who is this guy? I tried to kick him in the thigh, but he caught my foot and swung me in a circle that sent me flying across the room.

I figured I'd go back to the body shots, but he held his hand on my forehead so that I couldn't reach him. This is an old grammar school trick. Bear looked at his friends, who were howling with laughter. I knocked his hand off and kicked him in the nuts. This wiped the smile off his face. I hit him with a couple of jabs and then an uppercut, which had no effect.

"I'm tired of playing with you, piss ant."

He picked me off the ground and pressed me over his head. He then took two steps and threw me. I distinctly remember flying through the air and hitting the wall. I don't remember hitting the floor.

When I came to, it was dark. The bikers were still there. I slowly walked over to Bear.

"Hey man, I want to apologize. I'm having some chick problems."

I held out my hand. He shook it. "No sweat, pilgrim. You're pretty scrappy."

I bought him a few drinks and he bought me a few. "We're having a party tomorrow night. Come on by." Bear said. He drew me a map on a napkin. We shook hands again and then I stumbled to my motel room. The next afternoon I headed to Bear's.

Bear's place was way out in the desert. I had been driving on a dirt road for 1 5 minutes when I ran into a four wheel drive truck parked off the road. A biker was standing next to it with a shotgun. He waved me to a stop.

"Who are you? Are you a cop?" He had a video camera in his hand and was filming. "Don't lie. I'm recording it."

"No, I'm not a cop."

"Who invited you?"

"Bear."

He went to his truck and looked on a list. "What's your name?"

"Will Callahan."

"You're not on the list."

"Can you call?" He went to his truck and talked on his C.B. "He still doesn't know you."

"Tell him it's 'Piss Ant.'"

The biker broke into a big grin as he talked to Bear. "You're cool. Have fun."

It was another 30 minutes to get to the front gate. There was a big house, two warehouses, about six trailers and a swimming pool. Bear was waiting for me at the gate. He had his arm around a girl. She was completely naked. "Pull your truck in so I can close the gate."

I parked to the side of the house where there were at least 50 Harleys and 20 cars or trucks. There was a big wall around the whole place with razor wire on top. It almost looked like a prison. There were sensory devices and cameras in strategic areas.

Bear gave me the soul shake. "Dude, glad you came. This is Marilyn."

I held out my hand for a handshake. She pressed her breasts together.

"Do you want to feel them?" she asked.

I looked at Bear. I was embarrassed. He laughed. "Go ahead, or she will be insulted." I gave one of her breasts a handshake. A little voice was telling me to split. I was in over my head.

"Do you want to have sex?" she purred. I started to squirm. I was feeling very uncomfortable. This, of course, was great entertainment for Bear, who couldn't stop laughing.

"I'm sorry. I'm engaged," I lied.

Bear gave her a pat on the butt and said "Marilyn, run along. I want to show Will around. For your information regarding the girls you can screw any of them any time you want, unless she has an old man. "

"How would I know that?"

"She'll tell you."

I looked over at the pool where there were at least 20 naked women swimming, sun bathing or sleeping.

"Will, I'm going to be straight with you. We have a business that, let's say, is not exactly legal. So, we'd appreciate it if you were discreet."

"Why tell me?"

"You are going to find out anyway. Look around. Every body here is getting loaded."

I could see people smoking pipes, joints and doing lines of coke or crystal.

"We just want to party."

"Isn't it dangerous to bring me here?"

"I trust you. After last night, I know you're one whacked out dude. Let me give you the bottom line. If you did something stupid, we'd kill you, grind you into fertilizer and spread you in our garden. Anyway, let's take a tour."

He took me into the house. It was enormous. Eight bedrooms and in the kitchen was a Mexican cook making food. We went into the game room, which was equipped with two pool tables, a big screen television and arcade games that lined the wall. Bear opened a refrigerator and pulled out two beers. He reached under the T.V. and brought out a tray. He rolled a big joint, then chopped up two big lines on a mirror.

"This is coke. I hate crystal. You're up all night." He did half the line in one nostril and the other half in the other nostril. I followed his lead. Within a minute, I felt like I had drunk ten espressos.

"Here, this will take off the edge." He handed me a huge joint, after he had taken a big hit. I followed his lead except I coughed my brains out. He laughed.

"Good shit, huh?" I guzzled my beer down and he got me another. "Let's go. I want to show you the rest."

We smoked the joint as we walked, I was stoned out of my gourd. Everywhere we went, we would see 'The Lost Disciples' with the skeleton figure. Obviously, this was the name of their club.

"There are twenty of us that live here full time. Only the originals are in the house. We have maid service, a cook and a gardener/maintenance man. The rest stay in trailers. Next year, we're going to build another house. We just have to find a discreet contractor who can work with cash. The trailers were all hooked up to water, sewer and electricity. If you get too fucked up tonight, you can sleep in Weasel's trailer."

Bear pointed to the trailer on the very end. We went into a work shed that looked like a motorcycle shop. There were motorcycles in all stages of repair. A guy with long braided hair and full beard was working from his wheelchair on one of the bikes. Bear pulled out another joint, lit it and handed it to the guy in the wheelchair. He took an extra long hit and held his breath. He closed his eyes, said, "Mmmmmmmmm," then slowly exhaled. His eyes glassed over.

I held out my hand, "Will."

He shook my hand. "Jimmy."

Both of his legs were missing, one above the knee and one below. We smoked the joint. Bear went to the refrigerator in the work shed and got three beers, as well as a bottle of peppermint schnapps out of the freezer.

We all took long pulls off the schnapps bottle and drank our beers. Jimmy and Bear were talking about motorcycles, but I could barely hear them. I was toasted. After a while, it could have been two hours or two minutes, Bear showed me the warehouses. We did not go in. "Those are off limits."

A weird looking man wearing a long white coat and white pants came out the side door of the warehouse. "How's it going, Professor?" Bear yelled to him. The man took off his glasses, spun around three times to his left, once to his right, then went back in the door.

Bear shook his head, "Full on tweaker. He is going to need to be replaced. He was the best chemist we've had. But eventually they get on the shit and then they deteriorate. Did you know crystal causes schizophrenia?...true story. Hey, let's go party."

We headed back to the house. Bear stopped to talk to the maintenance man while I headed up to the pool. I was still ripped out of my mind. Even in this state I wasn't comfortable with the naked women. I guess I'm a prude at heart. I put on my sunglasses, sat in a lounge chair and attempted to desensitize myself. The sun started to set and the women, one by one, left and went into the house. A biker sat next to me and handed me a pipe. I have no idea what was in it. We passed it back and forth and he would occasionally fill it with what looked like clay. I later found it out was hashish. You could safely say I was immobile. I felt like I had been poured into my chair. My newfound friend got up without saying a word. I felt like I was a quadriplegic.

After a while, though I have no idea what that translates into in real time, Bear came and got me. "It's time to eat, Will." He pulled me out of my chair. There was a giant buffet prepared by the cook and her husband, who was also the gardener/maintenance man. This lady could cook. She had every type of Mexican food as well as steaks, spareribs, chicken, salads, potatoes, and homemade ice cream for dessert. I don't know whether it was all the dope, but I ate until my stomach hurt. What a spread! After dinner, most people headed for the game room. Drugs of all types were passed to me and I tried them all; at one point it didn't matter because I had reached a state of total vibration. I was humming like a transformer on an electric pole.

The next morning I woke up in Weasel's trailer. How I got there I have no idea. I rolled over in bed and looked at the back of a very large person. This person must weigh over 300 pounds, and his whole back was covered with tattoos. Some of the folds of fat made the tattoos hard to distinguish. I then realized I was naked. I slowly lifted up the blanket and saw he was naked. "Oh my God, I slept with a man!"

I tried to remember last night, but it was a total blackout. I had such a hangover that I couldn't really get a handle on it. My head was splitting. I felt nauseated and I had to piss really bad. The only way out of the bed was over the mountain of flab. I tried to climb over him, but my coordination wasn't awake yet and I ended rolling on top and then falling onto the floor.

"Hi, sweet cakes," she whispered. Thank God it was a woman, and what a woman. She must have been six feet tall. Each breast was bigger than my head and pointed south. She had tattoos on her breasts and her upper arms. Her hair was short and dyed blonde. Her face was pretty, but she was missing a tooth. After visiting the restroom, I sat at the edge of the bed. "I'm sorry I don't know your name."

"Well, it used to be Sweat Hog, but they now call me Coyote Arm."

"How did you get that name?"

"A coyote will chew it's leg off to get out of a trap. Any guy who wakes up in the morning and finds me in his bed laying on his arm wishes he could chew off his arm." She then let out an enormous and contagious laugh. If I weren't so hung over, I would have laughed. The most I could muster was a weak smile.

"Did we... you know.?"

She looked at me puzzled.

"Did we do it?"

She reached down to the floor and picked up a used condom and then another. She batted her eyes. "You were wonderful. In fact are you ready for another ride?"

"I'm not feeling too chipper this morning." Damn that Mr. Happy.

"I've got something that can cure that hangover, but only on two conditions. One...you do not tell Bear or anyone else what I gave you and two...we go for a ride." My head was pounding. This was the worst hangover I ever had. "Alright, but no ride unless my hangover is completely gone." I knew this wasn't possible, so I was safe.

She went into her purse and pulled out a little packet. She poured some on the counter top and made two little lines. "I'm not ready for any more coke," I said.

"This isn't blow. This is smack."

I slowly inhaled both lines. Within two minutes, my pain was gone.

"That's a miracle, what is that stuff." She did a couple of lines herself. "It's heroin. Don't say anything. The boys are down on this stuff."

She reached over and grabbed Mr. Happy, who snapped to attention. Coyote Arm smiled at me. "Let's rock and roll."

As I finished putting on my clothes, I looked at Coyote Arm, who had fallen back to sleep. I quietly closed the door to the trailer and headed for the house. The Mexican cook fed me breakfast. There were people sleeping everywhere on the couches and on the floor. Some were completely naked. In the morning light, it was not a pretty sight. I wandered over to the work shed where Jimmy repaired the motorcycles. He looked up from some part he was cleaning.

"Howzit?"

"I'm doing alright, I think."

"Crazy place, huh?"

"I've never seen anything like it."

"It'll mellow out after the party ends."

"When's that?"

"Probably a couple of more days." He answered.

"Hey, do you know a chick named Coyote Arm?"

His whole demeanor changed, he looked serious. He reached into a drawer and pulled out a 44-magnum handgun. "Did you ever see the movie 'Dirty Harry? Well, this is the same gun." He pointed it at my chest. I raised my hands.

"Tell me about Coyote Arm."

"I just met her."

"Did you screw her?!" I was breaking a sweat.

"Well?...DID YOU FUCK HER!!?!"

"Yeah." I mumbled. He shot three times in rapid fire. I fell backward over a stool and knocked a trash can flying. Jimmy started laughing uncontrollably. I put my hands on my chest, expecting gaping holes, but there was nothing. Jimmy was laughing so hard tears were running down his cheeks.

He gasped, "They were blanks."

"What kind of a weird joke is that?

"I pull it on everyone that bangs my sister."

# CHAPTER 4
# EL CAPITAN

Capitan Lorenzo Alphonso Baca was sitting in a squad car parked under a tree. He was eating corn tortillas with cheese and picante sauce. The Capitan pulled a cold cerveza out of his cooler that was sitting next to him on the seat and popped the cap off the bottle. Normally, the Capitan did not drive a squad car, but today he was waiting for the old fisherman, Arturo Cruz Miguel. Twice a week, Arturo drove to town to sell his fish. The Capitan was having a fiesta tonight and he needed some fish for his guests. Arturo always had the best fish. The Capitan was finishing off his beer when Arturo drove by in his old Chevrolet pick-up. The Capitan belched, threw his beer bottle out the window and started up his patrol car.

Arturo was not hard to catch since his pick up truck did not have a fourth gear, which forced him to keep his speed down. The Capitan waited for a nice level place to pull Arturo over before he turned on his red and blue lights. The Capitan slowly walked up to Arturo's truck, adjusting his gun belt under his tremendous belly and wiping his mustache with the back of his hand. "Buenas dias, Capitan Baca," Arturo said, "What can I do for you?"

Arturo knew exactly what the Capitan wanted, but he had to play the game, or the Capitan would get very angry. The Capitan took off his sunglasses and stared at the old man. Arturo removed his worn Denver Broncos cap and waited. Arturo's dog "Chupa" growled once from the back of the truck, then became distracted by a large iguana. Chupa was one quarter Doberman, one quarter Rottweiler and half Mexican mutt.

"Can I see the papers for this truck?"

Arturo reached into the glove compartment and handed the Captain a packet of papers. The Captain studied the papers pretending that he cared, then handed the papers back to Arturo. "Do you know why I stopped you, Senor Miguel?"

"For speeding?" Arturo said, holding back a smile knowing that his joke was going to cost him another fish.

"Please come to the back of your truck, so I can show you."

At the back of the truck, the Capitan pointed to the left tail-light that had a crack in it.

"Capitan, that tail light has been broken for twelve years." Arturo sighed.

"Let me have your driver's license. You can have it back when you pay the fine at the station."

Arturo looked at the Capitan and said, "Is it possible we can take care of this problem here without going to he station? I am a very poor man, but I do have some nice fish."

The Capitan watched as Arturo opened one of his four coolers of fish and pulled out two large Dorado. "Do you have a bag I could put these in, Capitan?"

"I have a cooler in my front seat."

"What a coincidence!" Arturo thought to himself. The Capitan sped down the highway.

Arturo got back in his truck and stared at the faces of Jesus, Buddha, and Krishna that he had taped to his dashboard. "Please, teach me patience and humility." he said as he looked at each face. As he drove, he began to chant," Thou art my life, Thou art my love, Thou art my sweetness, which I do seek. In the thought by my love brought, I taste thy Name, so sweet, so sweet. Devotee knows how sweet you are." Arturo sang his chant over and over again until he felt a peaceful calm. After selling his fish, Arturo visited his good friend Gilberto.

Gilberto's porch faced the highway and the two men rocked quietly watching the traffic go by. Chupa lay at Arturo's feet dreaming of big, fat iguanas. "Will your sons come to visit this year? "Arturo asked Giberto.

"I would like that very much, but it will most likely not happen. They are very busy in Los Angeles. Do you know, in the United States they have a law that you have to make over 50 pesos an hour? In one hour, you can make a day's pay. How is that possible? How can there be so many rich people? Arturo, didn't you work in California once?"

"Yes. People are in a big rush for everything, even insignificant things. They worship money as God and they will have others raise their children so they can make more money. They sacrifice their health for money, then they spend their money trying to get their health back."

"Speaking of God, who are those weird fellows in your truck next to Jesus?"

Arturo did not like to talk about his religious beliefs, it always became a debate.

"They are holy men. Did you know I heard once that if you took all the holy men and put them in a room, they would be in agreement because they all preached love. If you took all of the disciples of those holy men and put them in a room, they would kill each other in the name of religion." They both laughed. A big truck roared by and they watched it go over the hill.

"Where did you find these holy men?

"When I was in California, I became curious, so I studied at the library about all the holy men. I learned something from all the holy men."

"Arturo, what is the most important thing you learned?"

"It is very complicated, but mostly the holy men say to love God and man. You should love even your enemies. That a rich man is not the one that has the most, but needs the least. If you live too much for the future, you will live neither in the future or the present."

Gilberto thought loving your enemies was ridiculous, but decided it was not worth arguing over.

"How is Estaban's daughter doing?"

"It is very hard for her to live with her grandmother and me. She is young and we are old. Also, where we live she has no friends to play with because we are so far from town. At least she has her friends at school."

Gilberto slowly got out of his chair and went into the house. He returned with a pouch of tobacco and cigarette papers. He expertly rolled two cigarettes and handed one to Arturo. They leaned back in their chairs enjoying the quiet.

"I don't think I'll ever quit this horrible habit." Arturo exhaled a long stream of smoke.

"How is Isabella?" Gilberto was not going to let Arturo make him feel guilty about his cigarette.

"My wife and I have not had sex since Estaban and Herminia died."

"How long has it been?"

"Two and a half years. Most of the time I don't miss it, but sometimes I get very uncomfortable when I remember what it was like."

Gilberto went into the house and brought out a plastic container of Mescal. He offered it to Arturo, who declined. Gilberta took a mouthful and swished it through his teeth before swallowing.

Nasario, his neighbor, told him this would prevent cavities. Although he doubted it, he felt it might be possible.

"Arturo, are you afraid to die?"

"Well, since I have been studying the holy men, I feel safer but I have a lot to learn. A monk once said 'He had his bag packed', but what he really meant was that he was ready to go at any time. Right now, I feel I have found a bag, but it's not packed. Do you know what I am saying?"

"Yes. Tell me an inspirational story."

"I don't have a story, but I have a quote from a holy man in India, 'I am but a seeker after truth. To find truth completely is to realize oneself and one's destiny.'"

Gilberto pondered this for a moment. "But what is the truth?" Arturo shook his head.

"I do not know. If I find out, you will be the first to know."

Gilberto chuckled "You have always been my best friend." Arturo got up to leave.

"My supper will be getting cold if I don't go home now."

"Asta rapido, mi amigo."

"Peace be with you, Gilberto. Adios."

Arturo turned off the highway on to the dirt road to his house. He whistled for Chupa, who jumped out of the back of the truck and started jogging along side. Chupa was the best dog Arturo had ever had and he was grateful for his companionship. This was the time he always missed his radio, which had stopped working last rainy season. The road, which was heavily rutted, was not so tedious with music to listen to. It would take 45 minutes from the turn off to make it home. Arturo started singing a long chant to pass the time.

"O God beautiful, O God beautiful, at thy feet, I do bow, O God beautiful, O God beautiful, in the forest Thou art green, in the mountain Thou art high, in the river Thou art restless, in the ocean Thou art grave, O God beautiful, O God beautiful, at Thy feet, I do bow, O God beautiful, 0 God beautiful, to the serviceful Thou art service, to the lover Thou art love, to the sorrowful Thou art sympathy, to the yogi Thou art bliss, O God beautiful, O God beautiful, at Thy feet, I do bow. "

Half way down the road, Arturo saw an armadillo digging a hole. Chupa ignored it, he was only interested in the iguanas. Tomorrow I will come back and trap that armadillo. Arturo's mouth watered when he thought of how Isabella could prepare the meat marinated in her sauces. Tonight's supper would be leftover fish with rice, beans and tortillas and maybe that tomato in his garden that should be ripe today.

Arturo pulled his truck into a lean-to attached to the side of his adobe brick house. He looked at the two crosses in his backyard, the graves of Estaban and Herminia. In between the crosses was a shrine about four feet high with an opening in the middle. Inside the opening Arturo could see a candle burning, which meant Isabella had been to the shrine recently. She always lit a candle before praying. Estaban had been her last child and her favorite son. Ironically, Estaban had been Arturo's favorite too. Arturo bowed his head, made the sign of the cross and asked God that they may rest in peace.

Isabella was standing in the doorway waiting for him. "How much did that bandit, Alfredo, give you for the fish?"

Arturo handed her the money, which she promptly counted.

"You're joking. This is all?"

"My two best fish went to the capitan."

"The capitan is a robber and a disgrace! I hope he burns in hell!"

Arturo was glad she wasn't directing her wrath at him. He sat in his rocking chair and looked out the window trying to forecast tomorrow's weather from the cloud formations.

"You smell of tobacco have you been at Gilberto's?" Arturo continued staring out the window. "The generator's broken again, which means the pump is not working, which means I have no water, which means you have no supper."

Arturo walked past her out the door to the shed that held the generator. Arturo had a love hate relationship with the generator. He loved to hate it. Arturo had fixed the generator so many times, he knew every piece by memory. He found the problem immediately. The spark plug wire had vibrated loose.

The generator was a necessity for many reasons: It kept his freezer cold for storing his fish and it made the ice which he needed to transport the fish. The generator also ran the pump from his well and provided electricity for the house. Arturo knew that he had to run the generator at least twice a day to keep the freezer cold, as well as pump enough water into his holding tank on top of the house. Gravity from the tank gave the plumbing enough water pressure. Only on fiesta did he use electric lighting in the house, the rest of the time, it was kerosene lamps.

When Arturo walked back to the house, he could hear his wife yelling at Cecelia, his granddaughter. After Estaban's car accident, his wife had become very impatient, everything made her mad or sad. She had stopped shaving her legs and under her arms and sometimes she didn't shower for days. He felt differently about her now, but he didn't want to admit it because she had been a good wife and mother for many years. Arturo went back in the house and turned on the pump. Cecelia had gone into her room, so the fighting had stopped.

"Arturo come here so I can put the lotion on your hands." Isabella sat at the table with a jar of lotion. Arturo sat next to her with his hands held out. She rubbed a homemade concoction on his callused hands. The wind, sun and sea had turned his hands to leather and if he did not use lotion, they would crack and split open. Once they cracked, they would bleed and he could not get the cuts to heal for weeks. Arturo looked at Isabella. He could not help but remember how he used to feel Isabella's love for him as she rubbed his hands but that seemed like a long time ago. Now, it was just another task for her. To him, she was still beautiful. He squeezed her hand. She looked up to see him looking at her. "Arturo, I am very tired and your supper is almost ready. Maybe tomorrow."

Arturo nodded and squeezed her hand again. He went out to shut off the generator and make sure the chickens had enough grain. He put food in Chupa's bowl, who was gone probably chasing an iguana, his favorite pastime. He fed the cats, which he didn't care much for, but they were a necessity to kill the rats and mice.

After supper, Arturo and Isabella sat on the porch in their rocking chairs, listening to a transistor radio that played sad Mexican ballads.

"Where is Cecelia?" Arturo asked.

"She is doing homework."

"Why must you fight with her? She is lonely here."

Isabella looked up from the shirt she was repairing. "She's a complainer, just like her mother was."

"Isabella please do not speak ill of the deceased." Arturo said, making the sign of the cross.

The next morning, Isabella walked into the kitchen and noticed Arturo had forgotten his lunch. She had packed some tortillas, a piece of cheese and a cucumber in a bag and left it by the front door. It made her sad to think he wouldn't have a lunch, almost everything made her sad. She went in and woke up Cecelia for school. Isabella put bread with butter and a cut papaya on the table for Cecelia's breakfast.

Their house was simple but functional. It had a cement floor with Saltillo pavers, adobe block walls for insulation and a traditional clay tile roof. Arturo and his friend, Florencio, had built it. The house had three bedrooms, a dining area and a kitchen. To the side of the house was a large palapa with a table and chairs and a few hammocks, which were used when the weather was too hot to stay inside. There was no glass in the windows and the breeze off the ocean would filter through the house, keeping it cool. The house sat half way up a little ridge above a small bay with a white sandy beach. Arturo had found this place when he was searching for fishing spots.

Arturo had worked ten years in the United States to save the money to buy his two acres of land. He worked in the vegetable fields in California miles from his beloved ocean, dreaming of the day he could go home. He also learned English from one of the other workers. This enabled him to read the many American books on religion. Arturo and Isabella had raised four children in this house. It was never lonely when the family had been together but now Isabella resented the remoteness. It took an hour and a half to get to the nearest town, half the trip on a dirt road.

Isabella made sure Cecelia had not fallen back to sleep. She then shook out Cecelia's clothes looking for scorpions. Scorpions were a part of life here and they all had been stung. The sting was serious and sometimes could even cause death.

Isabella hung the clothes over the back of a chair and went outside to the graves. The sun was just coming up turning the clouds in the east pink. The wind was causing the palm trees that surrounded the house to rustle and rock. Isabella knelt before the shrine and cleaned off the old wax from last night's candle. She made the sign of the cross and lit a new candle. Isabella pushed the candle way back into the opening in the shrine so the wind would not blow it out. She said a quick prayer for Arturo, this wind could cause rough seas. She said a long prayer for Estaban and grudgingly a short prayer for Herminia.

Isabella had not approved of Herminia with her mini skirts and high heels. She told Estaban that Herminia looked like a whore, he only laughed. Isabella had wanted Estaban to go to college in Mexico City just like his older brother, Chuy, who now taught school in Guadalajara. Estaban was a good student and a handsome boy.

Isabella, like most mothers, wanted a better life for her son. That changed when Herminia got pregnant. After the wedding, Estaban dropped out of school and worked with his father.

Arturo was grateful for the help and companionship. Isabella was stuck at the house with Herminia, who complained constantly. It was too hot or too cold, too far from town, too boring, too lonely. Isabella could tolerate her after the baby came because there was a lot to do and because Herminia's attitude had improved.

On Cecelia's twelfth birthday, Isabella asked if Arturo would consider building a separate house for Estaban and his family. The next night Estaban and Herminia were dead, killed in a car accident. They had gone to town for supplies but a half-mile from the dirt turn-off, they were hit by an old semi truck that blew a front tire. They both died instantly. The truck hadn't been serviced in three years and the driver was too poor to buy good tires. The driver of the truck lost his right arm and part of his right foot.

Isabella and Cecelia cried constantly for a month. Arturo's pain was deep, but he didn't feel it was appropriate with all the grieving coming from Isabella and Cecelia. Sometimes when he was out at sea, he would cry. Chupa would come over to him and lick his face.

Isabella got up from the shrine. She would be back later to say a rosary. The wind gusted. She looked out to the ocean and thought about Arturo in his little boat. He was such a good man and she had loved him dearly, but something in her had died when Estaban was killed. She felt emptied of her capacity to love. It made her sad because Arturo deserved more; he had always been a loyal husband and good father. Sometimes she thought he might be better off if she had died instead of Estaban.

It was time to walk Cecelia to the paved road to catch the bus to town for school. As they walked past the shrine Cecelia made the sign of the cross and kissed the small crucifix around her neck. The crucifix was her mother's. Isabella knew it wasn't fair to have resentment towards Cecelia. She was not a bad girl. Isabella walked ahead of Cecelia, carrying a machete. They walked along a path that cut across two small hills and through an arroyo. This was the shortest way to the paved road, but there was no way a car could come this way. This route took 1 5 minutes.

Isabella would use the machete to knock down the spider webs that had been made the night before. The spiders were very industrious and every morning had made new webs. Occasionally, she would chop an errant tree limb out of the way. They waited for a boa constrictor to slither by. It was not unusual to see large creatures this time of year. It was the end of the dry season and the animals were in search of water. In the rainy season Arturo would have to come out and help machete because Isabella could not keep up with the vegetation. Some of the vines could grow a foot a day.

As they waited for the bus, Isabella looked at Cecelia. She was fourteen and a half and was starting to become a young lady. She had been having her period for two years. Her breasts were starting to grow. She was very immature for her age and didn't seem interested in boys. Isabella was glad that she was different than her mom in that regard. Cecelia was glad to see her friends from school on the bus and hurried up the stairs. Isabella watched the bus leave a trail of exhaust around the corner, then headed home.

Arturo had left home two hours before dark. He was half way to his destination when the wind got bad. He was planning on doing some long line fishing, but the wind changed his plan. Long line fishing consisted of dropping a weight with a float on a rope. The float was tied to another rope that could run for two miles. That line also had floats, usually plastic soda bottles, with baited fish lines every ten feet. The end of the rope was attached to another float that was attached to a weight.

All day long Arturo would hand pull himself down the long line, collecting fish and baiting the hooks. Today, he changed his plans. He would fish with his hand line. He knew of a shelf 10 miles south that should have some fish. Arturo felt comfortable in his 22 foot panga. He had built a little cover in front for Chupa so he could get out of the sun.

Arturo had always wanted to be a fisherman just like his Uncle Francisco. He didn't mind the hard work and he was at peace when he was out to sea. His Uncle had been a great fisherman, but then again, there had been more fish. Either from greed or necessity, the waters had been over fished. Arturo still had his secret spots, but it was a lot harder now to make a living.

Arturo thought about Isabella. He prayed to God to some-how help her become herself again. Arturo started to sing one of his chants. Chupa looked up at him without lifting his head, the chants always put Chupa to sleep.

"Door of my heart, open wide I keep for thee...Wilt Thou come, wilt Thou come? Just for once come to me?...Will my days fly away without seeing thee, my Lord?...Night and day, oh night and day, I look for Thee night and day." Arturo continued his chant over and over again.

After four hours of fishing, Arturo caught 2 chula, which were in the mackerel family and that he would give to Chupa and the cats, 2 Dorado, which he would take to market and a Washenango, which was like a red snapper that he would have for dinner.

Arturo put on his mask and fins, then dropped over the side of the boat. He found two conchs that he also would have for dinner. As he put the conch into his dive bag, he saw a movement in one of the cre-vasses. After getting a breath of air, he went back down and reached into the crevasse. It was a lobster, so he grabbed it. An eel came out with it its muscular head baring razor sharp teeth. Arturo said to the eel," Do not be concerned my friend. I will do you no harm." Arturo knew that if the eel bit him, he would be in grave danger. They were so strong they could hold a diver down until he drowned. About the only way you could get free is to cut off their head. The eel slowly re-treated back into its hole. Arturo nodded. "Gracias."

The ride home was very bumpy and the spray from the bow was causing Arturo's eyes to sting and get red. Chupa slept through all but the biggest swells, which caused the panga to get air under the bow and crash down with a thud. Tonight, I am going to read the Bhagavad Gita, Arturo thought. Arturo found the eastern religions fascinating and was drawn to his studies like he had been drawn to the sea. He was more interested in the original message from the gurus than in the rituals that followed.

Arturo cleaned his boat and his fish. He put the Dorado in the refrigerator and gave the other fish, conch and lobster to Isabella. Arturo sat under the palapa and tried to meditate, but he was restless. Arturo meditated for twenty minutes twice a day. He had also learned some basic yoga when he was in the United States. He pulled out his mat and went through his regimen. Isabella had never got used to this foolishness, but she had stopped criticizing him about it. The yoga helped Arturo stretch and relax his tired muscles and gave him an inner peace. He went inside, showered, fed the animals and ate dinner.

Cecelia talked nonstop about her friends at school during the meal. An hour after dark, Arturo was in a deep sleep, the Bhagavad Gita on his chest. Before he fell asleep, he had read a passage that stated," God does not appear necessarily through the lips of a form in a vision, or a materialized human body, but may intimate words of wisdom through the medium of the devotee's awakened intuition." Arturo had smiled at this. He liked to feel he could find God through his own devices.

Arturo and Cecelia were sitting on buckets, pulling weeds out of the garden. The soil was soft and rich and the weeds came out easily. Arturo was pulling out four weeds to Cecelia's one. Isabella sat on the porch, mending clothes and listening to the radio. Chupa lay in the shade with Isabella. Cecelia and Arturo were wearing tattered straw hats to shade them from the blistering sun.

"Grandfather, do you think we will ever move to town?"

"Do you think town could match this beauty?" His gaze swept the little bay with the white sand and the green blue water.

"Town has people and things to do."

He looked at her and smiled. "What? You don't like being with your grandfather?"

"Grandfather, I'm serious. Would we ever move?"

"I want to tell you 'yes' to make you happy, but the answer is 'no.'"

After a long silence Arturo, touched her hand. "Cecelia, in a few years you will be going off to college. After that you will settle down with a nice man and raise a family. Eventually you will remember this place and you will think of it and your grandparents fondly. You will even wish that you could come back and be here, but you won't be able to. So why not enjoy being here now?"

"Going away to school scares me. I don't want to leave you and grandmother."

"Changes are always scary, but you are a smart, friendly girl. You will make friends fast and you will also be busy with schoolwork and parties."

A weed hit him in the head. He looked up with mock surprise and indignation.

"Why is grandmother so cross with me, grandfather?"

Arturo frowned. "Cecelia, do you believe your grandmother loves you"

"Yes."

"Your grandmother is still suffering over your parents. Everyone handles heartbreak differently. For some reason, this pain has latched on to her and she can't let go. I pray every night for her to be released. Some day, she will be finished with it. Can you please be patient with her?"

Cecelia nodded her head. "What about your pain?"

"I feel it everyday, but life is for the living."

"Tell me a story."

"Alright. But if it is a good story, will you sing a chant with me?"

"Grandfather, the chants make no sense."

"They make me feel good."

"Okay, but only if it is a good story."

"This is a true story that happened over fifty years ago in India, there was this man named Gangi, I think that was his name." Arturo took off his hat wiped his face with a bandana and thought for a while. "No, it was Gandhi, that was his name. Anyway, this Gandhi fellow felt that if you took an eye for an eye, it would never end until everyone was blind. His philosophy was to return good for evil until the evildoer tires of evil. Now, the British ran his country, or maybe owned it. I'm not sure, except for the fact they treated the Indian people like dirt. Gandhi led a peaceful takeover of the country."

Cecelia had stopped weeding; Arturo wondered if this was why she wanted a story. "Listen while you work."

"How is it possible to have a peaceful takeover, grandfather?"

"It took a long time, many, many years. The Indians did not buy any more products from the British. They would commit acts of civil disobedience, but never with violence. The Indians loved their leader and even the British respected this man of God. One of the injustices of the British was their salt law. The Indians could only buy their salt from the British and the tax on the salt was equivalent to three days work for the common man. Gandhi decided in protest he would walk to the salt flats, which were twenty days away which was 240 miles.

All along the way, the peasants came out and joined him. At the salt flats, he was arrested for taking salt illegally. Gandhi told his followers that they would probably be beaten, but that they shouldn't resist, or even raise their hands to ward the blows. The police formed a line and the people came forward and were struck down without any form of resistance. Thousands were beaten, women too. The newspapers took pictures, and the world finally saw the injustice."

"The people would be beaten without fighting back? Isn't that stupid?"

"Cecelia, nonviolence is very powerful. Jesus said to turn the other cheek. If we resort to violence, aren't we the same as our enemies?"

Cecelia didn't answer.

"Anyway, when Gandhi was in jail, he would stop eating to get the British and the New Indian government to come to an agreement. He told them he would fast until he died. Neither side wanted to be responsible for his death. Eventually Britain realized they had lost control of the country and India became independent. The story is more complicated, but this all I can remember."

"What happened to Gandhi?"

"He never stopped working for peace. He said that he wanted the two religious groups in India to stop fighting and that he would fast in protest of their disagreements. One of the fanatics for one of the religions shot and killed Gandhi."

"Where did you learn all this, Grandfather?"

"Out of books in the United States. They have wonderful libraries. Well, was my story good enough?"

"The story is depressing. The man, this Gandhi, gets killed. He was against violence and yet he dies violently. Tell me another story. That story isn't good enough."

"Okay one more. This one is also about Gandhi." Arturo ignored Cecelia's groan.

"People would come to Gandhi for advice. A mother brought her child to Gandhi. She asked him to tell her son to stop eating candy. Gandhi told the mother that if she came back in two weeks, he would have an answer. The mother came back in two weeks. Gandhi looked at the child. 'Stop eating candy.' he said. The mother was upset. 'Why did we have to wait two weeks? Why didn't you tell him to stop before?' Gandhi looked at the mother.

"Because two weeks ago, I was still eating candy.'...do you get it? Gandhi couldn't tell someone to do something he wouldn't do himself!"

"I get it, grandfather."

"Now, will you sing with me?"

A nice breeze came in off the ocean and cooled down the temperature. Two Macaws landed in a tree behind them and squawked at each other like two old lovers. "Yes, but I want better stories next time."

Arturo started chanting and Cecelia joined in. She knew all of his chants, having heard them a thousand times. Arturo was always moved by her beautiful voice.

"Do not dry the ocean of my love with the fires of my desires, with the fires of my restlessness, for Thee I pine, for thee I weep, I'll cry no more, Thou mine evermore, Thee I find behind the fringe of my mind, hide no more, Lord, hide no more, leave me not, Lord, leave me no more!"

Isabella could hear them singing from the porch, she shook her head. Why can't he just be happy with being Catholic. What an odd man, she thought to herself. Chupa was having a dream about chasing something, so his paws were twitching and his lips were curling.

# CHAPTER 5

# DOWN THE RABBIT HOLE

Yeah, Rosemary's my sister. Did she do any junk?"
"What's junk?"
"Heroin."
"You're not going to shoot me, are you?"
He smiled. "No, that joke's over."
"Let me put it to you this way, she asked me not to say anything."
He shook his head. "She'll never kick that shit. Did you know she has a Ph.D. in Sociology from the University of Arizona?"
He rolled a joint, lit it, took a big hit, and passed it to me.
"Is there any hypocrisy in this?" I held up the joint.
"You don't know too much about drugs, do you?"
"I smoked weed when I was in high school. There were guys doing speed on the jobs. Ya' know, tweakers, but I never tried it."
He took a big hit and exhaled slowly. "Let me run it by you. It's all addictive. Marijuana is the least dangerous, unless less you get into the real powerful strains. Even then, you will just become lackadaisical. You never get violent. You can definitely lose your ambition. Then there's Hash and Opium, which are stronger than weed. The real dangerous drugs are the chemicals; methamphet-amine, also known as crystal, crank, or speed, is what they make in

the warehouses. Dangerous stuff! A lot of tweakers become violent. Cocaine, also known as blow, coke, devil dust, is very addictive, and quite frankly, a very overrated drug. Crack, which is cocaine in rock form that you smoke, gives you a high that lasts for a few minutes, then leaves you jonesing for more. People will sell their souls for that shit."

"Then there's the psychedelics, LSD, mescaline and PCP; only the hippies do that crap. It makes you way weird. And then, there's the big daddy of them all, heroin, also known as smack, junk, shit or 'H.' Once you're strung out, you are highly motivated to use more, otherwise you get sick. The irony is, after a while taking the drug doesn't make you high, it just stops you from getting sick. These drugs snatch up lives and spit them back out wrecked. Take my sister for instance, she was a straight 'A' student and also lettered on the girls basketball team until she started screwing around with the chemicals. She had a good job lined up, but never showed up."

I passed him the joint. He picked a roach clip out of his tool bucket and attached it to the end of the joint. "Why did she do it?"

"Well, she had problem finding men her height, so she hooked up with this loser, a guy named John Maynard. He was a good-looking guy and he was taller than her and he slowly introduced her to all the poisons. Heroin is her favorite, but she'll do any drug, anytime."

"What happened to her boyfriend?"

Jimmy wheeled over to the refrigerator and got a couple cans of beer. He tossed me one.

"Last I heard he was in jail, but I'm not sure. Bear told him if he ever sees him around here he'd kill him." Jimmy went back to cleaning a carburetor. "Hey, can I give you a hand?" I asked.

"Sure. See those chains? I need to get all that grime off them. You can use that solvent and that bucket over there." He put in a Bob Dylan tape. We worked in silence for a while, listening to the words...."Once upon a time you dressed so fine, do the bumping

87

jive, in your prime, didn't you? People called, say beware doll, you're bound to fall...you thought they were all kidding you. You used to laugh about, everybody that was hanging out. Now you don't talk so loud, now you don't seem so proud, about having to be scrounging your next meal. How does it feel? How does it feel, to be without home, like a complete unknown, like a rolling stone?"

He looked up. "So what's your deal?"

"I'm cruising."

"Give me the unauthorized version."

"Well, I killed my fiance's lover, so I'm a little confused."

"You didn't catch them in the act, did you?"

"Yeah."

"I'm glad you killed the son of a bitch. Shoulda' killed her too."

I avoided looking at his stumps. "What about you?"

"Well, at one time I was one tough hombre. I could out run, fight, fuck, jump, eat, ride, and drink any man in Arizona. Then I hit the back of a semi trailer one night when I was wasted out of my mind and woke up without my legs. I would have committed suicide if I could those first few months, but eventually with some therapy, I got past it. Motorcycles were my passion. Now I can't ride."

Dylan's music in the background filled in the gaps. "You know, Will, until it happens to you, you could never imagine what it's like to be a crip, or as the politically correct say, physically challenged. I took pride in the fact that I was a bad ass. Now anybody could kick my butt. I lost my identity. It wears on you. I hate sympathy. Hey, I got a joke for you this guy's jogging down the beach and he comes across this pathetic chick in a wheelchair who waves him over. She says to him, 'I've never been hugged.' So he thinks what the hell and gives her a hug. The next day he jogs down the jetty and at the end of the jetty is the same girl and she tells him,'I've never been kissed.' So he thinks this is a little too much, but he kisses her. The next day, he jogs on the pier and at the end of the pier is the same chick and she says, 'I've never been fucked.' So he picks her up and throws her off the end of the pier and says, 'Now you've been fucked!'"

Jimmy howls at this joke. I am disgusted, which is what makes it so funny to him. "Will, have you ever ridden a hawg?"

"Nope."

"It's the greatest feeling in the world. The wind is in your face and a powerful machine between your legs. Damn, it's good!"

Jimmy pulled out his stash bag and started rolling another joint. "We should make you a scooter." he said.

He handed me the joint and I took a big hit. I was becoming familiar with the high.

I finished cleaning the chains.

"What's next, Jimmy?"

"See those gas tanks and fenders. They need to be sanded for painting. These guys like to have nice paint jobs. We're talking forty coats of lacquer, all hand sanded."

He showed me the technique and I started sanding.

"Do you have a girl, Jimmy?"

"Before the accident, I was in love with a beautiful blond with big tits and a tight ass, but I chased her away after I lost my legs. She was in love with the old Jimmy. I got angry every time I saw her, she needed a man, not a crip.

She swore she loved me, but that was bullshit because I didn't even know who me was then and I sure as hell didn't love me. How could she? Now, I'm sort of in a Catch 22. If a girl likes me, I lose all respect for her, and obviously, I don't have a chance with the ones that don't like me. The ones that piss me off are the ones that want to take care of me. I don't need a mother. So, I smoke my dope, listen to Bob and bang a few of the whores that hang out. Could be worse."

I pondered this while I worked and listened to the music..."You got a lot of nerve to say you are my friend. When I was down you just stood there grinning. You got a lot of nerve to say you gotta' a helping hand to lend... you just want to be on the side that's winning. You say I let you down, you know it's not like that. If you're so hurt, why then don't you show it? You say you lost your faith, but that is not where it's at. You have no faith to lose and you know it."

I looked at Jimmy struggling in his wheelchair to change a tire.

"Do you have fake legs?" He pointed to the corner. There were two prostheses with arm canes that have elbow holders. "I use them occasionally, but they hurt my stumps. This chair is state of the art and it's easier for me to work on the bikes."

I sanded for a couple of hours, then went to get some lunch for Jimmy and me. In the kitchen. I met a clean-cut guy named Howard, who was very friendly and wanted to make sure I was having a good time.

When I got back I asked Jimmy, "Who's Howard?"

"Howard's the brains and Bear's the muscle. Howard is the CEO. Let me clue you in on a couple of things. There is a lot of money here, and some of it's legit. Howard has fish canneries in Canada, some real estate companies, some computer shit, stocks and bonds, and a few taverns. Let me tell you, Will, the less you know, the better. Wherever money's involved, there's always going to be problems. Especially if the money has an illegal source, if someone wants to take you over or rob you, what are you going to do? Call the cops? So you need protection, like soldiers.

Some of the guys in the club are killers, real psychos who do what Bear tells them without questions. As long as they are fed, given their drugs, maintain their scooters, and have a little pocket change, they'll do what they're told. One of the problems is some of these assholes get strung out on the product and become really tweaked. Bear has to kick them out of the club. Bear also hates heroin because guys will start stealing to keep up with their habit.

That's why it's a banned substance. Rosemary would probably get kicked out if Bear knew she was using."

Jimmy and I took a break and went up the swimming pool to check out the T and A. Some young girl was having sex with a crusty looking biker over by the poolside bar. Jimmy shook his head and laughed.

"It's weird how many chicks have a fantasy about balling a biker."

We drank some beers and smoked a couple of joints, we both turned down the lines of coke and crystal that were passed our way.

Jimmy told me it was time for his siesta. So I walked with him to his trailer. "You know, Will, you're safe here as long as the party's going but watch out after that. We're not as rigid as some of the other clubs with our rules, initiations and flying our colors. A lot of that shit is outdated but believe me, these guys are dangerous, especially a guy that goes by the name of Dragon. He has a long braided ponytail like mine, an ugly goatee, and always wears a bandana with an oriental dragon. He likes to fuck with people."

"What about Weasel? When will he be back?" I asked.

"He's got another two to four before he comes up for parole. He got busted for possession and firearms for his third offense."

I went into Weasel's trailer and was surprised to find a pretty extensive paperback library. I started reading "Lonesome Dove" and drifted off to sleep.

Jimmy and I worked on the bikes again in the afternoon. We smoked pot and we talked as we worked. The rest of the night was pretty much the same, except I gave the partying a night off and read in my trailer.

When I showed up at Jimmy's work shed the next morning, a lot of the people were gone. They had left late last night. The rest were in some form of packing or preparing to pull out.

"Party's over?" I asked Jimmy.

"Yup. I asked Bear if you could hang out and work with me. He didn't have a problem with it, but he said stay away from the warehouses."

"That's cool. Bear said something about building another house. I could do that if you got me the material."

Jimmy talked to Howard and Bear. They were stoked. They drew up a sketch of what they wanted. It was pretty basic. There were three bedrooms, dining room, rec room, kitchen, three bathrooms and a couple of fake walls for storing weapons. I could do it all with some helpers, but I needed someone to do the plumbing and the electrical. They had a plumber and an electrician in town, who they trusted.

Howard spared no expense. He bought me a new transit to level my forms for pouring the foundation. Two of the bikers had construction experience and they worked with me. I really wasn't used to working stoned and drinking beers, but that was the MO on this job. The job went at half speed. Since Howard and Bear had nothing to compare it to, they were real happy with the progress.

Sometimes after work, I would do heroin with Rosemary. I loved that shit. It made me feel great and helped me get past all my problems. I was missing Danni. I also hated her for what she did. Luckily, I had the house to build. That kept me occupied.

I decided to put a hip roof on the house with some dormers to spruce it up. Instead of buying trusses, I cut in all the rafters. This was old style, nobody appreciated how much skill it took. I put in a cathedral ceiling in the living room.

Bear and Howard came by one day when I was sheathing the roof.

"Damn! It looks good, Will. Where you'd learn all this?" Howard yelled to me. "From Ray Bartkowski."

"Who?"

"It's not important. How do you like those dormers?"

"They look killer. I wish you had built the other house. Anything we can do for you?"

"I have a list for the roofing material. We will need it loaded day after tomorrow."

"No problem. Keep up the good work."

I watched them walk off. I pulled a vial of coke out of my nail bag. I unscrewed the top, put the little coke spoon in and did a couple of toots. That, of course, made me want to drink a beer and have a cigarette. After I finished my beer, I needed another toot. Luckily, it was close to quitting time, so I just headed over to Rosemary's.

The roofing took forever. We put on a shake roof. The cedar smelled great, but I got bored with it after the second day. I'm about half the speed of a professional roofer when I'm sober. I was never sober, so it took a week and a half to lay the shakes, and that was with two helpers. I put some nice redwood siding on the exterior. Howard had to buy me some more tools. He didn't care.

I refused to paint or put in the insulation. The fiberglass from the insulation will make you really itchy. Howard had some flunkies do the insulation and stain the siding while I hung drywall. I used those same flunkies to sand the drywall and paint the interior. I hung baseboard while the plumber and electrician did their finish work. All it needed was carpet.

The cabinets in the living room had a hinge in the center and wheels on the ends. Behind the cabinets were the secret storage walls. The cabinets pivoted on the hinge and rolled away from the wall exposing the secret storage space. You could hide an arsenal back there, which they did. You could never tell by looking at the cabinets.

Howard and Bear were very happy. They gave me a big bonus. I gave it to Rosemary to buy some stash. I told Howard and Bear I was going to take some time off. I felt like getting fucked up.

A couple of weeks passed in a haze of smoke, liquor and more than an occasional line. Occasionally Rosemary and I were getting loaded on smack, which was my favorite. After a line of junk, I would drift off into a world without pain or concern. I could even reminisce about Danni without getting pissed off.

One day after lunch, I passed out on a lounge chair by the pool. Somebody kicked the bottom of my shoe. I opened one eye and saw four guys standing over me. The guy who had kicked me wore a bandana with a dragon on it.

"Who the fuck are you?" he snarled.

I tried to play it cool and pretended to go back to sleep. He kicked me again, harder.

"I'm talking to you, asswipe."

I sat up and rubbed the sleep from my eyes.

"Bear said it was cool that..."

He interrupted me. "Bear ain't here now, sweetheart. How do I know you ain't a narc?"

"Is Jimmy here?"

"Who cares? Do you need someone to rescue you?"

His buddies laughed at this. Everybody knew where this was going. Either I fight him, or back down.

"Did you have something in mind?" I asked him.

"Yeah, I want you for my bitch."

I took off my shirt, I hate it when I ruin my shirts.

I looked at him and said, "So you want to have sex with me. Is it because I'm so good looking, or do you have homosexual tendencies?"

He started circling me flexing his arms. I knew he was going to be a street fighter, so I prepared for his first flurry. He charged me with a wild assortment of punches and kicks; one of them caught me on my scarred eyebrow and opened it up again. His compadres were whooping it up and they could sense a quick victory.

I stayed mostly defensive while he repeatedly charged me. I waited until he was winded and I moved in. I methodically jabbed as I bobbed and weaved. I could tell he was surprised at my skill. Every punch he threw now, he telegraphed. I would avoid and then counter punch. Hard. I could have taken him out a couple of times, but I was enjoying this. His buddies were silent now. The only sounds were heavy breathing, the whacks as fists hit flesh and the grunts of exertion.

I was really starting to loosen up as I took Dragon to school. His eyes were starting to glaze over. He took another wild swing at me, which I side stepped. I then moved in with a jab to his solar plexus, a jab to his face, then a straight right and a monstrous uppercut that I started somewhere near my shoe tops. The uppercut hit his jaw with a loud crack. His eyes rolled back. Homerun! Amazingly, he wobbled on his feet for a few seconds, then started slowly going down. I couldn't resist and yelled, "Timber!!"

He fell flat on his back. Dust flew up into the air all around him and slowly drifted back down. I looked at his amigos. They were smiling and shaking their heads, then, one by one, came over to shake my hand and pat me on the back. I saw Jimmy in the background, who he gave me the thumbs up sign.

Two of the boys dragged Dragon towards the house, where one of the girls could tend to him. The others sat around me drinking and smoking. They rehashed the fight over and over again. Apparently, a guy named White Dog, who had gone to veterinary school, sewed up my eyebrow. I didn't let on, but it hurt like hell. I wanted to yell every time he jammed me with the needle.

I had two broken knuckles on my right hand. I soaked them in a bucket of ice. About two hours later, Dragon came out of the house with a girl under his arm to assist him. He was pretty wobbly. His face was swollen and his chin was discolored. He stopped by my chair. "You're a fucking dead man," he mumbled.

The other bikers couldn't help but snicker when he turned his back.

The next few weeks were pretty uneventful. Jimmy and I worked on the bikes and started building one for me out of spare parts. Jimmy was really excited about it and it was all he wanted to talk about. Lucky for me, Dragon was sent out of town on business, or we would have tangled again. Jimmy gave me a handgun and a large knife to keep in my trailer in case Dragon came by unannounced.

My motorcycle was finally finished and looked like what it was, a conglomeration of old parts. Jimmy was proud of it and so was I. The tank and fender were still primer gray because we had been too busy to paint them. I had ridden dirt bikes as a teenager, but this was a different story. These bikes were heavy and they hauled ass. I practiced riding on the dirt road to the compound.

I have to admit that it was very stimulating to have that much power. Jimmy put on some counterfeit plates. I asked him if he could do anything with my truck in case they were looking for me. He said, "No problem." He changed the plates from California to Arizona. He then called down to the DMV and a guy put them into the computer along with my motorcycle.

"Howard and Bear own a guy at the DMV, as well as a sheriff in the local station. The sheriff gives us advance notice, so they can truck all their stuff out before a bust happens. Even if we don't get advance warning, there's a watchman at the turn off that gives them forty five minutes to flush any incriminating evidence down some large drains. And they have some storage tanks in the desert that they can hide stuff in. The sheriffs haven't been out here in two years because every time they come there's nothing here. It's amazing what money can do."

Most of my days were spent working with Jimmy and riding my scooter. I made Jimmy take $500.00. It should have been more, but he grudgingly took that. After a while, I was burned out on all the biker chicks, all they cared about was the cocaine. They could do it twenty-four hours a day, everyday. They were extremely boring and most of them were not that hygienic, which was a real turn off. I would usually hang out with Rosemary in the evenings, unless she had a date. We would screw occasionally if we were really loaded, but we were mostly platonic. She had a brilliant mind and was well read. She was taking a lot of speed to lose weight. She was letting her hair grow out. I liked her in a puzzling sort of way. I stayed too stoned to analyze it. She also had the smack, which I loved.

One morning, she asked me," Do you want to shoot it?"

I hate needles, but I have to admit I was intrigued. She pulled out an eyedropper with a needle attached to the end of it by a rubber band. She added water to the heroin in a large spoon. She then heated it from underneath with a lighter to boil out any impurities. Rosemary put a little ball of cotton in the mix and then drew the liquid through the cotton to filter it. She wrapped a bandana around her arm and forced a vein to bulge. I could see previous scars. She inserted the needle, and when blood flowed into the eyedropper, she let go of the bandana and squeezed the little bulb on the back of the eyedropper. She leaned forward and exhaled, "ahhhhhhhh."

I watched her for ten minutes as her head kept nodding forward uncontrollably. I was beginning to get concerned. When she opened her eyes, her pupils were dilated and she smiled a contented smile. I was now envious of her high and couldn't wait for her to do me. "That feels ssooo good." she sighed.

I had to wait another ten minutes before she was ready to get me off. She took apart her outfit and washed everything in alcohol. "Do not share a needle with anybody," she said as she rubbed her nose, which was a sign of an opiate high. For some reason the nose becomes numb and itchy. "That is how you can get AIDS or hepatitis."

I thought that was a little ironic, since I was going to share her needle. Whatever. She went through the same procedure of cooking up the heroin. I held the bandana to my arm. She injected me slowly. The rush was immediate. A warm fuzzy glow came over me and my head kept bouncing off my chest. I couldn't help smiling. This was the best feeling. I was in total ecstasy.

After a few minutes, I tried to stand up, but got extremely nauseated. I couldn't help it as I lost my lunch right on the floor. Some of it sprayed Rosemary, who was so high she started laughing, which made me laugh.

"I think I gave you a little too much," she giggled. I lay down on the bed and fell in and out of a stupor. Whenever I got up, I felt nauseated again. Hours or minutes passed between each time I closed my eyes. I couldn't tell. The day turned to afternoon, then dusk. I was still immobile. Rosemary was gone. I felt a little remorse that night, but I got past it with a joint and a few beers.

The next day I rode into town with Jimmy. Jimmy had a three wheel Harley rigged up so the gears and the brakes were on the handlebars. It was the closest way he could get to riding again. I loved my bike. When I was stoned and going fast, it was like flying. What a rush!

Jimmy needed parts from the motorcycle shop. I watched myself in a store window. I looked different. I hadn't cut my hair in three months and I had a four-day-old growth on my face. All I needed was a bandana and boots and I would look like a biker. I went to a store and purchased my black boots and a blue bandana. Might as well ride the horse in the direction it's going.

An old conservative couple gave me a disgusted look, which made me laugh. Then, I got a long hard gaze by a young yuppie mom. I translated her look into one of lust and strutted past her. On the way back, I got pulled over and was given a ticket for excessive noise from my tail pipes. Jimmy told me we would exchange the pipes for some legal ones when we got back, as soon as we'd get the ticket signed off, we'd put the old ones back on. He did it at least once a week for the other bikers.

Jimmy and I were pretty much caught up on work, so he decided to visit his brother in Colorado. I spent the time with Rosemary. We would shoot up every morning and lay around waiting to come down, so we could shoot up again. I had my own needle that I got from a clean needle drop in town, one of the benefits of AIDS. I would play with my outfit all day taking it apart, cleaning it and sharpening the needle.

By the time Jimmy got back, I was pretty strung out and had spent over a thousand dollars getting high. I didn't want Jimmy to know I was using, so I went cold turkey and had my first withdrawals. I had flu like symptoms, audio hallucinations, insomnia and was in a very uncomfortable agitated state. I was jonesing hard to get high, but I hung tough. It took three days to get over it with each day getting progressively better.

Jimmy came by a couple of times and I lied to him. I told him I had the flu. Jimmy and I went back to work. We smoked weed all day, but the temptress was always in the back of my mind. No matter how buzzed I was, I never lost my craving to get toasted on smack.

The club was going on a run to some old silver mining town that had a once a year blow out for the bikers. Bear told me I could go, but that I had to ride in the back of the pack, as I wasn't a member. Dragon wasn't happy I was going, but he couldn't challenge Bear.

I have to admit it was a bizarre feeling to be in a pack of thirty bikers with the Harleys making a deafening roar as we drove down the highway. People stared and gawked as we filed by in sets of two, with me bringing up the rear solo. I felt like I was part of a thundering herd of outlaws, like Jesse James or maybe Genghis Kahn. I was ready to pillage. I could see fear in people's eyes, it was intoxicating. I put on my badass face like a mask. I should have gone into acting.

The town had a couple of thousand bikers in it. What a zoo. They were all trying to outdo each other, and the chicks were just as bad. I parked my bike off the main drag because it was really a piece of crap compared to the beautiful machines on display. I was lucky to rent a room from an old man, who lived one street back from the action. Most people were camping in the park because the hotels were booked.

There was every drug imaginable available at the park. I started snorting junk the day I got there and kept away from Jimmy and Bear so I wouldn't get busted. On the second night of my binge, Bear came up to me. I was sitting on a bench watching the cast of characters on Main Street. "Hey, Will! I've been looking all over for you. The Easy Riders challenged us to a bare fisted boxing match. Me, you, and Dragon are going to represent us."

I looked away. I didn't want him to see my dilated pupils.

"I don't think so, Bear. I've been drinking pretty hard all day. What about Apache, or Zig Zag?"

"You're better than them. I'm not asking you, I'm telling you. Be at the big elm in the park in a half hour." He grabbed my arm for emphasis. "Do not let me down."

I sat back on the bench. Shit! How was I going to get sober in a half hour? I bought some speed. The quality was so bad that it made me puke. My nervous system was traumatized. I slowly walked over to the park shaking my head trying to clear out the cobwebs. There must have been a crowd of a couple hundred people in a giant circle buzzing with anticipation. Bear told me I would fight after Dragon. He pointed to a guy on the other side of the circle. The guy was a Neanderthal with a shaved head and tattoos that went from both wrists up onto his neck. He blew me a kiss and laughed.

I watched Dragon fight his man. They charged each other like two pit bulls, neither one using any defense. It didn't last long as

Dragon finished him off with a viscous upper cut. I guess he retained something from our fight.

I was next. I went out and started bobbing and weaving. My opponent stood and waited for me. I felt like I was in slow motion. He blocked my first jab and hit me with a tremendous shot to the side of my head that staggered me. He moved in and started pounding me with body shots. I had my head covered up, but he was doing damage to my kidneys. Occasionally, I would come out of my tuck and try to jab, but he would beat me to the punch. I was too slow.

The sounds of the crowd were going silent. I knew I was close to being knocked out. I rallied and decided to go for broke and just slug it out with him. We stood toe to toe and hammered each other. He was rocking me with each shot to my head. I could see his head snap on a couple of my punches, but my punches had no pop. It was too little too late. I could taste blood in my mouth, and my eyebrow was cut again, the blood stinging my eye.

He hit me with a roundhouse right that staggered me. My legs were Jell-0. I refused to go down. I threw a feeble left that missed big. He wound up and hit me with another roundhouse. I fell back into the crowd. They threw me back into the circle. I was swaying like a drunk at closing time. He came running at me relishing the coup de grace. I feebly held my fists up. Bear stepped between us.

"It's over!" Bear declared.

I put my hands on my knees as blood poured out of my nose and mouth. Jimmy came out with his canes. I grabbed a hold of his arm and he led me out of the circle. It was hard to see with the blood and sweat in my eyes. Dragon came up to us. "Nice going, you pussy."

I tried to say something, but I gagged on the blood in my mouth. Jimmy took me to the twenty-four hour clinic. I got fourteen stitches inside my mouth, twelve on my eyebrow, and four on the bridge of my nose. The doctor told me I probably had a concussion, "No drinking or drugs for 24 hours." Jimmy grabbed a twelve pack and took me to my room. After four beers and two joints I passed out.

The next morning I wanted to die. My face was so swollen I couldn't talk. I was in extreme pain and also hung over from my binge. I lay in bed moaning. Around ten o'clock, Bear came by. "How you feeling?"

"Fine." I lied.

"You don't look so good."

I had no comment.

"I brought you some pain pills and some Valium." He tossed them to me. I chased a couple of pain pills down with a warm beer.

"So, how did you do yesterday, Bear?" I whispered through swollen lips.

"I made him pay for what that guy did to you. I hear he had to go to the hospital."

Thankfully, the pain pills were starting to kick in. Bear handed me a wad of money. "We're heading back home. Here's some dough to rent a hotel room and recoup." He stood at the door for a second, then left.

Around noon, Jimmy showed up.

"You look like shit! "

"Thanks."

"Will, is something going on that you want to talk to me about? I saw you fight Dragon and you were much quicker."

He knew. I knew he knew. He wanted to see if I'd lie. "I had too much to drink."

He couldn't be positive I was lying, but I still felt like a chump. Jimmy always was straight with me. Now I had lied to him twice. He patted me on the leg. "At least you didn't go down."

"Yeah, if Bear hadn't stopped it, I would have killed that guy."

He smiled. I tried to smile, but my stitches wouldn't allow it.

"Will, be careful."

"What does that mean?"

He stood up using his canes.

"You, my friend, know exactly what I mean. Dance with the devil, and you may end up in hell. See you back at the ranch." He quietly closed the door. I took two more pain pills and a Valium and waited to pass out. It took exactly seventeen minutes.

The next day, the swelling had not gone down, but the pain wasn't as bad. Maybe the three pain pills and a Valium had something to do with it. I checked out of the old man's house and gave him an extra fifty, he was grateful. I checked into one of the hotels, which were now almost completely empty.

From my room I called Rosemary and asked her to come and see me and bring the you know what. I told her Jimmy was suspicious and to be discreet and also that I was buying, so hurry up. With the money I had and the money Bear had given me we were toasted for nine days.

We never left the room and we did not allow maid service. The room was covered with fast food wrappers, pizza boxes, empty beer cans, and overflowing ashtrays. I had enough money for two more days at the hotel. We used the rest of the pain pills and Valium to come down off our binge, but we were still hurting when we finally went home.

I went to Weasel's trailer and hid for a couple of days. I felt like shit. Rosemary had helped me remove the stitches when we were stoned, but I still had a couple in my eyebrow. I was removing them when Bear came by. "I need you tomorrow."

Bear wanted me to make a run with him in my pickup. What he needed was more chemicals to cook up his speed. He bought them in industrial size barrels. He wanted me to drive and be his back up, which meant carrying a sawed-off shotgun. Bear must have been on the shit because he never stopped talking as we drove.

"So, Will, here's the dealio. We're going to pull up to their rig, which has a pulley system in the back."

I asked, "What's a dealio?"

Bear rolled his eyes." You know, deal....dealio...whatever.... listen up."

I was jonesing for a line of smack.

"Anyway, these guys are going to have a rig with a pulley system."

"You already said that."

Bear looked at me for a while. "Are you fucking with me, cowboy?" I didn't know what I was doing besides jonesing. I shrugged my shoulders.

"So these guys will have a pulley system on their rig." Bear waited for me to comment, then continued.

"They..." I interrupted, "You already said that."

Bear turned and faced me.

"Just kidding," I said with a stupid grin.

Bear hesitated then laughed, "I knew you were fucking around."

I thought to myself, "I wonder if he'll think it's funny if I do it one more time."

I decided against it and went back to thinking about heroin.

Bear rattled on and on about the chemicals needed to make methamphetamine as though I cared. He was proud that he could remember these long names as though he was a scientist or something. He snapped me out of my day dreaming by putting his hand on my shoulder.

"This is important, Will. You have to stay behind the truck. If any shit goes down, I don't want them to have a clear shot at both of us." He popped open his briefcase. I could see it was full of stacks of one hundred dollar bills.

"They will load our truck first before I give them the money. They will have one guy doing the same thing as you, standing by their truck as a back up. Nothing to it. I've been doing business with these guys for three years. I don't expect any fuck ups, but in this business, you never know. If they decide to rip us off, they'll take me out first. You make sure you plug the guy with the gray hair. He's the boss. Then haul ass. Howard will take care of the rest of them."

I stood by the driver's door with the shotgun pointing up, resting on the side of the bed of my truck. I was mimicking their guy, who had his weapon pointed up. I think he might have looked cooler because he had on mirrored sunglasses. I did my best Clint Eastwood imitation. They were halfway through loading when my shotgun went off by mistake. I must have leaned too far down on the trigger. It sounded like an atomic bomb and caused everybody to pull out their weapons and point at the nearest person.

The boom was still echoing down the desert when Bear said, "Keep cool everybody. Will, talk to me." Bear had his gun pointed at the gray haired guy, who had his pistol pointed back at Bear.

"Sorry Bear, it was a little malfunction. My bad."

"False alarm, everybody. Back to work," Bear said as he holstered his Glock.

On the return ride, Bear was studying me. "Are you using junk?"

"No." I lied to his face. I could hardly wait to get back and get high.

"That was bush league back there. You could have gotten someone killed. You know, you gotta' earn your keep. Jimmy says you haven't been showing up for work. If you don't contribute, you gotta' go. This ain't welfare."

"Sorry, Bear. I'll work with Jimmy tomorrow."

I worked with Jimmy for a couple of days. Then Rosemary and I went bingeing. She was still using speed and was down to two hundred pounds. With her hair growing out and her weight loss, she was looking better everyday. We weren't having sex too much. We were too wasted.

# CHAPTER 6
# LOCO JEFE

*A* *Mexican once told a gringo, "Thank God for bribes, otherwise noth-*
*ing would get done."*

Lorenzo Alphonso Baca was police Captain of the small town of La
Cruz de Chakala. He was familiar with the system, having learned
it from his father, the former Capitan. The Capitan was the most
hated man in the town. He had his hand in every pocket, even the
mayor, who had been indiscrete one night at the cantina where
Capitan Lorenzo had one of his men strategically positioned with
a camera. The mayor's wife's family was well connected and bought
the election for their son-in-law as a wedding gift. They would not
be happy to see his head between some whore's legs.

On this particular day, the Capitan was selling marijuana to
two gringos. He had been doing business with them for 12 years.
Part of the deal was to show the gringos where the drug road-
blocks would be and the alternate routes. Troy, one of the gringos,
asked Lorenzo, "Are you sure this stuff hasn't been sprayed with
paraquat?"

Lorenzo smiled. "I can assure you, it has not." Truthfully, he
had no idea.

"Why has the price gone up and the quality gone down?"

"It has been a bad year for rain."

The other gringo, Peter, said, "Okay, then we'll see you next month."

Again Lorenzo smiled, "I am going to need you to pay me up front next time. No more credit."

Lorenzo had found new clients who would pay more money. The next time Peter and Troy came down, he would collect the money they owed him and the money they were bringing and arrest them. He would then collect a big settlement from their families to get them out of jail. Life was good.

The two gringos walked to their truck. The truck had a zodiac tied to the top of a camper shell. This is how they bypassed customs at the border. One drove the zodiac in the ocean with the drugs and one drove the truck. The truck picked up the zodiac in Imperial Beach.

Peter whispered to Troy, "How stupid does that prick think we are?"

Troy shook his head. "What a fucking idiot. Now we need a new source."

"Simple. Find another cop."

They laughed and slapped high fives.

The Capitan had other business with some of the local businessmen who needed to make their monthly payments. They waited patiently outside his office while he gorged himself on his lunch. The Capitan had big appetites for food, sex, money and liquor. His lunch consisted of a whole chicken, rice and beans with corn tortillas. He liberally splashed homemade salsa on everything then drank three cold beers and had a shot of tequila.

The businessmen were terrified of the Capitan. The Capitan had killed a man eight years ago who had tried to cheat him. One day, he disappeared, never to be seen again. The whole town knew he had been murdered, but were helpless to do anything. There were also rumors of random beatings and rapes, but no one would press charges.

After his collection, the Capitan went down to his favorite cantina for more tequila and Lucinda his favorite whore. Tonight, he would have to be home at a reasonable hour because his wife was fixing carne asada for dinner in celebration of his fourth daughters' up coming First Communion. Carne asada was his favorite.

Lucinda batted her eyes at the Capitan, but to herself she groaned, "Why does this smelly pig of a man have to like me? Why not Juanita? She has much bigger breasts or Marie? She is younger. I hate his horrible breath. It smells like his teeth are rotten. His sweat is slimy and his armpits smell like a sewer."

Lorenzo got a bottle of Tequila and sat in the front table of the cantina so everyone would see him when they came in. "Here is where you sit, lovely one." he said to Lucinda and pointed to his lap. Lucinda gave him a big hug and sat on his lap. She laughed loud at all of his ridiculous jokes, the whole time thinking about getting a job in the cantina in the neighboring town.

When half the bottle was gone, Lorenzo led Lucinda into one of the back rooms. He told Lucinda to bend over and put her hands on the chair. He lifted her dress, pulled down her panties. He then dropped his pants and entered her from behind. His thrusts were angry and meant to hurt. Lucinda could not be hurt by the Capitan's smaller than average member. She cried out as if she was in pain, which would inevitably arouse the Capitan to completion.

He smirked, "I am sorry if I hurt you."

"It was worth it, Lorenzo."

He gave her 30 pesos, which was half her normal fare. "Gracias, Capitan."

Lucinda was glad he would be leaving early, otherwise he would want to go again. If he drank too much, he might have difficulty. This always caused him to fly into a rage, which frightened

Lucinda. When he left, Lucinda thought to herself, "God bless his wife. She is a saint."

The Capitan revved his engine to scare the chickens out of his way so he could park his car in front of his office. The Commissioner's car was in the Capitan's normal parking spot. What could the commissioner want? He had already paid him for this month. This was not good. He was already in a foul mood. His wife informed him that his oldest daughter was going to be going to college, possibly in the United States. She would need money for tuition and living expenses. "Why does a girl need to go to college?" he thought to himself. Once she gets married, all she's going to do is have babies and clean house. When it came to the children, his wife was adamant and nothing would change her mind.

He found the commissioner sitting in his chair drinking some of his prized scotch and smoking one of his cigars. 'You arrogant ass.' he thought.

"Jose Luis, to what do I owe the honor of your presence?"

The commissioner was bald on the top of his head, but had a ring of black hair not unlike a Franciscan monk. He wore thick glasses and he was thin in stature, giving him a studious look. His eyes gave away his intensity.

"I have come to talk some business with you."

He took a sip of the scotch and savored the smoke from the cigar.

"You received your payment, correct?"

"Yes. That reminds me. Do you remember the kidnapping of Carlos Hernandez?"

The capitan sat down. "Yes?"

"My sources told me there was a 100,000 peso pay off. Is that correct?"

"That is correct."

"I only received 1000 pesos."

The capitan leaned forward in his chair. "That is because I only received 10,000 pesos", he lied. He had really received 15,000 pesos. "All I did for the kidnappers was let them hide in the hills. They wouldn't give me any more money."

The commissioner knew he was lying, but he couldn't prove it. "I have a job for you, Lorenzo. Tomorrow afternoon, two Guatemalans will come through town with a shipment of cocaine. You will apprehend them and take their cocaine and their money."

"Who do they work for?"

"Diego Rodriguez."

"The Diego that goes by the name of Lobo?"

"The same."

"Are you out of your mind? He is in the cartel. He will kill us in a heartbeat. I have heard that he is ruthless and tortures his enemies before he kills them."

"That's why you must eliminate the witnesses."

"Why would they even come through this town? We are an half hour from the main road." Lorenzo was hoping this would dissuade this foolhardy plan. He did not want any part of Lobo.

"That is the brilliant part of the plan. I will arrange road work and detour the traffic this way. After they pass, I will remove the roadblock. When Diego's men disappear, he will search for them on the main road. He will never even think that they would be back here." Capitan Baca had to admit it was a good plan.

"What will we do with the cocaine?"

Jose Luis smiled "I already have a buyer."

Lobo's men, Miguel and Jesus, had made this run numerous times before. They knew if they got stopped, they could either bribe their way out, or mention the name of Lobo and be on their way. The detour was not shocking to them. Mexican roads were always under construction. Jose fell asleep while Miguel drove. Capitan Baca pulled them over. They were right on schedule.

He casually walked up to the car; he knew that they were armed. "Buenas Tardes, Capitan." Miguel said with a smile.

"Can I see your driver's license?"

Miguel handed him his license with a folded 100 peso note underneath it. The capitan handed back the license with the money. Miguel shook his head. "My, this capitan is greedy" he thought. He handed him the license with a 200 peso note underneath it.

"Do you know it is against the law to bribe a police official? I must ask both of you to get out of the vehicle."

The Capitan pulled his gun and made them lay spread eagle on the ground. He frisked them. They each had a handgun. He then hand cuffed them and put them in the back of his squad car. Lorenzo radioed to his cousin to come and pick up their car. Lorenzo's cousin would remove the dope and money, which were in the back fenders. He would then drive it to Mexico City, where he could sell it to a car ring. Miguel leaned up close to Lorenzo. "We work for Diego Rodriguez, also known as Lobo."

Capitan Baca started his engine, "Never heard of him."

Jesus said, "Capitan you are making a big mistake. Please, let us make a phone call."

Capitan Baca drove about 20 kilometers and then turned off the paved road on to a dirt road. The road hadn't been used much and was very rough.

"Lobo will cut your head off and feed it to his dogs, you fat swine." Lorenzo whipped Jesus across the head with his pistol, knocking him unconscious. Miguel knew now that they were going to be executed. He made the sign of the cross with his head and started praying..."Our Father, who art in heaven, hallowed be thy name"

Once they were deep in the jungle, Lorenzo stopped the squad car. He tied a rope around their necks and tied it around his waist so they couldn't run. He then made them walk for a kilometer deeper into the jungle. Miguel was crying and praying. Jesus was still in a daze from being pistol-whipped. Lorenzo removed their shoes and had them kneel on the edge of an arroyo. He removed the rope from his waist and shot them in the base of their skulls with one of their guns.

They dropped into the arroyo. He was too lazy to bury them. He could sell the guns to one of the local ranchers. The shoes he would give to the Padre at the church. The Padre would give the shoes to the poor.

When Lorenzo got back to his office, he was pleasantly surprised that the Guatemalans had been carrying five thousand American dollars besides 50,000 pesos. He decided he wouldn't tell the commissioner about the dollars. It looked to be about 40 pounds of cocaine. Lorenzo carefully cut open a bag and filled up a small glass jar for himself. He taped the bag back together. Unless you looked carefully, you couldn't tell it had been tampered with.

He loved cocaine, he could screw and drink all night. He really didn't know what the coke was worth, although he did know it was about a fifth the cost it would be in the United States. He also knew the Commissioner would not tell him the truth about how much he made on the coke, that justified not telling him about the dollars. "The hell with him," he thought.

He did a big line of coke and popped the top off a cold beer. If Lucinda the whore knew that the Capitan had coke, she would have left town. The Capitan was violent when he was doing cocaine.

# CHAPTER 7
# OLD SOUL

Arturo was mending his net under the big oak tree by the side of his house. Chupa was chasing crabs on the beach. Isabella had gone to meet the bus to make sure Cecilia was safe coming home from school. Last night's rains had cooled the temperature down. The clouds were stopping the sun's relentless heat. This time of year it was hard to be outdoors in the middle of the day.

For some reason, whenever Arturo mended the nets, he thought of his years in the Estadas Unitas, the United States. When Arturo was a young man, he would listen intently to the men who had worked in the United States. Unskilled labor there paid more than the college educated in Mexico. It seemed impossible, but they had the money to prove it. You had to live like an animal, but it was the only way out of poverty.

Arturo had watched his Uncle Francisco, a man he greatly admired, end up penniless after years of hard labor. Eventually, his uncle had turned to alcohol for solace. The alcohol had eventually given him peace. The peace came in the form of a premature death, but not before he had lost all self- esteem.

Arturo paid his life savings for a guide across the border and for showing him a place of work. The guide took Arturo and four other men to a farm in Oceanside, California. The pay was not as much as in Los Angeles, but they did not have to cross the immigration checkpoint before San Clemente. This was a difficult checkpoint because there were no alternative routes around it. The checkpoint was on the major freeway, Highway 5, headed north. The highway 5 runs through a Marine base that is sixteen miles long and five miles wide. The Immigration Department strategically located the checkpoint three quarters of the way into the Marine base.

Arturo worked for an Asian family of farmers named Takayama. They were decent people, but very frugal. They expected a full day's work, everyday. If you lagged, you were replaced. The farm grew tomatoes in the winter and strawberries in the summer. There were smaller crops of lettuce, broccoli and cauliflower. Sometimes, the Takayamas would loan out their workers to pick the avocados in the hills of Escondido and Fallbrook. Arturo was determined, he wanted to buy property and have a family. When his back ached and he felt he wanted to go home, he would talk to Uncle Francisco and ask him to pray for him. The souls in heaven were closer to God, so their prayers were easier to hear.

The workers had a camp in an arroyo a half mile from the farm. The men had scavenged all sorts of items to build their little shacks. In the summer, all they needed was shade during the day. The evenings were pleasant. In the winter there was rain and wind and sometimes the nights could get into the low forties. You had to have your blankets off the ground, or they would get wet. A lot of the men slept on pallets. You needed plastic to keep the rain out and at least two walls to keep out the wind.

There was an agreement to not urinate and defecate in camp, but if a man was sick or really drunk, he would break the rules. The illegal workers came from all over Mexico and even some from Guatemala. Even though they spoke Spanish, Arturo could not understand some of the dialects. No one in the camp went hungry; if a man was too sick to work, the other men would share their provisions with him. Although the men did not know each other, their cultures were similar. Now the gringos that was a different story.

Arturo never knew if they would be friendly, angry, or condescending. He only had to deal with the gringos when he went for supplies, or mailed his money home. Arturo was surprised that, in a country as rich as the United States, they didn't have a better bus system. In Mexico, the buses come by every half hour. Most of the time he would have to walk to the nearest town, which was an hour away.

No matter where the laborers were, in camp or working, they always had an escape route planned from the Border Patrol agents. At the first sight of their truck, someone would yell, "La Migra!" Everyone would scatter running in opposite directions. Usually, they would catch one or two workers. The workers would be back in two days.

The rules of the game were you could run until you were caught and then there was to be no resistance. The illegals once caught were very cooperative. The agents respected them for that, so they tried to be considerate. The agents were in a no win situation. The growers needed the laborers and the laborers needed the work but the border patrol's job was to keep the illegals out. It was not like the workers were criminals.

Arturo made friends with two men in the camp, Juan Acero and Manuel Gallieraga. Juan was the oldest man in camp. He had come because his wife and his mother had become seriously ill. He was deeply in debt. Manuel, who liked to be called Manny, was a young man who loved to have money. He wanted to buy a nice car.

One evening after work, Manny came by Arturo's shack.

"Arturo, I have a business proposition for you."

When it came to money, Arturo was leery. With every dollar he saved, he was closer to his goal. He studied Manny. Manny wore gold chains when he wasn't working and would spend a week's pay on fancy tennis shoes. Yet, he trusted Manny since he had never misled him.

"What is the proposition?"

"I will teach you English."

"I did not know you knew English. Say something in English."

Manny smiled and said, "You are the stupidest and ugliest beaner this side of Texas. Your mother sleeps with the chickens and your father is a low life son-of-a-bitch."

"Very impressive. What did you say?"

"You are an intelligent and handsome man, who comes from excellent parents."

"How much will this cost me?"

"Fifteen dollars a week."

"That is three hours work! Anyway, I am eventually going back to Mexico. Why do I need English?"

"You will be here for many years. It is beneficial to know the language.

Besides, what else do you have to do with your free time?"

"This is true. How about ten dollars?"

"Twelve dollars and fifty cents. You will need a pad and pen to keep notes."

"It is a deal." They shook hands.

Manny taught Arturo English after work everyday but Sunday. Sunday everyone went into town to do their laundry, get supplies, and mail their letters. The language was harder than Spanish. In fact, sometimes it was not logical. Manny was a good teacher and some days while working in the fields they would talk only in English.

Arturo would go home once a year, usually around Christmas. He looked forward to these trips, but they made him very homesick. Arturo's English had gotten to the point where he could understand what the gringos were saying, but he did not feel comfortable speaking it yet. One day at the market while he was waiting in line with Juan, he heard two women talking about them.

The first one said, "Look at those poor illegals. They have to sleep in the bushes. They work bent over all day. What a horrible life."

The other one said, "Don't be ridiculous. They love it here. They would rather sleep in the bushes than have to go back to Mexico. My husband hires them. He says they're good workers, but you can't treat them too good or they will expect it. This is the best they ever had it in their lives."

Arturo wanted to turn them and say, "Do you think I would be in your country for one second if I could earn a decent wage at home? No! I miss my people, my family and the Mexican way. Do you not think I get cold, hot, tired, hungry and sad. We are not animals, even though you use us like animals. We have our pride and dignity. You either look at us with pity, or disgust. My government should be ashamed that it makes its young men go through this humiliation. We are an honest, hard working, God fearing people, and you are lucky that you have us. None of your spoiled children would ever stoop to do such a lowly job." Of course, Arturo said nothing.

One night, during a violent rainstorm, the plastic that Arturo had covering his shack tore in half, dumping ice-cold water on him. The rest of the night he sat in his wet clothes, shivering and waiting for the sun to come up. The next morning was cloudy and windy. Arturo was chilled to the bone.

Everything in his shack had gotten soaked. Juan loaned him some dry clothes.

Manny loaned him some shoes, so he could go to work.

The cold wind blew all day. Arturo could not get warm no matter how fast he worked. At noon, another storm came. The men put on trash bags as raincoats. Their legs and feet still got wet. By quitting time, Arturo felt light headed. Without the sun, none of Arturo's clothes or blankets could dry. Arturo had forgotten to bring plastic to patch his shack. He felt so tired. He lay down on his pallet and feel asleep.

Juan and Manny noticed Arturo was not at the campfire cooking his supper. They went to his shack and found him sleeping. "Arturo wake up. You can't sleep like that. You haven't eaten your supper." Juan said.

"I am very tired." Arturo mumbled.

Manny and Juan pulled Arturo to his feet and walked him to Juan's shack. They pulled off his wet clothes and shoes. The only dry clothes Juan had were caked with dirt. They put him in the dirty clothes. He lay down in Juan's bed and immediately fell asleep.

"I have room in my jacal, Juan," Manny offered.

"God bless you, Manny."

The storm lasted all night with blowing rain and thunder. Arturo had a fever and would alternate from sweating to the chills. One time in the middle of the night, he called out for his mother to bring him water. The next day, as Manny and Juan looked in on Arturo before work, he did not look well.

Juan asked, "How are you, my friend?"

Arturo smiled weakly, "I am fine, I feel much better. I have been much sicker than this before. This is nothing."

"We will see you after work, Arturo."

Arturo started coughing not long after they left. He forced himself to sit up and drink water, his head pounded from the effort. Most of the day, he drifted in and out of a restless sleep. He dreamt he was back in Mexico. They were having a fiesta in his honor. All of his family was there, including his aunts, uncles and cousins. His Uncle Francisco was cooking a goat and everyone was laughing and dancing. When he opened his eyes, he was in Juan's shack and he couldn't stop coughing.

Arturo sat up. His head and all of his joints ached. He had never been this sick before. He slowly made his way to his shack and looked through his bag of medicine. He had one aspirin, but nothing for the cough. He lay back down, the walk had made him weak. The wind started blowing, so he wrapped himself in Juan's blanket. After a while, he woke up sweating. His shirt under his jacket was soaking wet from perspiration. Arturo pulled off the blanket and unzipped the jacket. He came out of a deep sleep, freezing from the chills. His teeth were chattering. His hands were shaking so bad he could hardly zip his jacket. Again, he wrapped himself in the blanket. Over and over again he would alternate from freezing to burning up.

When Juan and Manny came back to camp they were discouraged to find Arturo had deteriorated. Juan held Arturo's head so he could drink water.

"What are we going to do, Juan?"

"We have to get him to a hospital."

They made a stretcher out of tree limbs blankets and ropes. Two of the other workers in the camp volunteered to help carry him out. Even with the four of them, they had to rest a couple of times. Arturo kept saying, "I'm sorry."

Manny said," Arturo be quiet. We know you are sorry. We need to go to the pay phone by the Laundromat. I have an idea."

When they got to the Laundromat, the other two men headed back to camp. Manny dialed 911. When the operator came on, he yelled in English. "Please send the Border Patrol. There are two drunken illegals at the Laundromat."

He then gave the address.

"Well Juan, you better leave before they get here."

"You're a good friend, Manny."

They gave each other a soul shake, and Juan left with the stretcher.

The Border Patrol arrived in fifteen minutes in a green four wheel drive Ford Bronco. They flashed their spotlights on Manny, who was standing, and on Arturo, who was lying on the ground.

"Buenos Noches, Officers."

"What's going on here?" the driver asked in Spanish.

"My friend is very sick."

"How does that concern us?"

"Well, we are illegals and, by law, your hospitals can not refuse us. My friend is very sick, so he will have a lengthy stay, which could cost thousands of dollars or there is an alternative."

"Which is?"

"Deport us. Then he is Mexico's problem."

The officers looked at each other.

"Get in."

The Border Patrol Bronco raced south in the fast lane of the freeway with its lights blinking. When they got to the border, they had a quick talk with the Mexican border guards before they were waved through. The agents dropped Manny and Arturo at the front door of one of Tijuana's hospitals. Manny shook their hands.

"Mucho gracias, mi amigos."

The agents smiled. "De nada."

Manny put Arturo's arm around his shoulder and hoisted him to his feet. "Help me, Arturo. Try and walk." Arturo shuffled his feet. When they got inside the door, two nurses helped Manny lay him on a gurney. After they wheeled Arturo away, Manny headed for the door. He was headed back to Oceanside. If he was lucky, he would be back to work by tomorrow afternoon. He thought to himself, "I should have asked the agents for a ride back." The thought made him chuckle.

When Arturo became conscious two days later, he was amazed to find himself in Mexico. He was being fed intravenously. He was so weak he could only keep his eyes open for a short while before he would fall back to sleep.

Three nurses worked in Arturo's ward. The nurse on the first shift, eight a.m. to four p.m., was a woman named Marta. She was forty-eight and a great-grandmother. She had seen it all in the hospital, so nothing shocked her. Over the years her people skills had diminished, but she was a good worker. Ernestina had the second shift, which started at four p.m. and ended at twelve midnight. This shift was ideal for her because her husband got off work at three and could take care of the babies. On the last shift, midnight to eight, was Isabella.

Isabella had always dreamed of being a doctor, but her parents were so poor that that was an impossibility. After her father died, she moved with her mother and her older sister north to Tijuana to be near her grandmother, as well as her Aunt and Uncle. Isabella had been a surprise to her parents. They thought Esperanza, Isabella's mother, was in menopause. She hadn't had a period in three years. To say Isabella's father was disappointed would be an understatement. He had five daughters already. He had married off three of them and thought he had only two to go until Isabella was born.

Esperanza was delighted with Isabella. She loved children. In fact, her life was starting to feel meaningless with all the children grown or teenagers. Isabella became her pet and she protected her from all discipline. "She's my princess." she would say to Isabella's father. He was too tired and old to fight her. His youngest daughter was pampered. She also was intelligent. Isabella was used to getting her own way.

When Isabella had come to work the first night Arturo was brought in, Ernestina had approached her.

"Have you seen the handsome young man in ward three?"

Ernestina was always looking for a husband for Isabella.

"Ernestina, will you stop your matchmaking? You know I am dating Dr.Benitez."

"Dr. Benitez is a pompous burro. He will treat you like dirt. If you want good treatment from Dr. Benitez, be his mistress."

"I will never be anyone's mistress! I have no more time for this foolish talk."

Isabella's curiosity took her to ward three. She went straight over to Arturo and picked up his hand to take his pulse. She had to admit he was attractive. His hand was large and callused. His arms were thick with muscle. He didn't have a mustache, she liked that. Isabella was looking at her watch, timing his pulse when he spoke, startling her.

"Are you an angel?"

Before she could reply, he had passed out again. Isabella read his chart, he had pneumonia. She was sorry for him, but glad that he would be in the hospital for a while. For some reason, Isabella thought about Arturo the rest of the night.

Arturo looked forward to seeing Isabella. He would try and sleep during the day so he could stay up all night watching her. She was the most beautiful woman he had ever seen. Her hair was so black it looked to have shades of blue. When she looked into his eyes, he could barely breath.

One night while she was taking his temperature, he said," It is almost worth getting sick to meet someone like you."

"Do not talk with the thermometer in your mouth."

"When I get better, will you go to dinner with me?"

"Hush! I have a boyfriend. Anyway, I don't know you."

"I'm Arturo Cruz. I am working in the United States so I can buy my own land and start a family."

"You must stop talking!"

She held his wrist taking his pulse. With her peripheral vision, she could see him smiling at her. She ignored him, but she did like his confidence.

Arturo started asking the other nurses about Isabella. Marta was ambivalent. However, Ernestina encouraged him since she hated Dr. Benitez. Everyday, Arturo was gaining strength. His infatuation with Isabella grew with his strength.

Isabella was having dinner with Dr. Benitez. She started to notice all of his idiosyncrasies. He chewed with his mouth open. He blatantly looked at other women while he was with her. He listened to her halfheartedly. His hands were very thin and frail, almost feminine. The only time he paid attention was when they were having sex, but even that was very controlled. There was a procedure to be followed, it was never spontaneous. He was talking when she starting thinking about Arturo.

"Isabella! I was talking to you, but you weren't listening."

"I'm sorry. What were you saying?"

"It's not important. Never mind. "

Isabella thought, "You're right. It is not important."

The next night at the hospital, Isabella went up to see Arturo. His bed was empty. She almost ran to the desk.

"What happened to Arturo Cruz?"

"He was released this morning. Why?" asked the clerk.

"No reason."

Isabella was disappointed in herself. She had played a game with him and now he was gone. It was the longest night of her career. After she clocked out, she went out the employee door.

"Buenos dias, senorita."

It was Arturo. Isabella smiled at him and then quickly caught herself.

"Senor Cruz, how are you feeling?'

"I'm feeling better, not totally well, but soon. Can I buy you breakfast?" He walked along side her.

"I really don't know you."

"Let me buy you breakfast and I will tell you all there is to know."

"Alright, Senor Cruz. I know a nice little cafe around the corner."

They sat in the back. She found Arturo to be very amusing. To impress her, he started talking to her in English. Isabella had learned some English in school. They conversed a while in English, which made them laugh. Arturo ate his breakfast slowly, not wanting her to leave. Isabella looked at her watch.

"I must go. My mother will be concerned." Arturo stood." When can I see you again?"

"Arturo, you must be patient."

He looked into her eyes, "Why wait when I know you're the one?"

Her heart skipped a beat. She made herself frown.

"That's ridiculous. You don't even know me!"

"My heart does. I listen to my heart."

Isabella turned away. "I must go."

"Isabella!"

She turned back and looked at him.

"I'm going back to work in California. How can I find you when I return?'

"I go to the Saint Joseph Catholic church every Sunday for the ten o'clock mass."

She started walking down the street.

"Isabella!"

Isabella whirled around, "Arturo, I must leave!"

"One last thing could you give me something of yours to remind me of you? It would help me get through the long, lonely nights."

She reached into her purse and pulled out her rosary. She threw it to him. He caught it and with a big smile kissed the crucifix.

Arturo returned to his job with a new energy. He felt he had found the woman he would marry. He would visit Isabella every other Sunday. He became adept at riding the buses in the United States. If he left early Sunday morning, he could make it down there in time and then make it back for work on Monday morning.

Isabella was pleasantly surprised to see Arturo waiting for her outside the church the first time he came. They had lunch in the park. Arturo was really good with children and it wouldn't be long before they were crowded around him in some form of play. One

Sunday, Isabella was watching Arturo and she realized she was smiling. He made her feel good.

One Sunday, Dr. Benitez decided to go to church with Isabella. He was holding Isabella's hand as they walked up to the church. Arturo could see them coming. He tried to make eye contact with Isabella. Isabella felt terrible and looked away. Dr. Benitez noticed Arturo's stare. Arturo turned and left. When they were in the church, he asked, "Did you know that man? He was staring at you."

"Yes."

"Who is he?"

"Just a patient.

Isabella was confused. Dr. Benitez guaranteed her a secure life. Arturo reached into her soul. When she asked her mother about this confusion, her mother was definitive.

"Love will come and go. You need to think who can best provide for your children."

Back at the camp Arturo was crushed. He moped all day. Manny and Juan tried to make him laugh, but he was inconsolable. Arturo did not go back to the church.

Sitting by the campfire one night, Arturo asked Juan, "Have you ever been in love?

"Of course."

"Did she love you?"

"In her own way, but not in my way."

"I don't understand?" Arturo said stirring the coals with a stick.

"You love her in your way, but you are a man. She might love you, but it is a different love."

Arturo remained silent. Juan continued.

"The biggest mistake men make is thinking that the woman thinks similar to them."

"Well, how do they think? "

Juan laughed, "How the hell would I know? I just know it is different."

"Juan, what should I do? I haven't seen her in three months, but I can't stop thinking of her."

"Trust me. I am no expert. I know most things in life that are important don't come easy. You gave up. Fight for her."

"He's a doctor. I can't compete with that."

"Money can't buy love. Go back and you will know."

"Gracias mi amigo."

Isabella and Dr. Benitez were already in church when Arturo got there. Mass had not started. Arturo made the sign of the cross with holy water. At the pew, he genuflected and sat on the other side of Isabella. Dr. Benitez leaned forward and glared at Arturo. Arturo looked forward. He could smell her perfume. Isabella could not help but smile.

After church Arturo walked along side Isabella. Dr. Benitez locked arms with her on the other side.

"Isabella, can I talk to you."

"She is my fiancee and no, you may not talk to her!"

Arturo looked at her, "Is this the type of man you are interested in, one that talks for you?"

Dr. Benitez stepped between Isabella and Arturo. "I am telling you to leave, or else!"

Arturo for the first time looked at the Doctor, "Or else what?"

Isabella grabbed Dr. Benitez and turned him around. "Give me five minutes alone."

Benitez said, "Five minutes, that's all. Any more and you can walk home."

He turned and stormed off.

Arturo smiled at Isabella. "Why would you choose to spend your life with such a man?"

Isabella didn't reply.

"Isabella, I love you. I will share my life with you. I can not offer you any more than that."

Isabella still did not reply.

"Listen. Isabella. Sometimes you have to take a gamble in life. You have to have faith that I can take care of you and our children. I have two strong arms and a strong back, I will do it."

Isabella looked bewildered.

"Isabella, your heart won't lie to you. Hold out your hands. If you don't feel it when I touch you, then I will walk out of your life forever."

She held out her hands. Arturo took a hold of them and she felt the electricity run through her body. She still didn't say anything. Arturo dropped them and walked away. Isabella knew that this decision would affect her for the rest of her life.

"Arturo!" she yelled.

Arturo turned and ran back. He picked her off her feet and swung her in a circle. He slowly put her down, then kissed her. It was the happiest moment of his life.

Arturo came to see Isabella every other Sunday for the next eight months until the wedding. The bride's parents were supposed to pay for the wedding, but Isabella's mother had no money. Isabella and Arturo paid for it. Isabella's mother, in the eight months, had grown to love Arturo. His devotion to Isabella was obvious.

The winter sun was rising over the hilltops. Arturo had already been up for an hour. He had fixed his own breakfast, as well as breakfast for Juan.

Manny had gone to Chicago, he heard they paid more there. Juan came up to the fire. Arturo handed him a plate and a cup of coffee.

"Gracias, amigo." Juan said.

"You're welcome." Arturo answered in English. "Do you think we will get rain?"

"I don't feel it, but maybe."

Arturo looked to the red clouds in the sunrise, then scrapped his plate and wiped it with a cloth.

"I have to go."

Juan said to him with a mouthful of food, "You are the best supervisor I have ever had."

"Juan, you are my best friend. What else would you say?"

"No. You are fair and you work harder than any one else."

"Thanks, Juan. Asta luego."

Arturo went into his shack. He had a picture of Isabella and his son, Cholly, hanging on the plywood wall. He kissed two fingers and put his fingers on their lips. Arturo had grudgingly taken the supervisor position. He did not like having to answer for other men's work, but the supervisor's job paid two dollars an hour more. Arturo figured those two dollars an hour would take a couple of years off his timetable.

Isabella paid her mother to watch Cholly when she worked. She had given up her dream to be an administrator. She now shared Arturo's dream of owning property. When she and Arturo had visited his parents, he had taken her to the property. It was gorgeous and she loved it instantly. The picturesque bay was imprinted into her mind and she would occasionally think about it for inspiration. Being away from Arturo was very difficult, but she agreed that they needed to make the sacrifice. She did not want to be like so many of her people, so poor that they could barely feed their families.

Hard working men in Mexico make five dollars a day, sometimes less. That is not enough for a family, so the young boys are forced to work at an early age. This means no education for the boys. Without education, they are destined to a life of poverty. The circle goes unbroken.

Mr. Takayama liked Arturo since he was the best supervisor he had ever had. Mr. Takayama rewarded Arturo for his hard work by giving him work on Sundays around his house. When Arturo went to visit Isabella, he would give Arturo clothes and shoes for Cholly and Isabella. Mr. Takayama let Arturo drive his pick up truck around the farm, he had never done this for any other supervisor. Mr. Takayama was hoping Arturo would bring his family up from Mexico to live permanently. Arturo told him that was impossible because he loved the ocean and that he was a fisherman.

Late Saturday afternoons, a Catholic padre would come into the camp to say mass and give communion. Father Peter did not know very much Spanish, so he would give his sermons in English. The men would listen attentively, but they had no idea what he was saying. Sometimes Arturo would translate for Juan. Father Peter figured God's message in English was better than nothing.

That night, sitting by the fire, Arturo asked Juan, "Was Jesus God?"

"Well, if he wasn't, he was one of the holiest men to walk this earth."

"I don't know, Juan. Some things are hard for me to believe. How come you cannot go to heaven if you're not baptized? What if you're a newborn baby and you have never sinned? God is supposed to be all loving, but he sends souls to hell to burn for eternity. Doesn't that seem vengeful?"

Juan lit a cigarette and shared it with Arturo.

"I think there are things about the church that didn't come from Jesus." Arturo handed the cigarette back. "What do you mean?"

"Jesus lived almost two thousand years ago. All of his teachings had to be passed down through the centuries. Is it possible that people could have added or subtracted something?"

Arturo was silent.

Juan continued. "For example, do you think Jesus would want the crosses in his church to be made out of gold and jewels, while the babies went hungry? Remember, this is a man who owned nothing. Would he want his churches to be giant monuments, while the children wore rags? Would he want his priests to live better than the parishioners? Would he want the Catholic Church to be as rich as some countries? I say, 'No.' You must remember, whenever the common man is involved, it will be flawed. Jesus's message was simple to me: love God, love your fellow man, and no violence."

"That sounds simple."

"But is it simple to do?"

"No." Arturo shook his head.

Juan said, "Arturo, I have always been curious about the other religions. Would you travel to the library with me, so we can learn about them?"

"I would like that."

Three times a week, Arturo and Juan would travel to the library. Arturo would drive Mr. Takayama's truck to the end of the property and then they would walk to the highway. After a short bus ride, they would be at the library. Juan soon lost interest in the religions and would read the magazines and newspapers that were printed in Spanish. Arturo, after some searching, became interested in the Indian yogis and the practice of Yoga.

"Juan, have you heard of Yoga?"

Juan did not look up from his magazine.

"It is very interesting. There are breathing techniques, meditation techniques and even some exercises."

Juan hadn't heard a word, "Uh, huh. Did you know they have built a toll road all the way to Mazatlan? The only people that can afford it are the gringos and the rich."

"So Juan, these yogis can perform incredible feats through this yoga. By controlling their heart rates, they can stay under water for over ten minutes."

Juan thought Arturo was ridiculous. He thought to himself, 'Why waste your time with such foolishness?', but said, "sounds interesting Arturo."

Arturo was reading from one of the books he had piled in front of him. "Listen to this story, Juan. An elderly monk was making a pilgrimage through the mountains. Stopping to drink from a brook, he chanced to find a large nugget of gold gleaming under the rippling stream. He filled his water vessel, put the gold in his bag and sat by the path to rest. Just then, a young man came huffing and puffing up the trail. Approaching the monk, he said, 'I have eaten nothing this day and a long journey lies yet before me. Have you any morsel for a fellow wanderer?'

'You are welcome to share my bread,' replied the pilgrim and pointed to his bag, gesturing to the youth to help himself. The gold nugget dropped out and the monk casually set it to the side. While they ate, the young traveler gazed at the gold and spoke wistfully of the older man's good fortune, the freedom and security imparted by such wealth. As he rose to leave, the monk smilingly dropped the precious nugget into the traveler's hand. Astonished at his good fortune, the young man made off with his prize. But nagging thoughts pulled at his steps and soon he found himself back with the pilgrim at the brook side. Placing the treasure before his benefactor, the young man bowed and said, 'I know how valuable this stone is, but I perceive you have something even more precious. I pray you, bestow on me that which is within in you, that which enables you to give me this gold!'"

Arturo smiled at Juan, "Isn't that a great story?"

Juan looked puzzled. "Wouldn't that gold nugget help you buy your property?"

"Of course."

"So, you would keep it?"

"Of course."

"Then why is this a great story?"

"Because the pilgrim has achieved a higher awareness. That is what I would like to achieve also."

Juan did not say anything, but he wondered if Arturo was going to start preaching to him. Juan had seen conversions before. Every one of these people became insufferable with their holiness. On the ride home when Arturo was not looking, Juan would look at him and try to picture him with a shaved head and wearing a robe. Every time, he looked ridiculous.

Arturo started going to a temple on Sundays. The service consisted of an opening prayer; the opening prayer was to Jesus, Krishna, saints of all religions, and to God. Then, there was a fifteen-minute meditation, using ancient meditation techniques. Then, there was a sermon by one of the monks who lived by the temple. The services were simple, but Arturo loved the message.

After one service, Arturo was replaying the sermon in his mind. The monk had said, "Yoga is the art of doing everything with the consciousness of God. Not only when you are meditating, but also when you are working, your thoughts should be constantly anchored in Him. If you work with the consciousness that you are doing it to please God, that activity unites you with Him. Therefore, do not imagine that you can find God only in meditation. Both meditation and right activity are essential, as the Bhagavad Gita teaches. If you think of God while you perform your duties in this world, you will be mentally united with Him." Arturo liked God as his constant companion. Arturo was lonely for his family. Isabella was pregnant again.

Arturo held Cholly's hand. They looked through the window at all the cribs holding the newborn babies.

"Which one is she, papa?"

Cholly was two and a half years old and everything he said was in the form of a question. Arturo picked him up and hugged him. Cholly pushed Arturo's whiskered face away.

"Which one is she, papa?"

Arturo pointed to the back row. "Over there."

Arturo was proud that Cholly was smart like his mother. He hoped all the children inherited her brains. Isabella had gone to school after work and learned some computer skills. She was now working part time in the office of the hospital, which paid more. The rest of the time, she was still a nurse. When she was a nurse, she worked with the terminally ill which also paid more. Isabella tried not to get close to the patients, but sometimes it was inevitable. Some nights she would cry herself to sleep.

Arturo was grateful for Isabella's mother and aunt. They would take care of Cholly while Isabella worked. Sometimes, Cholly mistakenly would call his grandmother "mama". Fortunately, the aunt and Isabella's mother loved children and were happy at the birth of a daughter.

Cholly pointed his chubby finger at the crib, touching the glass. "What's her name, papa?"

"Vivianna."

"Why?"

"Because that was my grandmother's name."

"Why is she a girl, papa?"

"God decides that, Cholly."

Cholly squirmed to be put down. Arturo kissed him on the cheek and lowered him to the floor. As soon as Cholly's feet hit the ground, he ran. Arturo had to hustle to catch up to him. Arturo laughed at how fast Cholly's little legs were. "Let's go see mama."

Isabella was half asleep when they entered her room. The doctor had given her something for the pain and it made her sleepy. Cholly climbed up on her bed and put his head on her chest. She smiled and wrapped her arms around him. Arturo never ceased to be amazed at his wife's beauty. He felt blessed to have such a beautiful wife. Arturo brushed back her hair from her forehead and kissed her. "How are you?" Arturo asked.

"Just tired. When are you going back?"

"The day after tomorrow. We are starting to harvest then. I am going to take Cholly to the beach this afternoon. I want him to see the ocean."

"Do you miss the ocean?"

"It is my second love after you."

Isabella squeezed his hand. "A few more years and we will be in our own home."

Arturo nodded. A couple of more years seemed like a long time. It was very difficult living away from Isabella and Cholly.

Isabella looked serious. "Arturo I have something I want you to consider." She reached out and took his hand

"What is it Isabella?"

"I would like for Mama to come with us to live when we buy the land." Arturo didn't hesitate. "Of course."

Isabella smiled. "You are a wonderful man, I am glad you are my husband."

"Cholly, let's go and let your mama rest."

Cholly jumped down and ran out the door.

Arturo yelled over his shoulder as he ran after Cholly, "Goodbye, Isabella!"

Arturo sat at the dinner table with Mr. and Mrs. Takayama. They were eating pizza and spaghetti. For the last two years, Arturo was sleeping in a room Mr. Takayama had built in one of his garages. Arturo missed the camaraderie of the camp, but the room was much better for his health. This would be their last meal together; Arturo had finally acquired his land. He had purchased the land a year earlier, but needed money to build his house and buy his boat. Mr. and Mrs. Takayama were sad to see Arturo go, he was the best worker they ever had.

"How is Isabella doing?" Mrs. Takayama asked.

"She is anxious to make the move."

"And how are the children?"

"Cholly and Vivianna are in school. Rosa starts school in two years and Julia is out of diapers."

Mr. Takayama ate a piece of pepperoni pizza.

"Arturo, Mrs. Takayama and I want to give you a couple of gifts for all your years of hard work."

"Mr. Takayama, that is not necessary. You have always been more than fair."

"We would like to give you the pick up truck."

Arturo could not believe his ears. The truck was six years old, but it was in excellent condition. Arturo was speechless.

"We want to show you something." Mr. Takayama got up from the table.

"Follow me."

They went out to one of the warehouses. Mr. Takayama swung the door open, and there was a brand new outboard motor and a camper for the back of the truck.

Arturo felt overwhelmed.

"I have nothing to give you."

"You have made our farm a lot of money and we are appreciative. Accept our gifts without guilt. You have earned them."

Arturo hugged Mrs. Takayama and shook Mr. Takayama's hand. It was hard to believe he was leaving for good. His friend Juan had gone back to Mexico last year, so he really didn't have any friends to say good-bye to.

Mr. Takayama helped Arturo put the camper on his truck. He handed Arturo the registration that had been signed over. The camper had a small kitchen and three sleeping areas. Arturo pictured his family staying in the camper while he built the house. He could build a palapa for sleeping outside in hammocks when the weather was nice.

"I will not be able to sleep tonight, so I am going to leave after I pack."

Mrs. Takayama said, "We will miss you, Arturo." She hugged him again. Mr. Takayama started to shake Arturo's hand, but instead gave him an awkward hug.

"Good luck, Arturo."

As Arturo drove out the dirt road for the last time, he looked back at the fields. It seemed like he had been here all his life. He said a prayer of thanks. One of the monks at the last service had said the most important word for him was 'gratitude'. Arturo agreed. God had blessed him and he started singing a chant as he pulled on to the paved road headed for his new life.

"I am Aum, I am Aum...Aum, Aum, I am Aum... Aum, Aum, come to me, come to me, come to me!"

Arturo and Isabella turned off the road at the turnout to their property. The children were all asleep in the camper.

"Do you mind if we sleep here in the truck? I am too tired to set up the tent," Arturo asked.

"This is fine. I cannot believe we are finally starting our new life. I am so excited. We will not have to be apart ever again."

She smiled at Arturo. He was already asleep.

When Isabella awoke the next morning, Arturo was gone. She checked in on the children, who were still asleep. She could see a hole cut through the jungle. Arturo was searching for the old road to the property. It had been four years since they had been down the road and the jungle had reclaimed it. Isabella got out the small propane stove and started preparing breakfast.

She made coffee, eggs with chorizo, tortillas and cereal for the children.

The children, one by one, woke up and came and sat by her. They were good children and got along well with each other. Cholly rubbed his eyes, "Where are we Mama?"

"This is the way to our new home."

"I only see bushes."

"Your father is looking for the old road. Eat your cereal."

Arturo came back carrying his machete and axe. There were leaves stuck to his hat. Isabella handed him a plate of food and a cup of coffee.

"Did you find the road?"

"Yes, but it is completely overgrown, I will need your help. Even with your help, it is going to take a couple of days."

"As long as we are together, I don't care what we are doing."

Arturo squeezed her hand, "You are the best."

Isabella and Arturo cut an eight-foot path with machetes. Occasionally, Arturo would have to use the axe on a small tree. The old road was fairly easy to follow as it was not as dense as the rest of the jungle. Cholly and Vivianna wanted to help, so Arturo let them drag the branches to the sides of the road. He made sure that they were careful with the ones that had sharp thorns. Julia and Rosa preferred to sit in the truck and play house with her dolls.

At noon, they stopped for lunch. Isabella made sandwiches. Arturo sang one of his chants with the children. They loved singing with their father, even though they did not understand the words.

"We are making good progress. How are you doing Isabella?"

Isabella had leaves and twigs stuck in her hair. The day had turned hot and humid. "Can you park the truck under that tree for shade? I am going to take a siesta with the children. I will be able to help you again when I wake up."

In the afternoon, as they worked, the children were delighted to see snakes, iguanas, and even a fox. Isabella was not as happy about the snakes. Arturo was strong and never slowed his assault on the jungle. Periodically, he would stop and sharpen his machete. He could take out most limbs with two swings.

At dusk, Arturo set up a tent for him and Isabella to sleep. The camper was packed with their possessions. There was barely enough room for the children to sleep. After dinner, Arturo and Isabella sat by a small fire. The children were put to bed. Isabella caught Arturo staring at her.

"Don't even think about it."

"But you are so beautiful."

"Trust me. Until I have a shower and wash my hair, you will not touch me."

"Tomorrow, I will work twice as fast!"

Isabella laughed, then leaned over and kissed him lightly on the lips.

The next day, after about three hours of cutting, they came to a thin ditch that had been caused by a heavy rain in the rainy season. It was too wide and deep for the truck.

"What will we do, Arturo?"

"We must go back to the dry stream bed and collect rocks to fill in the arroyo."

Arturo had to laugh to himself because the rocks piled in the back of the truck were in direct proportion to the person carrying them. Isabella's were medium, Cholly's small, Vivianna's smaller and Julia's were the size of an egg. Rosa didn't participate since one of her dolls was having a crises.

"Good job, Julia. You are a good worker!" Arturo said to Julia as she went by him with two small rocks in her tiny hands.

"What about me, papa?" Cholly asked as he struggled with his biggest rock yet.

"Very good, Cholly, but do not strain yourself."

"Will we make it through today, Arturo?"

"No. Tomorrow for sure if there are no more arroyos."

That night while Isabella was putting the children to sleep, Arturo walked into the jungle.

When Arturo came back, Isabella asked, "Where did you go?"

"Are the children asleep?"

"Yes."

"Follow me. I must show you something."

Arturo took the lantern and led her down a little trail that had been just cleared.

"Arturo, where are we going?"

"Be patient it is a little farther."

Arturo led her into a little clearing. There was a small stream running into a pool of water. Arturo had a towel and a lantern hanging in a tree. On one of the rocks by the pool was some shampoo and a bar of soap. Arturo bowed deeply.

"I have your bath ready for you, madam."

Isabella laughed. "You are determined."

They bathed together and washed each other's hair.

"We must get back and check the children."

"You go Isabella. I will pick up and meet you there.

When Arturo got back, Isabella was waiting for him in the tent.

In the early afternoon of the next day, they broke through to the beach. The children squealed with delight. Arturo took them for a swim. They loved the water. Isabella started setting up a camp under some tall trees. After the swim, Arturo and Isabella discussed a plan for building their house. They wanted to make sure they had the perfect location.

One of the reasons Arturo wanted this property was because it had a well. Apparently, the original owner dug the well, then ran out of money and sold the property. The well needed work. It needed to be cleaned and to have a new pump installed. Arturo was hoping Isabella would pick a place close to the well. The closer to the well, the fewer trenches he would have to dig for the water pipe.

Isabella and Arturo cut paths through the jungle so they could check the view and feel the afternoon breeze. They finally found a spot halfway up the hill by some big trees. They both agreed it was the all around best.

Arturo had enough money to build one room and a kitchen. They would add the other rooms later. After Arturo cleared the area for the foundation, he went into town and paid for materials. He had to pay double for delivery because his road was so remote and rough.

The truck could not get up the last two hundred yards of the hill, so they unloaded the bricks, cement, sand and re-bar. Arturo, Isabella and the children loaded Arturo's truck. Arturo would haul it up to the site. Arturo would smile at Isabella when he saw the little ones carrying the bricks to the truck. Isabella was satisfied she had made the right choice in men.

Arturo's father's friend, Florencio, helped Arturo build the house. Florencio was a retired bridge builder and a magician with cement. Florencio had a bad back and could not lift, so Arturo was his back. Florencio would sit in the shade drinking cold beer and tell Arturo what to do. All of the cement was mixed by hand. Isabella and Cholly helped, the girls had become tired of it.

Sometimes Arturo would take the morning off and fish with Florencio.

The only thing Florencio loved more than fishing was eating fish. Florencio couldn't believe how easy Arturo caught fish. He had a real talent. "Fiorencio, I am sorry I cannot give you more money."

"Arturo, do not worry about the money. I enjoy getting off my porch. My wife cannot count how many beers I drink when I am out here."

"How is your wife doing?"

"Getting fatter and meaner."

"What about your sons?"

"One half are in the United States and the others are in Mexico City. They do not like the country life, or maybe their wives do not like the country. We see them on Christmas. They all make good money and are very generous. They take care of me and their mother."

Arturo and Florencio fished another hour in silence. Arturo looked at Florencio. He was overweight, his wife was miserable and his children had all left home. Arturo wondered if his was to be a similar fate.

It took three months to build the rooms. When the house was finished, Arturo and Isabella had a celebration with Florencio. They drank a beer with him after supper.

The bedroom was crowded with all the children and the kitchen made the house hot after cooking supper. Nothing could dampen Arturo's and Isabella's thrill of their first house. They built a porch in the front and hung swings from the trees for the children. They would sit on the porch holding hands watching the children play.

"Arturo, I think I am pregnant."

Arturo got up and kissed her forehead.

""You are such a good wife to give me so many children."

"If it is a boy, I would like to name him Estaban, after my mother's father."

"That is fine. All the names you have chosen have been good." Arturo looked at the setting sun and said a prayer of thanks.

By the time Estaban was born, Florencio and Arturo had added another room. Estaban was born with a midwife at home. It was Isabella's easiest delivery. Watching Isabella give birth always made Arturo cry. Part of it was the miracle, part of it was the pain for Isabella and part of it was holding one of his children for the first time. All the other children wanted to hold little Estaban. Cholly kept saying, "Now there are two boys, now there are two boys!"

When Isabella went to the doctor's to have a check up, he told her he thought she should not have any more children as there might be complications.

"That is fine." Arturo, said, " I will get a vasectomy."

"The Pope says no birth control."

"Isabella, the Pope is celibate. I am married to the most beautiful woman in the world and I am getting a vasectomy. If something happened to you, I would never be the same."

..Thank you, husband...

With Arturo's fishing money they were able to build another room. Now, they could separate the boys from the girls, who were in constant conflict over their territory. All of the children loved school. They liked making friends. They excelled· in their schoolwork and the teachers were impressed with their manners. At home they swam, fished and explored the jungle.

Isabella and Arturo loved to watch the children play. Arturo would join in the soccer games and the swimming. He would take the boys fishing. They were so proud of the fish they caught. Arturo would lead the children in singing the chants. They all liked the melodic songs. Isabella tolerated it as long as Arturo also went to Catholic Church with the family on Sundays. Arturo enjoyed the service on Sundays. Church brought the family together.

Arturo was working in his garden on a Sunday afternoon when Isabella came running with baby Estaban.

"Arturo, Estaban has been stung by a scorpion! "

Arturo ran and grabbed Estaban. "Isabella, get the children we must get to the hospital."

Arturo took Estaban to the truck. He laid him on he seat. He was crying, which was a good sign. Arturo ran to the house and got some ice out of the freezer. Isabella loaded the children in the car. She held Estaban on her lap.

"Where was he stung?"

"On the leg."

Isabella was trying not to cry. "Put this ice on it."

Arturo was driving as fast as he could down the dirt road without breaking the truck. The other children were standing on the seat hanging on. They were silent. They knew something was serious.

By the time they got to the hospital, Estaban was struggling for breath. Isabella ran for the emergency room while Arturo parked the car. Arturo made the children hold his hand as they walked.

"Will he die, Papa?" Cholly asked.

The girls looked at him. He stopped and kneeled down.

"God loves him as much as we do, but if He needs him, he will take him. Let's hope it is not time."

They sat in the waiting room. Isabella came out crying.

"The doctors are doing a tracheotomy. He can't breathe."

The children stood around their mother, holding her dress. They were scared. Arturo squeezed her hands, "Be strong, Isabella, it is out of our hands. I am going to take the children to my sister's."

On the ride to their aunts', the children were silent. Arturo hurried back to the hospital. Isabella was not in the waiting room. She came out of the operating room with one of the doctors. When she saw Arturo she ran to him.

"He is going to make it They gave him a shot of antidote and a shot of antihistamine, and he is breathing much better!'

Arturo shook the doctors hand.

"Gracias, mi amigo, gracias."

The doctor smiled. "We will need to leave him here for the night."

The doctor talked to them and then went on his rounds. Isabella took Arturo's hands in hers.

"I don't know what I would do if I had lost him."

"I know."

"No, Arturo. I felt crazy. It was scary."

Arturo took her in his arms and held her tight.

# CHAPTER 8

# I'M SINKING

I was deep underwater and the water was pitch black. I was very comfortable and relaxed. I could hear my name being called. Since I was underwater, I could not hear very well. I slowly started drifting to the surface. My name was starting to become clearer.

"WILL! WILL! WILL!"

Bear was shouting as loud as he could and shaking me. I groggily opened my eyes. My eyes involuntarily closed again. I started sinking underwater again.

"WILL! WILL!".

Bear was calling my name again. I was getting a little perturbed with this. Let me swim. I surfaced again. Now, I could see Jimmy, Howard and Bear standing in front of me. My head nodded again. I sank down.

"WILL! WILL! "WILL! WILL!"

I opened my eyes again. "Damn. What are you shouting about?"

It was hard for them to understand me. I was still not all the way out of the water. I heard Howard say," Give him some speed. Wake him up."

They stuck a straw in my nose. Jimmy was holding my head up. I inhaled. The crystal burned my nostril. After a few minutes, I came to the surface and, lo and behold, I wasn't in the water. I was in Weasel's trailer. Bear was standing by me. Howard and Jimmy were sitting at the table.

"Hey, Will. Welcome back." Howard said.

I didn't like the look of this.

"So Will, are you using?"

"Using what?"

Bear grabbed my face in his hands. "Smack, junk, H, heroin, whatever the fuck you want to call it."

"Of course not. That shit's not cool."

I could see Jimmy shake his head in disgust.

"Then whose is this?" He held up my eyedropper and needle.

"That's Rosemary's." I lied.

Howard said, "Then whose is this?"

He held up Rosemary's kit.

I looked around the table. Is it possible I am a bigger loser than my old man?

"Let me explain."

Howard got up and left the trailer.

Bear crouched down so we were eye level.

"Will, I need to make this perfectly clear, so focus. I am giving you until nine o'clock tonight to get your gear together. After that, I will put a bullet right here." He pushed his finger hard between my eyes.

"Are we clear?"

"Yeah, Bear. Sorry."

"Fuck you, asshole." He slammed the screen door.

I sat across the table from Jimmy. He lit a cigarette and gave me one. "I fucked up, didn't I, Jimmy?"

He blew the smoke towards the ceiling.

"We all gotta' do it sometime."

"Do what?"

"Hit bottom. I just hope this is your bottom."

"I'm really sorry, Jimmy. I feel like I let you down."

"No worries, dude. Shit happens."

Jimmy rolled a humongous joint and we smoked it.

"Where's Rosemary?"

He pointed to the back room. I could see her laying naked on the bed.

"I really like her, you know."

"Will, some people bring out her self destructive side. Unfortunately you're one of them."

"Jimmy, I appreciate everything you've done for me."

"My pleasure, pardner. Oh, by the way, Bear told me not to tell you because he's so pissed at you, but fuck him. There's warrants out for you and the sheriffs know you're around here. You better take the back way out. Bear's buddy at the sheriff's department let him know last night."

He gave me a soul shake and a hug. "Happy trails."

I packed my gear and loaded my bike into the back of my truck. When I went back into the trailer, Rosemary was awake and brushing her hair.

"Ready to get high?" She smiled.

I made us some baloney and cheese sandwiches.

"Well, Darling, I got expelled."

She looked at me while she was eating. "What do you mean?"

"The principal and the vice principal were here today with your brother."

"Howard, Bear and Jimmy?"

"Bingo."

"What happened?"

"I lied to them and they busted me. I have until nine o'clock."

"Shit! What a bummer! What are you going to do?"

"I think I'm gonna go to Mexico. Wanna' go?" She shook her head no."

"We could use a break from each other, Will."

I had to admit I agreed. We got high, but not incoherent and made love. We had fun. I kissed her tenderly on the forehead.

"Until we meet again."

"Bye, lover."

She gave me the rest of her stash and I gave her some money to replace it. I went the back way out and headed for the border. I'm sure they wouldn't be looking for people to smuggle drugs into Mexico.

I wish I could tell you about my travels in Mexico, but I don't remember them. I parked my truck in the back of a shopping mall on the U.S. side and took my bike across the border. I had a change of clothes and a toothbrush in a backpack. I had stopped shaving and cutting my hair months ago.

Once I crossed the border I would drive, eat, get high and get drunk, and not necessarily in that order. I met a lot of lowlife gringos hanging out in the cantinas, a lot of them hiding from the law in the States. I can't remember anybody specific. They all blended into a hazy blur of blubbering idiots with nothing much to say. Since I was at their level, it was a good way to pass time. Everyday, I got deeper into Mexico. The weather and scenery turned tropical. I had no idea where I was going.

I had been in the tropics for a week when I needed to score some more dope. All the gringos in the cantinas knew where to get weed, but nobody knew anything about smack. I ended up waiting for the bartender to close the place so he could show me where to score. I rode in his car to some filthy little town and some filthy little house. I went in with him and he woke somebody up in a back room. The place smelled putrid. The bartender's friend came out in his underwear. He was squinting and holding a gram bag of cocaine.

"No, I need heroin."

He pushed the bag at me. I shook my head no. I turned to the bartender, who spoke English.

"Tell him I need heroin."

The bartender said something in Spanish. The man shook his head "no" and answered in rapid fire Spanish.

"He says come back tomorrow."

My hands were starting to twitch. I pulled out two twenty dollar bills. I pointed at each of them, insinuating one for each if they could score. The man put on some shorts and an old tank top and they left. I sat on a chair and watched giant cockroaches crawl all over some dirty dishes in the sink. I had brought a bottle of tequila. I didn't have anything to mix it with, so I started drinking it straight. If these guys couldn't score, I was going to be in a world of hurt in a few hours. I was a third of the way into the bottle when I heard them pull up.

The bartender's friend had a big, proud, grin on his face. He showed me a bag of brown heroin. He said something in Spanish. I looked at the bartender.

"He wants two hundred dollars and the twenty for going to get it."

This guy was ripping me off, but I would have paid twice that. I gave him his money and twenty to the bartender. The bartender gave me a ride back to the cantina and my motorcycle. I asked him if I could go to his house so I could shoot up.

"No senor, I have a wife and family at my house, but I will open up the cantina for you for ten dollars."

I handed him ten dollars. He drank a beer and watched me get off. The heroin was stronger than I was used to. I immediately started nodding. I could feel the bartender putting my possessions in my backpack. He then walked me around the back of the cantina and sat me down, propping me up against the wall.

I didn't come to until late morning. There was a scrungy dog sleeping next to my leg. I shooed him away. The dog looked like it had mange. The fur had fallen off the back half of him and he had open sores. I needed to get high and get something to eat. I followed my nose to an outdoor grill. A Mexican lady was selling chicken tacos. I sat in one of her plastic chairs at one of her plastic tables under a blue tarp. I ate five of her tacos and a plate of rice and beans, which I washed down with two ice-cold beers. I bought a taco for the mangy dog that had followed me. He swallowed the taco down in two gulps before any of the other mangy dogs could get any. The other dogs had magically appeared when the taco hit the ground, but my sleeping partner wasn't into sharing.

Since I had no place to shoot up, I discreetly snorted some of the junk. Man, this was some good shit. I rode out of town, slowly going over speed bumps and avoiding potholes. Some of the little children waved to me. I guess they don't see many Harleys down here. I was feeling good.

My binge continued through more dirty little towns and dark cantinas. I knew I was strung out, but I wasn't ready to pay the piper. Well, it was more like I was afraid of coming down. There was going to be hell to pay once I came down.

I was sitting at a table drinking tequila and chasing it down with beers. I wasn't in a cantina, it was more like a converted living room into a bar. An old Mexican lady was bringing me the beers. Her husband was passed out in the next room and he was snoring.

I was ripped out of my skull. I had shot up a big load earlier and mixed in some cocaine, so I was buzzing. I was going to have to score some more dope tomorrow, but that was tomorrow. Tonight I was flying. I don't remember leaving.

I don't remember driving, but I must have because I woke up lying in the hot sun on a beach. I lifted my head and groaned. I had a hangover from hell. My head felt like it was split in half. I had sand stuck to my face from when I passed out. I felt like I was going to vomit. Sweat ran down my back causing my shirt to stick to my skin. With a mighty effort, I sat up and looked around. There was an empty tequila bottle lying in the sand. The sun was blinding, driving sharp stabbing pains deep into my brain. Where were my sunglasses? Where was my bike? Where the hell was I? It looked like jungle everywhere. To my horror, I saw my stash bag lying in the sand. I must have tried to get into it last night when I was wasted. I crawled over to it. It was emptyl I could see some brown granules mixed into the sand. I must have spilled it. I desperately tried to sort through the sand and retrieve enough for a line. I could hear myself saying frantically, "Oh my God, Oh my God." I was getting nowhere when a shadow blocked out the sun. I looked up to see an old Mexican with a puzzled look on his face.

"Can I help you?" he said in perfect English.

"Yes! Help get this brown powder out of the sand!"

A wave of nausea washed over me and I vomited right into the remains of my stash. The vomit tasted of tequila and I retched until my stomach was empty and then some. Mercifully, I passed out.

# CHAPTER 9
# BOUNCING OFF THE BOTTOM

Arturo dragged Will up to the house. Isabella saw him coming and came out to meet them.

"Who is this person?"

"I don't know. He is sick. Help me carry him into the house."

"Arturo, he is not going into my house. He is dirty and he has vomit on him."

"Isabella! I'm telling you he is ill."

Isabella put her hands on her hips and stood blocking the door. "You must clean him first."

Arturo shook his head. There was no point arguing when it came to the house.

"Okay. Help me get his clothes off." They removed Will's clothes.

"Look at all these bruises. His arms are covered with scabs."

Isabella was disgusted. "He is so dirty. I think those scabs are from drug addiction."

Arturo was washing Will with a cloth that he dipped in a bucket of soapy water.

"Isabella get me some shampoo, a towel, and some clean clothes."

"He is like a hippie. How did he find us?"

"Isabella, go now. Hurry."

They washed his hair and beard. Occasionally, Will would moan.

"He is like an animal."

"Isabella help me carry him into Estaban's room."

"No, he cannot sleep in Estaban's room."

"Where then?"

"In the shed."

Arturo was getting angry.

"Doesn't your religion teach you any compassion?"

Isabella was silent.

"Remember when Jesus said, 'If you give a thirsty man something to drink, you give it to me.'"

"He did not say anything about dirty hippies."

Arturo grabbed Will under the arms and dragged him past Isabella. Isabella grudgingly picked up Will's feet. They laid him down on Estaban's bed. When Cecelia got home from school, she looked at Will from the door.

"What is the matter with him?"

"Your grandmother thinks he is a drug addict."

"Is he?"

"I don't know."

"Grandfather, he scares me."

"Sleep with your grandmother tonight. I will sleep in your bed."

"Thank you, grandfather."

Cecelia hugged Arturo. He patted her on the head. When they were eating supper, they could hear Will softly moaning. Arturo was concerned about the stranger too. He didn't let on to Isabella or Cecelia. When they went to bed, he tied Estaban's door shut with some rope. If the man was dangerous, he would not get out with out waking Arturo.

In the middle of the night Arturo woke up. The stranger was screaming and pulling on the door. Arturo stood by the door.

"What is your name?"

"Open the fucking door!"

"What is your name?"

"Who fucking cares what my name is?! Open the fucking door!"

"I will not open the door until you calm down and tell me your name."

Arturo heard the stranger beating on the door with a chair that was in the room. Isabella touched Arturo on the shoulder.

"Now, are you glad you let him in?"

Arturo gave Isabella a stern look. "Do not start that, Isabella! Go and get me my small throw net and more rope! Hurry!"

Arturo could hear the chair breaking apart as the stranger pounded on the door. The door was made of hard wood and the stranger would never be able to break it. Isabella came back with the net and rope. Arturo waved her into the kitchen and he followed her.

"Listen," Arturo whispered, "when I open the door, we will turn out all the lights. I will throw the net over him and he will fall. Cecelia will turn on the lights and we will tie him up with the rope." Isabella and Cecelia nodded in agreement.

The stranger yelled from the room," My name is Will. I am in pain.

Please let me out." His voice was quivering with tension. Arturo positioned himself by the door. The voice from the room desperately asked, "Please, please let me out. I'm begging you. PLEASE!"

Cecelia blew out the lamp. Arturo untied the door and stood back with the net. "The door is open."

Will swung open the door and barged out. Arturo threw the net over him. Will let out a horrible scream and tried to run which caused him to crash to the floor. Arturo jumped on top of him. Will was thrashing around like a bucking bronco. Arturo was barely hanging on. Cecelia lit the lamp.

"Isabella help me!" Isabella jumped on the pile. Will was yelling obscenities that were for the most part incoherent. Even with Isabella and Arturo on top of him, they could not control the violent thrashing.

Isabella yelled, "Cecelia help!"

Cecelia added her weight on to the pile. The four of them bounced around the room. Everyone was grunting from the exertion. Eventually, Will started to tire. Then suddenly, he stopped altogether. He lay underneath them panting from the effort.

"Isabella hold him," Arturo said as he got the rope. Arturo first roped his ankles then his wrists. Will offered no resistance. Arturo pulled off the net. They all sat on the floor, trying to regain their strength.

Will looked at Arturo. Will's body was convulsing. Will's eyes were wild.

"Listen man, I'm in deep trouble, I need heroin. I am strung out and I am going through withdrawals. Please, help me. I am having audio hallucinations. I am going crazy. Please help me. I cannot go through this cold turkey." Will was perspiring and looked pale.

"We have no heroin. You are an hour from the nearest town. It is the middle of the night."

"Do you have any sleeping pills?"

"No."

"Do you have any alcohol?"

"No."

Will whimpered. "Please, let me go."

"You will never find your way out."

"You fucking untie me right now!"

Will's eyes looked crazy.

"I don't trust you. I think you are going to have to let your body clean itself of all the poisons you have put in it."

"Listen! Look at me! I'm shaking! I might die. Now, untie me! I could go into seizures!"

Arturo shook his head no. Will started screaming, then crying and then moaning. "Isabella help me, carry him outside." They tied him into a hammock. He was delirious. Spit was running down his chin and he was sobbing. Arturo put his hand on his forehead, it was clammy. "God, please ease this poor soul's pain." Arturo and Isabella went into the house.

Early the next morning Arturo checked on Will. He seemed to be asleep, but he was twitching as if he were having a bad dream. Arturo touched his forehead, it was still clammy. Will's eyes opened but did not seem to focus. "Mom? Is that you? Why did you leave us? We needed you. I tried to be good, but I couldn't. I'm sorry. Don't go, please don't go."

Will's body shook and he closed his eyes.

Arturo and Isabella ate their breakfast looking out at the hammock. "Arturo what will we do?"

"I don't know. I am going to work. Do not untie him until I get back."

When I became coherent, I was tied up in a hammock. I felt like I had a bad flu. I was very thirsty. "Hello! Hello!" I yelled. A nice looking older Mexican lady came out of the house. She seemed frightened of me and approached cautiously.

"I need water, please."

"No comprendo. " she answered.

"Water, water."

I licked my lips.

She went back into the house and came out with a glass of water, which she held to my lips. I thirstily drained the glass, so she brought me another. "Thank you." She turned and left. The water made me nauseated and I had to concentrate to not vomit. I fell in and out of a restless sleep. In the afternoon, an old Mexican man approached me. He looked familiar.

"Do you speak English?"

"Yes." he nodded.

"Why am I tied up?"

"You do not remember last night?"

"Parts of it."

"You were violent."

"I am sorry. I am tired and still sick. Could you untie me? I will not cause any more trouble."

"I am warning you. If there is a problem, I will tie you up again."

"I do not want to cause any more trouble. I am very weak."

After he untied me, I tried to stand, but was unable. He grabbed me before I fell.

"What is your name?"

"Arturo."

"Thank you, Arturo. Where am I?"

"This is the Bahia de Costa Azul, the bay of the blue coast. All of the locals know it as Scorpion Bay."

"Scorpion Bay?"

"Yes. This area has many scorpions. Beware the sting is very strong."

Arturo helped me into the house and into a bedroom. There was a broken chair in the corner. "Was that me?"

"Yes."

"I am sorry. I will pay you."

"We will talk about it later."

I collapsed on the bed and immediately passed out. When I awoke, it was late at night. I was still feeling bad, but better than earlier. I had a craving for heroin, but it passed. I had no idea where I was, where my backpack was, where my bike was, or really what I had become. Was I destined to go through hell over and over? Where do I start?

I made a resolution to stay off the smack, at least until I could figure a few things out. I drifted into another restless sleep filled with nightmares of dark scary places and men and creatures that wanted to kill me.

I awoke to sunlight in my room and a young girl staring at me from the doorway. I smiled and waved to her, but she left without acknowledging me. I still felt hungover from the withdrawals, but I felt well enough to get up. I walked into the kitchen. The older lady was there, but the young girl was gone. I waved hello. She nodded without a smile. She put a cup of coffee on the table.

I said, "Thanks. I mean, Gracias."

She nodded again. The smell of the coffee made me ill.

I pointed to myself and said, "Will.'

I pointed at her and raised my eyebrows.

"Isabella".

I smiled and repeated," Isabella."

She did not smile back. I went and sat on the porch. The view was magnificent. There was a small bay with a large rock in the left corner. The beach was brilliant with white sand. The color of the water was turquoise. The bright green jungle trees grew right to the water's edge. Palm trees swayed in a soft breeze from the north. It was a postcard that had come to life.

A huge lizard at least a foot and a half long climbed one of the poles holding up the porch roof. It kept going all the way up and on to the roof. I walked down the trail to the beach. There were spiders everywhere along the trail, big, beautiful, colorful spiders in intricate webs that spanned five to six feet.

I walked on the sand, it was so clean it squeaked. I felt really antsy and detached. I hoped I hadn't done permanent damage to myself. My usual withdrawals were a couple of days. I always felt sick, but I had never been this strung out. I probably was having some alcohol withdrawals combined with the heroin. I was really depressed. What had I become? What did I have to live for? I had no job, a little money. Warrants for my arrest. What a mess. I needed some smack to ease the pain. That was not the answer, but it sure would help. Temporarily. Would any one care if I killed myself? Would I?

I felt like I was going crazy. I couldn't swallow. I felt like I couldn't breathe. I started to hyperventilate. I took off running down the beach like a lunatic. I wanted to scream. Finally, I couldn't take it any more and I jumped in the water and started swimming out to sea. Fuck it. I'm going to kill myself. What a LOSER!

I swam straight out until my arms ached. I lay on my back until I caught my breath and swam again. I kept repeating this process. Once I looked back, I could barely see the beach. I kept swimming until I couldn't swim any more, even after resting. I lay on my back and drifted with the current. I looked at the clouds. All the exercise had calmed me down. I actually felt better than I had felt in a long time. I closed my eyes. I would have fallen asleep if I wasn't floating in the water. I felt some peace. It felt good.

I don't know how much time passed, but when I opened my eyes the color of the sky had darkened as it had become afternoon. Suddenly, something very large bumped me hard in the side, startling me. I straightened up, treading water. What was that? A shark? I couldn't see anything. Whatever it was, it was big and aggressive. I looked to land. I must be at least two miles offshore, maybe more. I wasn't sure I wanted to die anymore. I knew I didn't want to get eaten. I started swimming for shore slowly. I knew I did not have enough energy to make it, but maybe I could get away from whatever bumped me. Maybe I could get in a current that would pull me into shore. Luckily, I was too tired to panic. I was resolved to accept my fate.

After about an hour, I was no closer to shore. Now, I knew I wanted to live. I tried to pace my swimming stroke, but I really had nothing left. When I want to die, I don't. When I don't want to, I am. What a loser.

I was about ready to let myself sink into the water when I heard an outboard motor. I looked up and saw a fishing panga a half-mile away that was headed for shore. I waved my arms. It turned towards me, I couldn't believe my luck. The panga pulled up alongside me, it was Arturo.

"What are you doing out here, Senor Will? These waters are very dangerous. There are many sharks." He held out his hand and helped me into the boat. We headed for shore. Arturo pointed behind us. Two large fins were swimming in our wake. "Tiburon... shark."

I looked around Arturo's boat; it was about twenty feet long and five feet wide. Arturo's dog was under a piece of plywood that Arturo had installed for shade. The dog was sleeping even though the boat was bouncing in the swells. It smelled of gasoline and fish. There was an anchor, net, and fishing line up front. I was sitting in the middle of the boat next to buckets of fish that had been cleaned. The outboard motor was so loud there was no chance for conversation. Arturo was cleaning fish as we drove in. He threw the guts in a separate bucket. Arturo had a peaceful demeanor and I felt envious. Arturo gunned the motor and we flew up the sandy beach about twenty feet from the water.

I think Arturo knew that my swim was not just for exercise.

"You know Will, one of God's tools is misery. When a person is so miserable he can hardly stand it any more, he turns to a higher source for relief."

That's all he said. He tied his boat to a tree. Arturo had built a shed above the high tide line. He unloaded his gas tank and stored it in the shed. His nets and fishing lines he spread over a rope that was tied between two trees. This made for easy access for repairs. We both carried buckets to the house.

I am not a fisherman so I had no idea what type of fish these were. Arturo's dog, Chupa, followed behind me. Chupa loved to kill the iguanas so he was always searching for signs of the big lizards. When we got near the house, three cats appeared out of nowhere and started following Arturo. Chupa tried to chase one, but it turned and swatted him. He backed off.

When Arturo got to the porch, he put the buckets down. He threw some fish guts on a flat rock. The cats quickly surrounded the rock, gobbling up the scraps. Arturo gave a fish to Isabella and put the rest in a refrigerator. He handed me a glass of water and drank one himself. We sat on the porch, Chupa laid at Arturo's feet.

"What are you going to do, Will?"

"Arturo, I thank you for your help. I would like to stay for a while and get healthy. Could I help you fish to pay for my room and the food I eat?"

"I need to talk to Isabella, but I think that will be okay."

Isabella brought out a plate of sliced mangoes. They were the sweetest fruit I have ever eaten. The juice ran down my chin. Arturo got up. "I am going to work in my garden. Supper will be ready in an hour."

"Thank you, I am going to look for my motorcycle."

I started down the dirt road that led to the highway. Giant macaws were squawking in the trees. For some reason, Chupa followed me. He was ever vigilant. I felt safer with him along. Something crashed in the bushes alongside the road. Chupa jumped into the bushes and gave chase. He disappeared into the growth. I picked up a stick and used it a walking stick. I really wanted it as a weapon. The jungle looked prehistoric.

After twenty minutes I found my backpack. Everything was there, including a half bottle of tequila. I took it out and looked at it. I started salivating. I opened it and poured it out. That made me feel strong. I have no idea how long it had been since I was not drunk, stoned, hungover, or jonesing. I thought of Danni. I still had feelings for her. I wondered what she was doing. Chupa came back out of the jungle startling me. I held my stick up ready to swing it at the enemy. Chupa studied me, puzzled at my behavior.

Fifteen minutes later, I found my motorcycle. The front fork was severely twisted and it was laying on its side. When I got closer, a snake darted out from underneath it and disappeared into the jungle. Chupa gave a halfhearted chase. I would have to get Arturo to come back with his truck to help me get it back to the house. I doubted I could fix it, but maybe.

When I walked into the house, Isabella said something to Arturo in Spanish. "Isabella says you must take your shoes off on the porch. You also need to wash your hands for dinner; it will be ready in five minutes. We do not allow drugs or drinking in our house. This is my granddaughter, Cecelia."

He pointed to Cecelia. She stared at me without a smile, just like Isabella. I must have been really bad. I washed up and looked in the mirror. I was scary looking. My beard and hair were out of control. My eyes were sunken and bloodshot. I looked like a junkie. I had lost a lot of weight, so my arm and chest muscles had atrophied. I was disgusted with myself. Why would I hate myself this bad?

When I came back to the kitchen, the food was on the table: fresh fish, beans, rice, corn tortillas, onions, tomatoes, avocado, green salsa and red salsa. "Will, please stand for a prayer." They held hands. Arturo reached for mine, I reached for Isabella's. She gave me her hand without looking at me. Arturo first said a prayer in Spanish, then one in English.

"Lord, help me to be calm...I am spirit...though I dwell in this body, I am untouched by it... relax and cast aside all mental burdens, allowing God to express through me His perfect love, peace, and wisdom...please bless these bountiful gifts that you have put on our humble table...peace...aum... Amen."

I knew Arturo was directing the first part of the prayer for me and I was glad. I'll take all the help I can get. The food was delicious. Everything was so fresh. The fish melted in my mouth. They spoke in Spanish while I filled my stomach. I was feeling better. When everyone was finished, I asked Arturo to translate for me.

"First of all, I must say that this was the best meal I have ever eaten." Isabella almost smiled. "I also want to apologize from the bottom of my heart for my behavior. I broke up with my fiancee. I loved her very much. I was in a lot of pain. I am not making excuses. What I did was very wrong. I thank God that you found me and saved my life..."

I would have to wait for Arturo to translate. Isabella would look from me to Arturo and then back to me. "I promise you I will not take drugs or drink. I will work hard if you let me stay. I have nowhere to go. I am not violent. Please do not be afraid of me. I thank you for giving me a chance."

Arturo and Cecelia smiled at me. Isabella got up to do the dishes, she needed proof. I helped clear the table. Arturo went out on to the porch. Cecelia started her homework. I joined Arturo on the porch, he was smoking a hand rolled cigarette.

"Thank you Arturo for letting me stay."

"The work is not easy. You will earn your keep."

"I'm not afraid of hard work."

"What are you afraid of?"

I thought about it.

"I am afraid that I am weak."

"Are you afraid for your soul?"

"Arturo, can I be honest with you? I am not a religious person. I went to church when my mom was alive. I don't even know if I believe in God, heaven, souls or any of that stuff. I hope this doesn't offend you. I am not ready."

"This is fine, Will. We will talk about it when you like."

Arturo told me what we would be doing in the morning and what to expect. I asked him to reserve some time to help me get my motorcycle. Arturo came and got me while it was still dark. We quietly dressed and left. Arturo brought the bag of food and jug of water that Isabella had left by the door. On the porch, Arturo lit a lantern and we walked down the path with Chupa out front. A couple of times, Chupa crashed into the bushes, but always came back without anything.

Arturo was singing a chant over and over again. He had a good voice..."O thou King of the Infinite!... behold Thee in samadhi...in joy and in more joy...in thy light of mellow joy..."

When we got to the shed, Arturo gave me a list of things to do. He told me he was going to meditate for twenty minutes and that then we would leave. He disappeared into the darkness. I went into the shed to get the gas tank for the outboard. There were crabs everywhere. The biggest ones were about four inches across. When they saw me, they would scramble away holding their pinchers in the air. Chupa would catch them and crunch them. He came up to me with a claw hanging off his top lip. The crab had got him good before he had been crunched. I knocked the claw off with a stick. Chupa went back to work.

I loaded the nets, fishing lines and bucket of replacement hooks. I had just finished my list when Arturo came back. He untied the panga. He brought out four small logs. We put them behind the panga and used them as rollers to get the boat to the ocean. Chupa jumped in while Arturo and I guided the panga through the small waves breaking on the shore. When I was waist deep Arturo told me to get in. The motor started on the first pull.

"We are going to place I know that will take an hour to get to, so relax." With that, he gassed the motor and we headed out to sea. Since it was still cool out, Chupa stood in the front of the boat. I arranged the net into a bed and went to sleep.

The sound of the motor slowing down woke me from my sleep. The sun was coming up. I could not see land. Arturo threw a weight over that had a rope tied to it with a plastic jug as a float. He tied another rope to it, then slowly let out the rope while I steered the boat. Every ten feet, there was a plastic pop bottle that had a fishing line coming off the main rope. At the end of the line was a baited hook.

We let out a mile of rope with hooks every ten feet. This took two hours. The sun was getting warm and there was no breeze. Arturo threw me an old baseball cap that had a marijuana leaf emblazoned over the flag of Mexico. The hat smelled like rotten fish. I washed it in the ocean and put it on. For the rest of the day, I pulled the boat along the rope. Arturo would take fish off the hooks, re-bait the hooks and replace missing hooks. My arms and back were getting a workout. Arturo sorted the fish as we went. The only fish he released were the puffer fish; apparently they were not edible, not even for the cats.

It looked like we were in the middle of the ocean. "Why did you pick here to fish?" I asked. Arturo kept working as he talked. "Underneath us is a ledge that is only twenty feet deep. On the other side of the ledge, it drops down a couple of thousand feet. The fish come out of the deep water to feed. Let me show you."

Arturo grabbed a couple of masks out of his bag. "Have you ever dove before?"

"Yes. Are there sharks here?" I asked. I was tentative after my last swim.

"Of course there are sharks everywhere. If it is your time, it is your time."

"That doesn't make me feel any better."

Arturo pulled off his shirt. "Come on, pollo."

"What's pollo?"

"Chicken."

He fell over backwards holding his mask. I watched him disappear down into the deep blue water. I waited to make sure he was coming back before I went in. He surfaced holding a big lobster. "Look. There are no claws. I want you to catch one. Come on, pollo."

I entered the water and did a three hundred and sixty degree scan before I let go of the boat. I could see Arturo on the ledge, reaching in a hole and grabbing another lobster. The water was clear. The view was spectacular. The ledge was like a plateau under water. It was only about two hundred feet wide, but looked like it ran for miles. The water dropped off into deep black water on both sides. The deep black water was eerie and I was waiting for some sea monster to swim out of the deep. Along the ledge were thousands of fish of all sizes and colors. It was beautiful. Arturo surfaced with another lobster. "I left one down there for you. Do not take the small ones. They have to be this big, at least." The one he held in his hand had a tail that was twelve inches. I took a deep breath and swam down to where I had seen Arturo go. The fish were curious about me and barely moved out of my way. I saw fish of every size, shape and color. It was a wonderland. I got down to the hole where Arturo was pulling out the lobsters. I saw some movement and reached in. I could feel the lobster. It had a spiny back that hurt my hand. I tried to pull it out, but it dug in and I couldn't budge it. How did Arturo do it? I gave one more yank and gave up. Arturo laughed at me when I surfaced. "Too strong for you?"

"No. I'll get him."

I started back down when Arturo grabbed my leg. I looked at him. He pointed to the north. A huge hammerhead was swimming up out of the deep. I don't understand the function of the head, but it gives the effect of some alien out of a science fiction movie. Arturo and I watched the shark slowly swim by us. It went to one of the fish caught on our line and snapped it in half, leaving a trail of blood. I jumped into the boat. Arturo followed. "How big do you think it was?"

"About five meters."

I started pulling us down the line again. We brought in the half fish the shark had eaten. Arturo cut off the frayed part.

"The hammerhead is usually not aggressive. It is looking for fish."

"What sharks are aggressive?"

"Tigre. The tiger shark. The tiger has killed many, many divers in this area. It will come after you. It is like a great white shark, but it is in warm water."

"What else do I need to know? What will kill me?"

Arturo and I worked as we talked. "The sea snake has poison for which there is no antidote. Fortunately, they have a very small mouth, so it is hard for them to bite."

"Arturo, when you say no antidote, what does that mean?"

"You have minutes before you die, then let's see, there are the jellyfish. People have died from them."

"You mean, Portuguese Men of War?" I asked.

"Yes. The sea urchins on the bottom have venom in their quills. On land, there are many poisonous spiders and snakes. The coral snake is the worst; with no antidote, supposedly, you die in ten minutes. The doctors tell you to bring the snake with you after you've been bit. This way they can tell how to treat it. When I was growing up my father was bit by a snake. He killed it and took it to the doctor. The doctor told him he was going to die. After a half hour, he was still alive. The doctor asked if he was sure it was this snake? He said he was sure. So, they cut open the snake and it had a rodent in it's belly. The doctor figured the snake must have injected all of its venom in the rodent just prior to striking my father." I shook my head. "That is lucky."

Arturo re-baited a hook. "There's rattlesnakes, boas, fire ants and wasps. You have to be careful of the scorpions. If you are allergic, a sting can be fatal."

"Anything else."

"The jungle is alive with defenses. Some plants have thorns, some have toxic sap. Everything has to be tough to survive. My favorite spider is the Concha. If you measured its legs, they can stretch out to sixteen inches. It has venomous fangs and eats scorpions among other things."

"What happens if it bites you?" I asked, not sure I wanted to know.

"You pass out and go into convulsions for four hours then you wake up. No problem."

Arturo looked at me and laughed. We fished another four hours until my arms and back ached. We retrieved the line and headed home. Arturo showed me how to clean the fish, so we cleaned the fish on the way back. I was asleep a half hour after supper.

Arturo and I fished everyday but Sundays, which were a day of rest and religion. Arturo would go to mass with Isabella and Cecelia, then he would meditate twice for an hour. He would do two hours of yoga stretches and exercise. I would do nothing but lay around and read. I needed to recover from the work week. I was feeling better and stronger everyday physically. Mentally I was still a wreck. I had trouble sleeping. I had vivid nightmares. One was recurrent.

I was a small boy at the house I grew up at. It was a moon-lit night. I was locked out of the house. Someone was after me. I would hear him coming and I would run to the next door and it would be locked. I would shake the handle and call for my parents to open it, but nobody would help me. Then, I would hear the bushes rustle. I knew that the monster was coming. I would run to the next door, but it would be locked. Nobody would help me. I would wake up in a cold sweat.

Arturo had helped me get my motorcycle back. It wasn't easy with the forks broken. Arturo rigged up a pulley system. He cut two big limbs with his machete and roped them into a brace so we could pull the motorcycle into the back of the truck. The motorcycle was heavy. After we had the bike in the back, I looked at Arturo, who was in great shape. His arms and chest were muscular. He must be in his sixties, yet he was strong as a bull. He was one of the nicest people I had ever met. Everyday, he woke with a smile. He never said a bad word. He laughed all the time. At first, I thought it was not possible for some one to be so happy, but it was sincere. I was curious.

We lowered the motorcycle out of the truck and Arturo helped me take the forks off. The tire rim was also bent. As we worked on it, I asked him," Arturo why are you always so happy?"

"Why not Will? Why not choose to be happy? I am a wealthy man. He pointed to the bay. Look where I live. I have a wonderful family and a beautiful wife. I love the ocean and fishing. All of these things are priceless. I am rich."

"There are so many things to bring you down. It is hard to be happy."

"It is not hard if God is your best friend. Then, you can share his bliss."

"Arturo, put it in a way that I can understand."

"Will, if you live solely in the material world, you will never be happy. Money will not make you happy. Neither will sex, power, drugs or alcohol because you'll get bored with it. If you want to be happy, you need to love. The love for God and others can only grow better and better."

"If you give your life to God, how is it still your life?"

"I don't understand."

"It's like it's God's life. You have no control."

"What is the greatest gift you can give? Your life. It is not God living my life. I choose to give myself to God, my family and helping others. Is this not what Jesus said to do?"

"I am not ready."

Arturo touched my arm so I would look at him. "That is fine. Your day will come." We tried to straighten the forks out but they were too bent.

"I have a friend in town who is a mechanico. Possibly he can fix them." Arturo said. We worked in Arturo's garden for the rest of the afternoon. Arturo happily sang his chants.

The next time Arturo went to town, I went with him. The town was not big by United States standards, but there was a surprising amount of people who lived there. We dropped the forks off at the mechanic. He talked to Arturo in Spanish.

"He says possibly next week, which means next month."

Arturo went to sell his fish. I wandered around the town. The streets were made from cobblestones. The people were quick to smile and wave. The children were beautiful and a parent was always close by. I passed a butcher shop, tortilla shop, pharmacy, market, doctor, hardware, taco shop, liquor store, beer store, beauty shop, clothes store, vegetable stand, and numerous other shops that had a little of everything. All the people were busy cleaning, sweeping and working.

I went by the town center. It had a giant cross in a garden in the middle. The benches were made of concrete and a lot of them were occupied by old Mexican men wearing straw hats, cowboy hats and sombreros. They smoked and had animated conversations. There were stray dogs sleeping everywhere. The dogs looked pretty neglected, some had sores.

I was sitting on a bench when the local sheriff came up to me. "Buenas tardes, mi amigo."

"I'm sorry. I don't speak Spanish."

"I said, good afternoon, my friend."

"Good afternoon to you."

The sheriff was tall with a big belly, his clothes were finely pressed. He had a thick black mustache and eyebrows. His eyes were dark brown, almost black. He did not have a good vibe. The hairs on my neck were prickling a warning of danger. The sheriff sat down next to me.

"My name is Capitan Lorenzo Baca."

He stuck out a hand. I shook it.

"Will Callahan."

"What are you doing? You don't look like a tourist."

"I came in with Arturo to get my motorcycle fixed."

"Arturo the fisherman?"

"Yes."

Something caught the Capitan's eye. He got up and started walking away.

"Pleasure to meet you, Senor." He didn't wait for a reply and I didn't give one. On the drive back, I asked Arturo, "What do you think of the Capitan?"

"Isabella hates him. I think he is like all of our police and government officials, corrupt. Why?"

"I get a creepy feeling from that guy."

Arturo didn't respond.

The weeks passed. I got into a routine of fishing, gardening, beach combing and swimming. My arms and chest were hard as rock and my hair had turned blonde from all the sun. Isabella had trimmed my beard. I tied my hair back in a braid. Isabella thought this was very strange, but Cecelia liked it and would braid it for me. Cecelia and I had become friends, she reminded me of my sister Evangaline. Isabella was friendlier, but I think she didn't trust me after my freak out. I could understand that. I still felt lost, but I tried not to think of the future.

I forgot to shake out my sandals one morning and got stung by a scorpion. It felt like an electric shock. My foot was sore for a week. If you get stung in the neck, you can be in real trouble since it can cause asphyxiation. If you're allergic, you can die. The clear color scorpions are the worst, but the brown medium and the black are not so bad. I found a concla under my bed. This is an amazing creature. A spider with eight inch legs. It is jet black and armed with fangs that fold back and have spines on them. It also has a toxic spray. It is something you have to see to believe. Arturo talked me into not killing it. He scooped it into a box and took it out into the jungle.

A couple of days later Arturo found a coral snake in the shed. I was becoming real jumpy. I shook out my sheets every night. I shook out my clothes. I looked under my bed.

Arturo, Cecelia and Isabella decided to play a trick on me. They bought a big rubber spider and put it under my pillow. They left it so a little bit of his legs were sticking out from under my pillow. After supper, I washed up and went to bed. I was going to shake my sheets when I saw the legs.

"Oh, my God!!" I screamed. "HURRY! GET IN HERE!!" They all ran into my room with straight faces.

"What is it, Will?"

"THERE IS A GIANT SPIDER UNDER MY PILLOW! I ALMOST LAID MY HEAD ON IT! NOW, LISTEN! WE MUST KILL THIS MONSTER! SOMETIMES THESE THINGS ARE VERY FAST, SO WE NEED A PLAN! CECELIA GO GET TWO BROOMS AND A STICK! HURRY!"

I never took my eyes off it. This thing could not escape in my room. I would never be able to sleep. Cecelia came back with the brooms and the stick. "OKAY HERE'S THE PLAN! ISABELLA, YOU TURN OVER THE PILLOW! ARTURO AND I WILL KILL IT WITH THE BROOMS! WE CANNOT MAKE A MISTAKE! ON THE COUNT OF THREE!" They all looked at me with serious faces. "OKAY! ONE! TWO! THREE!

Isabella flipped the pillow off the bed. I had so much adrenaline going, I swung my broom like a madman. The fake spider was bouncing on the bed like a hockey puck. If I had been rational, I would have realized it was fake. I was expecting it to squish. So, I kept swinging faster and faster until I heard the laughing. Even then I hit it a couple of more times. Then I got it. I had been had.

I slowly turned around and saw that they were laughing so hard they were rolling on the floor. Isabella had tears running down her cheeks. I started swatting them with the broom. They got up still laughing and ran outside with me chasing them. It felt good to be a part of their family.

# CHAPTER 10
# COCK FIGHT

The Capitan had a bad hangover that not even menudo would cure. He would have stayed home, but today was the day he handed out ticket books. Every police officer had to buy a book of twenty citations for four hundred pesos, equal to forty US dollars. They would get their money back through bribes, the mordita. They could usually get forty pesos per ticket. If a policeman was good, he could get the bribe before he wrote the ticket however, he would still have to get rid of his tickets because the Capitan made them buy a book a week.

Most officers worked late Sunday afternoons when you could pull almost anyone over and catch a drunk driver. Besides the bribes, police officers were paid one hundred and fifty peso a day, equivalent to fifteen US dollars.

Rafael, one of the new officers, was complaining to the Capitan.

"I still have over half of my tickets from last week. How am I going to feed my family if I lose money?"

The Capitan looked up through blood shot eyes. "Maybe you are not cut out to be a police officer."

"But I finished high in the training class!" All the other officers laughed at this.

"Capitan, I could not find twenty violations where I worked."
Again everybody laughed.

The Capitan looked around the room. The laughing subsided.

"Officer Rafael, are you pulling over gringos?"

"If they break the law."

"Do not waste your time. They do not understand our ways. They don't know about mordita. Ask Officer Ce'sar for some help. He goes through two books a week and only Jesus Christ knows how many other bribes he doesn't report."

Ce'sar had a big smile.

"Everyone dismissed except Roberto and Felipe."

The men got up and headed for their cars. Roberto and Felipe went up to the Capitan's desk. The Capitan was feeling nauseated. He couldn't sleep last night, so he had kept drinking until the late hours of the night.

"Roberto and Felipe, take the prisoners to the court house. When Guerrmo Martinez comes before the judge, come and get me."

The Capitan went into his office and laid on the couch. Roberto and Felipe went to the holding cells in the back of the police station. There were three cells along each wall. The cells were six feet by eight feet. There were no beds in the cells and only a toilet. Half the toilets were not working. The prisoners received no food unless it was brought in by family or church members. The prisoners by law could only be held here for seventy two hours. Most went before the judge within twenty four hours, unless they were arrested on a Saturday and then the judge wouldn't be in until Monday.

Today the cells were packed. Some had standing room only. It was also unusual because almost half were women. The women were in their own cells.

Roberto and Felipe felt like covering their ears, there was so much shouting and cursing coming from the cells, mostly from the women. Yesterday afternoon, there had been a big wedding.

Gustavo Hernendez had married Rosa Ramierez. They were in love, but their mothers were not. After everyone had too much to drink, the two mothers got in a discussion that quickly escalated into scratching and hair pulling. This fight started a chain reaction that ended in a brawl between the two families.

Almost everyone that had been arrested from the wedding fight had torn clothing and some physical injury such as scratches, bloody noses and lips, or bruises. The sad part was that most of their best clothes had been torn during the brawl. Shirt sleeves were missing, pockets torn and dresses ripped. One older lady was arrested in her bra and panties. Fortunately, one of the officers had loaned her a jacket.

The only two prisoners that weren't involved with the wedding were a teenage boy and a middle age man. The teen had been arrested for shoplifting. The middle aged man, Gustavo Lopez, had hit a cow with his car.

The prisoners sat before the judge, who, one by one, called their names and gave them their fines. Just before Gustavo came before the judge, Felipe went and got the Capitan. The Capitan stood in the back of the room when Gustavo was called before the judge. The judge looked at the Capitan, who nodded. The Capitan then handed an envelope to Felipe to give to the judge when the judge was done with court. The Capitan headed back for his couch.

"Gustavo Lopez?" asked the judge. "Si." said Gustavo. He was trying to think how much the cow could cost, maybe one hundred dollars. No more than one hundred and fifty. It was an old dried up cow.

"Three months in the penitentiary."

"But why? I will pay. I have money. Please!"

"Court dismissed."

Officer Roberto led Gustavo to his police car. Felipe went to give the judge his bribe. What Gustavo didn't know was his neighbor had paid off the Capitan and the judge to get Gustavo sent

174

away. The neighbor wanted to put a water line across Gustavo's property and he knew that Gustavo would never agree. This was the easiest solution. By the time Gustavo got out of the penitentiary, the water line would be complete.

Capitan Lorenzo was searching through a drawer in his bathroom in his house. He had hidden a gram of cocaine in a band aid box and now it wasn't there. He was wondering if maybe he had already used it. No, it was in there somewhere. "Looking for this?" Lorenzo looked in the big mirror on the wall at his wife, who was standing behind him holding up a bindle.

"No. I was looking for an aspirin. I have a headache."

"You have a headache because you drink too much. Can you explain this? It was in the band aid box. I told you no more cocaine, Lorenzo! I will divorce you!"

"I didn't even know that it was there. I do not do cocaine any more, I promise on my mothers grave. Look. I will flush it down the toilet."

He took the coke, opened the bindle and dumped it in the toilet. Inside he winced.

"See? I do not do coke."

He flushed. His wife turned and left. Lorenzo watched the powder go round and round then disappear. "Damn bitch." he mumbled to himself. He would have to buy some more. He needed it for himself, but more importantly, he needed it for his prize roosters. Tonight was a big fight.

Lorenzo drove out to the ranch where he kept his gallos. His handler Marteen, walked with him to the pens.

"I want you to drug Diablo Rojo tonight."

"Capitan, I always give the Red Devil cocaine before his matches."

"No, Marteen, I want you to give him a sedative to slow him down."

"That means certain death. He has been your best cockfighter. You have won mucho dinero on him. Why would you want to kill him?"

"Because I am going to bet against him."

"Then everyone will know."

"Here's the plan. I will wager on the Red Devil. When people see me bet, they will bet also on the Red Devil. Your cousin, who is visiting you, will wager triple that against him. The Red Devil always gets odds of three to one, so we will make good money."

"Do you not feel anything for the courageous cock?"

"Don't be ridiculous. Who is next in line?"

Marteen pointed to another rooster. "I call him the 'Terminator'."

Lorenzo handed him a bindle of cocaine and a stack of pesos for betting.

"The coke is for the Terminator. Make sure the Red Devil does not win."

"Besides the sleeping potion, I will dull his blades. He will not win."

"Asta Luego."

"See you later, Capitan."

The Capitan needed some extra money because he was being blackmailed by his sister in law whom he had gotten pregnant a long time ago. She aborted the fetus, but threatened to expose him if he didn't pay her. Lorenzo promised himself if his wife ever did divorce him, he would kill the sister in law and relish it.

The bleachers were full for the cockfights. Tequila bottles were circulating the stands. Cold beer could be bought everywhere. Smoke from cigars and cigarettes rose over the crowd. Saturday night meant no work on Sunday, so it was time to get drunk and crazy...barrache y loco.

The main event would be the Capitan's Red devil versus a gallo all the way from Guadalajara. The roosters had razors taped to the spurs to assure death. Some of the fights were over in the first flurry. Others were so close that the crowd had to wait to see which bird would die first. The birds would lay motionless, both of them mortally wounded bleeding to death. The one still breathing last won.

Cock fighting is illegal in Mexico unless you have a permit. The police will break them up. Since the Capitan of police and the mayor were in attendance it was safe to say the police were not coming.

Before each fight, the bookies patrolled the stands taking wagers and changing the odds to balance the bets. They took ten percent of the winnings. For the people high in the stands who, they would throw a tennis ball with a slit in it. The bettor puts his money in the ball and throws it back. With his hand he signals which cock he wants. The crowd is almost as much a show as are the birds.

The Capitan had loudly proclaimed his bet and he had gotten the result he wanted. Red Diablo went up to four to one. Marteen's cousin put in his wager and it was so large it dropped the odds to two to one. Marteen entered the ring with Red Diablo. He had at first had given him too much sedative. It would be obvious, so he had to give him some cocaine to make him appear normal. The razors had been dulled, so the rooster had no chance.

Two handlers held the gallos in front of each other, riling them into a frenzy. At the appropriate signal, they let the cocks go. They charged each other with a vengeance. Red Diablo was cut to ribbons and lay dying in the middle of the ring. The crowd looked to the Capitan for some emotion. In true macho tradition, he showed nothing. He walked down and picked up the dead rooster and threw it in the pile of other dead cocks. The crowd nodded in appreciation. Lorenzo headed home, knowing he had made a lot of money. He wished he could tell his wife how smart he was, but she had banned cockfights also. He snorted some coke out of a little vial. The hell with her anyway, he thought. I'm going to the whore house.

# CHAPTER 11

# WAVE WALKER

When Arturo and I got back from fishing we could see a white VW van parked by the house.

Arturo smiled. "The Surfintistas are here."

"Who?"

"The people who ride the waves. Wavewalkers."

"You mean surfers?"

"Yes. That is it."

We cleaned up and headed for the house. The surfers were sitting at the table with Cecelia and Isabella speaking Spanish. The table was piled high with goods. The two surfers jumped up and hugged Arturo.

"Como esta, Arturo? Que paso?" one asked.

"Very good, thank you. This is my friend, Will."

The two surfers gave me an elaborate handshake that I was not familiar with. Everyone sat down at the table. The surfers had brought gifts, new pots and pans, ladles, big spoons for Isabella. They brought Cecelia a jacket, art supplies and magazines. For Arturo, a sledge hammer and a socket set. They also had surfing T-shirts for everyone. It was like a fiesta.

Cecelia brought out a drawing she had done of the bay. It was beautiful. She gave it to them. Isabella gave them each a giant conch shell. Arturo went out to his shed. He came back with two pieces of driftwood that he had carved on. One looked like a shark, the other a dolphin. The surfers were happy with their gifts.

We held hands while Arturo said grace. The two surfers were in college. Steve, blond and blue eyed, was planning on going to med. school. John, long dark haired and lanky, was studying to be an engineer. We sat down to our normal supper of fresh fish, rice and beans. For our visitors Arturo cooked a couple of lobsters. Three years ago the surfers had come down Arturo's road looking for remote surf spots. Arturo knew the coastline better than anyone and had taken them to a headland ten kilometers north, which had good waves. The surfers claimed it was a world-class wave that no one knew about. It was a secret spot, accessible only by boat. A place to surf good waves without crowds was a real commodity for surfers. They were indebted to Arturo.

The next morning, the surfers were excited with anticipation. They loaded their supplies, surfboards and camping gear into Arturo's panga.

"Will, why don't you come with us? We will teach you how to surf." Steve said. Arturo agreed. "You need to have some time off. You have been working very hard." Isabella put together some food for me. I brought my snorkel, spear mask and a fishing pole.

The surfers talked to Arturo about storms and swells as we rode the panga to the secret point. When we neared the point, we could see white water from waves breaking. The surfers went nuts, hooting and howling in joy. They slapped five and pounded Arturo and me on the back. The point was beautiful. It arced for about four hundred meters into a dark sandy beach. The point itself was rocky with jungle and trees growing right up to the high tide line. The waves were hitting the end of the point and wrapping all the way to the beach.

We beached the panga on the sand and unloaded our gear. The surfers couldn't stop looking and talking about the waves. Arturo was going fishing, so he left. He said he would check in every two days. The surfers left their gear in a pile and started waxing their surfboards.

"Will, we're going surfing. We will fix camp later. After we surf, we will give you a lesson. Okay?"

"Sure. I'll work on the camp while you're out there. Where do you want to put the tent?"

Steve pointed up the beach. I could see an old lean-to that the palm leaves had blown off. John and Steve sprinted to the water, hooting again. They were like heroin addicts. I had to laugh. What could make a person that excited? As I set up camp, I watched them surf.

From my limited perspective, they looked good as they would climb and drop on the wave surface, sending giant sheets of spray over the back of the waves. They achieved great speed turning along the wave sometimes they would lean over like water skiers. No matter how many waves they rode, they cheered for each other as though it was the first ride ever. I could hear their hoots echoing down the point.

I set up their tent and reinstalled the palm leafs on the lean-to. I set up my hammock between two trees and hung my mosquito net off a branch above the hammock. All of the supplies I put in the tent and closed it up. Afterwards, I walked up the point. There were many birds in the trees. The parrots squawked at me.

The point along the water consisted of large round rocks worn smooth from the constant pounding of the waves. I got halfway down the point, found a comfortable spot and watched John and Steve perform. John rode with his back to the wave while Steve rode facing the wave. I had no idea why they faced different ways. They both had amazing balance. They would zig zag down the wave then reverse direction in a one hundred and eighty degree turn, then bounce off the wave and keep going. I was impressed with their ability. It seemed like they were attached to their boards. Sometimes they would stall their boards and let the wave break over them, disappearing inside of it, then reappearing in a burst of speed.

Steve and John lasted for about three hours before coming in. They were excited and recounted ride after ride, slapping five and doing their handshake. After a lunch of peanut butter and jelly sandwiches, they started my first lesson. They pulled out a large round board, which looked way different then the speed shaped boards.

"Will, you need to start on a long board. This board is nine feet long.

John and I ride these long boards on small days since they have good glide. The short boards turn sharper and are more radical on bigger waves. They are not as stable as the long board. You need stability, flotation and easy paddling, which is why you need a long board. Understand?"

"Yes."

He laid the board down on the beach and showed me where to lie when I paddled. He also showed me how to stabilize the board with my hands when I stood up after catching a wave. He made me jump to my feet from a lying position on the sand to get the feel for it. After a few tries, he deduced that I was putting my right foot forward.

"You're a goofy foot like me. John's a regular foot. He has his left foot forward."

Steve smiled. "Goofy foot's rule, dude."

We put our boards in the shallows. Steve showed me how to roll over and grab the front of the board if a wave was going to break on me.

"Okay. Attach your surf leash to your left foot, your back foot. If a really big one comes, bail your board. Your leash will bring your board back to you. "Let's go."

He jumped on his short board. The long board felt very unstable, I couldn't imagine what the short boards were like. We paddled to the left of the breakers in deeper water. Some of the waves looked big.

"The hard part, Will, is to time your take off. If you paddle too late for a wave you miss it. If you paddle too early, then you get in front of it and it breaks on top of you. So try and look over your shoulder and see what the waves are doing. You have to paddle really fast to catch them. Once you feel the wave pick you up, lean forward, which will cause the board to slide down the wave. Then you jump to your feet, s this making sense?"

"Sure," I lied.

John and Steve positioned me at the end of the point. They were excited for me.

"Okay Will, here comes one! Paddle hard!"

1 paddled hard, but the wave went right by me.

"You have to paddle faster than that to catch one."

They got me back into position. I missed another wave, then another and another. They were getting a little frustrated with me. On my next try, Steve paddled behind me and gave me a shove into the wave. I was so excited about catching the wave, I forgot to stand up. The board went straight down and kept going. The nose went underwater and then flipped over. I was catapulted over the front of the board so that I landed on my back just in time to see the lip of the wave land on me. I bounced off the rocky bottom, thankfully the rocks were smooth. I was swirled around and around like I was in a washing machine. I was concerned about how much air I had when I surfaced. Another wave broke on me and I was held down again. This time, I relaxed and waited to surface. John was waiting for me when I came up.

"You okay dude?"

"I'm fine."

"Good. Let's give it another try."

My arms were aching from the paddling. I knew I was in good shape, but these were different muscles. Steve flew by us riding a wave. It looked amazing from the water. It looked great. I was determined to get the hang of it. I caught a wave without being pushed; again, I was too slow and got pitched over the front. This sport was difficult.

John paddled up next to me. "Once you feel the wave pick you up, you need to lean back to stop the board's nose from going straight down. You have to be quick."

I caught another wave. When I felt myself sliding down the wave, I leaned back and made the drop. Unfortunately, I was now going too fast to stand up. The board raced along the wave with me in a prone position, hanging on for dear life. Steve and John were hooting. Water kept splashing off the board and blinding me. It felt like I was going a thousand miles an hour.

It was almost like a toboggan on water as I raced down the point, laughing like a madman. The wave stopped in the shallow water in front of our camp. I had nothing left in my arms, so I went in. I drank some water and watched Steve and John rip apart the waves. Now I could appreciate how good these guys were. They had it wired. They surfed for another three hours.

"You did great, Will."

"I didn't get to my feet."

"You will. Now you know how to catch them. Tomorrow, you'll be going off."

They took a siesta. I went fishing and caught a nice fish off the point.

They went out for an evening session. That night we sat around the fire after dinner telling surf stories. I didn't have any, so I just listened. These guys could remember swells from years ago. They both had been to Fiji, Hawaii and Indonesia.

"This spot's the best."

"Why is that?" I asked.

"No crowds. If this spot was in California, there would be a hundred guys out there. There would be fistfights in the water and on the beach. It would be a zoo," said John.

"Will, did you know they have surf camps now where you have to pay to ride private breaks?" Steve shook his head in disgust. "Really."

"This point is perfect the way the waves peel down the point. You can get two hundred yard rides. Longer, if it's bigger."

They were recounting their waves for the third time when I went to sleep. The next morning, I was ready for my first standing ride. The boys were hurrying through their cereal, apparently the surf had come up. We paddled out. I felt strong. On my first two waves, I blew the takeoff. On my third wave, I got in early because Steve was screaming at me to get up. I jumped to my feet and almost fell, but I recovered my balance, bent my knees and raced along the face of the wave. Steve and John were yelling encouragement. The feeling was incredible.

Not only was I moving, but the wave was moving. Faster and faster I went. It was like running on water. I was laughing like a kid on an amusement ride. Halfway down the point, I lost my balance and fell. I was stoked. When I paddled back into position at the end of the point, Steve and John were beaming.

"Cool, wasn't it?"

"Unbelievable. I can't describe it."

"We hear you, brother."

I slowly learned that you could turn the board by leaning. To go faster on a long board, move towards the front; to turn, move to the back. The majority of the time, I was taking spills, underwater, or paddling. The few waves that I was successful on were out of this world. I only went in for lunch. That night I felt complete.

The next ten days were all about surfing, surfing and more surfing. My takeoff percentage was better than fifty percent. I could make the board do small turns and I was riding them all the way to the end of the point.

One of the days got big. The boys told me it wasn't wise to go out, that it was too dangerous. I paddled out and sat in the channel watching them surf. They were incredible. They would ride waves that were two stories high. The speed was almost twice as fast as the smaller days. After an hour, I paddled into the line up position.

"Will, are you sure?"

"No guts, no glory."

John gave me the thumbs up. I paddled into a huge wave. I had so much adrenaline, I tried to turn too fast. I fell and skipped down the face of the wave. Underwater, I felt myself being lifted into the wave so that I was actually a part of it. As the wave broke, I was trapped inside. The concussion was tremendous and knocked the wind out of me. I was cartwheeling under water with out any air. I started to panic and clawed for the surface, but got sucked down again. I had started to pray when I miraculously broke the surface. I gulped air and foam. I sat in the channel for long time watching them surf, but had to give it one more try and paddled back to the line up. "You got huevos, dude. You got drilled."

I explained to them how I had actually been trapped in the wave when it broke. They both nodded in complete understanding. Steve said, "Happens to everyone. It's called 'going over the falls,' and it's the worst, except for getting speared by your board."

They both caught huge waves. I waited for one that was just big. I made the drop and my first turn. The wave felt enormous and I had to crouch for balance. The section in front of me looked like it was going to collapse on me and I inched forward to gain more speed. The wave threw out in front of me. I was going through a tunnel of water. It was my first tube ride. The roaring water echoed like in a cave. The sun was blocked out and I could see the lip of the wave breaking in front of me as I raced along.

I came out of the barrel on the shoulder and pulled out of the wave.

John and Steve were hysterical. They paddled up to me and pounded me on the back like I had just won the Superbowl. I was spellbound. That was the most amazing experience I had ever had. I paddled in. I sat and thanked God for the experience, which made me think of Arturo. That old fisherman was having an influence on me.

Arturo picked us up a couple of days later. When he came, the surf had dropped. I now had my stories to tell on the ride home. Steve and John started their long drive home early the next morning. They left the board with Arturo. I went back to fishing but inside me burned the fever of the wavewalker.

# CHAPTER 12

# DON JUSTO

F our pelicans glided by us. Pelicans have a big beak for catching fish, yet they are one of the most graceful birds in flight. They catch the air currents off the swells and can glide for hundreds of feet without flapping their wings. Arturo always took time to marvel at their ability. Arturo was childlike in his admiration of nature. I was still cynical; life for me was a war, a war in which I had lost many battles.

Arturo was an exceptional fisherman. His many years on the ocean gave him an almost psychic feel for the fish. Some days we threw a net, other days we fished with just a single line. We also snorkeled for lobster, octopus and clams. Arturo never took more than he needed. He could easily catch twice as much as he did, but he was an environmentalist. Respecting the planet was logical and easy for him.

A lot of Mexicans did not share his view, we would constantly see trash floating in the water. Plastic was the most prevalent. It washed up on the beaches. We would see plastic bottles floating miles from shore. A lot of towns would dump their trash in the dry riverbeds. When the rains would come, it would wash the trash down the river and eventually into the sea.

On this particular day, we were long line fishing. The line stretches for a mile with hooks every ten feet. It was the same technique Arturo used on the first day I fished with him. Arturo knew every ledge, shallow spot and canyon basically, all of the best fishing spots. How he found them I have no idea. There were no markers because most of the time we were way out to sea.

Arturo was telling me the rainy season was coming in a few weeks. He said it would give us some relief from the humid heat. He described the lightning storms with booming thunder that come with the rain. He had seen lightning hit a hundred yards from him. It turned the water red for a split second. Giant balls of white light floated down after the bolt hit. He was telling me like it had been a good thing, although it sounded hairy to me.

By late afternoon we had gotten our quota. Arturo started pulling the rope to start the outboard motor. It wouldn't start, which was not unusual, the thing looked like it was a hundred years old. I made myself comfortable while Arturo took the case off the top and went to work. He knew every detail of that motor. I think he could probably fix it blindfolded since he had rebuilt it a thousand times. I pulled my hat over my face and prepared for a siesta. I was almost asleep when I heard Arturo curse, "Damn." I lifted the hat off my face. This was not good. I had never heard Arturo say "damn" before. "Que pasa, mi amigo? "Arturo held up a part that was broken in half.

"This needs to be replaced."

I am embarrassed to admit that I took stock of what was in the boat for the first time. I had been riding in it for months and I never noticed there were no life preservers. There was one old weathered paddle, but no oars. I could feel a rush of adrenaline.

"What's the plan?"

"Will, it is very simple. I have been in this situation once before. We are drifting in the current to the south. Eight miles from here there is a small island. We must reach the island."

*Scorpion Bay*

"And if we don't?"

"We will be in a current that will take us out to sea."

"You mean, like lost?"

"Si. We have one problem."

"Just one?"

"We are not in a direct path of the island, so we need to paddle six miles west. Also, I recommend that you conserve on water. We can always eat the fish but the island has no water."

I looked at our water supply. We had one plastic jug three quarters full and another one that was half full, not good. Arturo grabbed the paddle, got in the front of the boat and started paddling.

"I will paddle until I am tired then you take over. I don't want to worry you, but last time I had oars. I don't know whether we can do it with just this paddle. We have to hit the island directly. The current is so strong going around the island that if we are even a hundred yards off, we will be pulled by."

"That's great! Anything else?"

"Not that I can think of."

Arturo paddled hard and soon the sweat was glistening on his arms and his shirt was soaking wet. Chupa knew something was different and came out of his shade spot to look around. When he didn't see anything of interest, he went back in the shade and fell asleep. When my turn came, I was amazed at how fast Arturo had been paddling. It took a lot of energy to keep the boat moving. My arms and back were strong from the fishing. At least we controlled our own destiny. I paddled as hard and as fast as I could. When I handed the paddle to Arturo, he smiled. "Well done, hermano. If we can keep it up, we have a chance."

The length of time for each paddler shortened as we tired. The sun was setting and I could not see an island.

"Are we on course?"

Arturo kept paddling. "I think so. Pray for a clear night, so I can see the stars."

I was becoming weary. Arturo was picking up my slack. He was like a machine. An hour after sunset, we started seeing stars. "If I remember correctly, we need to make an adjustment. We are going a little too much west."

There was no moon, so we could paddle right by the damn thing without seeing it. I was dehydrated from the sweating. I took a swig of water, rinsed around my mouth and slowly swallowed it. I became in a trance like state, paddling then resting, paddling then resting. It was pitch black out. It would be impossible to find anything in the dark. I felt like gulping down the water, might as well be comfortable if you're going to die. I pictured myself pouring the water over my head and laughing hysterically. Arturo touched my shoulder, signaling me to stop paddling.

"Listen."

I listened. "I don't hear anything."

"Will, you must keep quiet and listen."

I listened, but all I could hear was the slapping of the choppy water against the boat. This was ridiculous. All of a sudden Arturo pointed.

"There! Did you hear it?" I heard nothing. Arturo started frantically paddling to our left. It was the sound of a wave.

When my turn came, I paddled with renewed energy. After a short while, Arturo started tapping me on the back he wanted his turn. He grabbed the paddle and quickened his pace. "We are close, but we are going around the side." He panted with the effort. "Will, get two ropes about ten feet long. Tie one around your waist and one around mine, then tie them to the front of the boat. We are going to have to swim for it. It is our only chance. Hurry!"

I could hear the waves and see the island. We were two hundred yards away, but in a strong current. I secured the ropes. Arturo threw the paddle down and dove over. I followed. The strength of the current was amazing. We were being pulled sideways. I swam and kicked as if my life depended on it, which it did. I forced myself to swim faster than I have ever swum.

We hit shore a hundred feet from the end of the island. Arturo and I stood in waist deep water and hugged each other. Arturo whispered, "God has blessed us. Praise the Lord."

We secured the boat. Arturo had a couple of candles that we lit. We needed to prepare the fish for smoking. This is the only way we could preserve the fish. Arturo got the fire going and we strung out the fish. Arturo spread out a piece of plastic to trap any dew overnight. I was exhausted.

"We will sleep by the boat tonight. Tomorrow, we will find a suitable place to camp," Arturo said.

I could barely keep my eyes open. "How long before another boat comes along?"

"Last time I was here for just two days, but it was the tourist season. The tourists like to come here to snorkel and dive. Sometimes fishermen come here, but not often. The tourist season is over, so it may be a while. Be prepared for the worst. Be patient. Tonight we will enjoy being alive, my brother."

I muttered, "Amen to that." I fell asleep sitting up.

The next morning was cloudless and hot. Arturo retrieved a tablespoon of water off the tarp. That was not going to be enough. We rationed ourselves to a half a glass of water a day. Just the fact that I couldn't drink the water made me thirstier than I really was.

On the other end of the beach from where we landed was a cave. Since there were no trees on the island, we would use the cave as our shade. We pulled the boat down there by wading in the water. I could see the current racing by just outside the breakers. It was a miracle we made it. If I had seen how strong it was, I might have given up.

Chupa was thirsty too and it was hard to ration his water. He didn't understand. Once we were organized, Arturo said, "Will, if we get a rain, I have cleaned out all my buckets. We will need to hold the tarp to drain into the buckets as fast as we can. We should not do anything in the middle of the day. It is too warm and we need to slow ourselves down to conserve our liquids."

I nodded. "I'm going to have a look around before it gets too hot." I said.

The island was mostly lava rock with sand on its perimeter. It had a couple of hills a hundred feet high. The island was probably two miles by four miles. How Arturo found this on a pitch black night was incredible. There were tons of birds on the island, the majority were the big frigate birds. Because of the lava, the island had a lot of caves. The only vegetation was some form of scrub brush.

When I got back Arturo was deep in meditation. The cave was thirty feet long, about eight feet deep and twenty feet high. I went to the other side of the cave so I didn't disturb Arturo. I looked at him in meditation. He was sitting cross-legged, his hands were on his knees with his palms turned up. His index finger was touching his thumb forming a circle. He was absolutely still. He had a very tranquil expression on his face. I looked at my watch and noted the time. I took a little siesta. When I awoke, Arturo was still meditating.

Arturo started to slowly moving after three hours, he stretched himself out.

"How long do you usually meditate, Arturo?"

"At home, I only have time for twenty minutes a couple of times a day. I am going to make the most out of this opportunity to meditate and pray."

"I am very bored. Will you teach me?"

"It would be an honor, my friend. Right now, I am going to do some yoga postures. They also are beneficial to your health."

Arturo explained every pose and its benefits. Breathing was also something we focused on. Arturo was at least forty years older than me, but he was much more limber. I could only go two thirds of the way on some of the stretches.

"Where did you learn this?"

"In California."

"What does Isabella think about it?"

"She thinks it is nonsense, but she knows it is important to me, so she does not try and make me stop."

"I always saw this stuff as for weirdos."

"Were you raised Catholic?"

"Yes, Irish Catholic."

"Do you find believing in the Immaculate Conception, purgatory, walking on water, original sin, Resurrection, Baptism, or any of the other things odd?"

"No."

"Of course not. You grew up with it but what if there was more than one path. What if there was more than one Christ?"

"There seem to be so many cults and liars. Who would know what the truth is?"

"Exactly! That is why you must find what is right for you. Do not be afraid to search my friend."

"I think I will just try the yoga and meditation for now."

"I am at your service. The meditation is extremely simple, but incredibly difficult. What you want to achieve is to have no thoughts. That sounds simple in reality, but it is not. One of the techniques and there are many is to use a mantra. A mantra is a word that you repeat slowly over and over again with your breathing. One of the ancient mantras is 'Ham Sa' as you inhale you say, not out loud, 'Ham,' and when you exhale you say, 'Sa'. Your eyes should be closed and lifted to the place between your eyebrows, your Christ center. When you get a thought, gently guide it out of your consciousness. Eventually, you will quiet your mind and allow your spirit to surface through the calm. Let's take some deep cleansing breaths and give it a try."

We breathed deeply a couple of times and then I closed my eyes. My mind was racing like an out of control computer. Eventually, with the mantra technique, I achieved a tremendous calm. When thoughts surfaced, I gently returned to the mantra and the thoughts drifted away. I felt like I was down deep in my subconscious. I started to surface, feeling like hours had passed.

I opened my eyes. It was only four minutes.

Arturo smiled at me. "Good start."

"I didn't last long."

"It takes time. You will have plenty of time to practice."

After eating our fish dinner, I lay looking at the stars. Chupa was lying with me. I felt calmer than I have ever felt. The heroin seemed like a distant nightmare. Thoughts of Danni came back. If we get off the island, I should call to see if it was possible to start over. Arturo was one of the best things that had ever happened to me. I drifted off to sleep and for the first night in a long time, I had no nightmares.

We passed the days in meditation and yoga. The yoga was really stretching me out and I felt good. The water was a problem though. We had enough for two days, maybe. The dew on the plastic was not enough and even Arturo was concerned. We cut back to two swallows a day. My tongue felt swollen. I tried not to think of my thirst, but it was impossible. That night I fell into a restless sleep. In the middle of the night, Arturo shook me hard.

"Will! Rain!"

I sprang to my feet. We held the plastic so it would drain into the buckets. The storm was strong but brief. We filled three buckets. We were ecstatic and started doing an Irish jig, swinging back and forth on each other's arms. Arturo, Chupa and I all had a long drink and then celebrated with some more fish.

The next day, in the middle of the day, I was doing some cave carvings. It was day number six.

Arturo said calmly, "Boat." I turned and looked where he was looking and could see something on the water. It was still way out to sea. I was afraid to ask.

"Will it come here?"

"Yes. There is no other destination."

I gave Arturo a high five.

"Thank you, Lord!" I heard myself say.

This made Arturo smile.

The boat was huge and very expensive, some kind of luxury yacht. They didn't see us and went to the other side of the island. We were waiting on the sand when they dropped anchor. The back end of the yacht lowered down to make a launching platform. A zodiac inflatable was put in the water by a winch off the back of the boat. A man in a white uniform got in the zodiac and came into shore. He sat in the boat while we stood by the side. Arturo spoke to him in Spanish. Arturo signaled for me to get in. We climbed in and he took us back to the yacht.

We stepped on to the platform. Another man in a white uniform signaled for us to follow him. The air conditioning felt too cold. The yacht was plush and made me feel self-conscious. I looked at Arturo, who having not shaved or changed clothes in six days, looked like Robinson Crusoe.

The man had us wait in what looked like a living room. After a few minutes, a thin gray haired man in his seventies appeared in a robe.

"Hello. My name is Don Justo. I am on my honeymoon. My wife is still sleeping. How can I help you?" Arturo introduced us and told him of our plight.

"Please you will be my guests. I am going to be diving on this island for a couple of days, then I will give you a ride back. I will have one of my men accompany you back to your panga. He will bring it back here and secure it. I have a suite you can stay in and I will have them bring you clothes and toiletries. Feel free to make yourselves at home. The only rooms that are off limits are my master suite and the sitting room next to it. Since it is my honeymoon, do not be offended if I am sometimes not available. I would like to request your company at dinner tonight."

He shook our hands again and then nodded to the man in the white uniform, who had been standing up against the back wall.

We went back with one of the attendants and brought back the panga and Chupa, who we had tied to the boat. The attendant, whose name was Luis, told us that Don Justo owned the Pepsi distribution for all of Mexico. The yacht was one hundred eighty three feet long and two stories high. There were twelve employees, including the captain. We secured the panga. Luis showed us to our suite, then took Chupa off for a bath and some food and water. The suite was like an expensive hotel room. Luis had measured us for clothes and said he would bring them back when he was done with Chupa.

I took a bath, it was the first one I had had in over a year. I lay in the tub drinking ice cold Pepsi, which was in a little refrigerator in our room. This was heaven. Arturo was singing a chant while he shaved. I heard myself singing along with him. I had heard this chant so many times, I knew the words by heart.

"Do not dry the ocean of my love with the fires of my desires, with the fires of my restlessness...for Thee I pine, for Thee I weep...I'll cry no more, Thou mine evermore...Thee I find behind the fringe of my mind...hide no more, Lord, hide no more...leave me not, Lord, leave me no more!"

I can't remember ever feeling this good. Life was good. I was still not sold on this religious thing, but I liked the meditation and the stretching. I had to admit that for today, God was good.

Arturo was in the shower when Luis came with the clothes. He brought two pairs of pants for both of us. The pants were the white uniform that all the employees wore. He brought us three shirts each. They all had tropical designs on them.

"Where did you get these, Luis?"

"These are the Don's son's shirts. He is close to your size."

"Do you mind if I go to the kitchen?"

"You are welcome anywhere on the ship except the master suite and adjoining sitting room. "

The pants fit perfectly. The shirt was a little tight in the chest. I walked around. The ship was decadent. I had never been around this type of money. It was staggering. Everything was clean and polished. There was expensive art on the walls. Arturo and I must have been quite a sight when we first came on board.

In the kitchen I persuaded one of the female cooks to braid my hair and trim my beard. My hair had grown past my shoulders. Luis told me we would be dining with the captain, Don Justo and his wife at eighteen hours. Arturo and I walked around the yacht until dinner. There was a workout room, entertainment center and a spa. Arturo and I were blown away. It didn't seem possible.

At six o'clock, we went up to the dining room where the captain introduced himself. We sat and told him of our adventure. At six thirty Don Justo and his new bride arrived.

"My apologies for being late. Christina was slower than usual." said Don Justo. Christina held out her hand.

"I am sorry I was late."

Christina was a tall blonde in a slinky evening dress that pushed her large breasts together. She was stunning. I was speechless. She bowed when she shook my hand so I got a good look at her ample chest. Mr. Happy came out of hibernation and yawned. Christina had her hair pulled up in an intricate hairstyle with an emerald brooch in her hair. The emeralds matched the color of her dress. She had hazel color eyes. I couldn't tell if she was Mexican. Her wedding ring was a massive diamond. Don Justo was very proud of her and paraded her around like a prize racehorse. A waiter appeared with oyster hors d'oeuvres and glasses of champagne.

"Let us toast to your adventure." The Don raised his glass.

We clinked glasses. I would have been satisfied with the hors d'oeuvres, which were oysters in a half shell with spinach and garlic. After some meaningless conversation, we sat down for a Caesar salad, followed by the main event. We were served New York steak wrapped in crisp bacon, mashed potatoes that had a creamy cheese sauce and asparagus in a spicy concoction. Arturo and I reached nirvana. The food was so good I actually forgot about Christina's breasts for a few minutes. Desert was melt in your mouth flan, a Mexican specialty. While the others opted for brandy, Arturo and I drank coffee.

Arturo and the captain talked fishing while I listened to the Don tell me how much money he had and what he was doing with it. Something bumped my foot and I moved my leg back, thinking somebody had inadvertently kicked me. I then felt something on my other foot. Christina was playing footsie with me! She never changed expression as we listened to her husband drone on.

She had her shoe off and she was running her big toe up my leg. It was very distracting. Mr. happy let out another yawn. I really did not want to wake him up. He was a troublemaker. Christina's toe was up to my knee. I was trying to concentrate on the Don, but I was having difficulty. I also was having a problem with the fact that I was playing footsie with the wife of the Guy who had just saved our lives. I discreetly reached under the table patted her foot and then removed it from my leg.

Arturo and I were used to going to sleep at dark. We politely excused ourselves. The Captain and the Don were going to go fishing with Arturo in the morning.

"Will, would you be so kind as to go diving with Christina tomorrow?" the Don asked me. "She hates fishing. I promised her I would go diving with her, but I want to see this fishing spot Arturo knows of."

"I could never refuse any of your requests, Sir. I owe you my life."

"Please. All I did was show up."

"That was more than enough and your hospitality is over whelming. I would be glad to take Christina diving."

I was having a bad premonition about this whole thing.   It was decided that they were going to leave at daybreak and take their breakfast to go. I was to meet Christina for breakfast at nine o'clock. I slept like a baby in my clean sheets.

The next morning, I looked at my watch, it was eight o'clock. I got up and took a shower. When I stepped out of the shower, Christina was standing in the doorway checking out my merchandise. I tried not to be embarrassed and grabbed a towel.

"I didn't hear you knock."

"I did. You were in the shower. I brought you a cup of coffee. I wanted to make sure you were awake."

"I'm awake."

"I'll see you in the dining room."

She turned and left. She was wearing a mesh shirt over her bathing suit, her back side was as good as her frontside. She was the complete package. Lord have mercy on me.

I savored my breakfast, which was huevos rancheros. Christina was actually very witty and we had a nice meal. I followed her down to the storage room and we had one of the attendants get our gear. After suiting up, we sat on the edge of the platform with our finned feet in the crystal clear water.

"Have you ever dove before, Will?"

"No."

"You'll love it."

"Do I need a lesson."

"It's simple. Just breathe through your mouth piece. Do you know how to clear your mask?"

I nodded.

"Just don't come up faster than your bubbles and pressurize your ears. Let's go."

With that she jumped in. I followed. It was a wonderland of color and fish. The lava made for underwater tunnels and arches. There were small canyons that dropped down a hundred feet. There were different size fish at all levels on the side of the canyon. Christina pulled the strings undone that held on her bikini, stashed it in her weight belt and then swam nude. Her pubic region had been shaved leaving a small triangle of hair. She was definitely not a natural blond. What a body. She was perfect. Mr. Happy was waking up. I tried to look at the fish, but I kept coming back to Christina, who was having a great time going through the tunnels. This chick was dangerous.

She dove down and shook one of the underwater plants. Fish flocked around it. Apparently, it released some kind of spore that the little fish eat. They were all around her. Soon, bigger fish started swimming around the perimeter of the little fish. I was watching the food chain in action. Christina swam up to me, turned me around and looked at my air gauge. One of her breasts was touching the back of my arm. She swung me around and gave the okay sign. I guess that meant I had air. She made a biting motion with her fingers and pointed behind me. I turned and saw a five foot barracuda about twenty feet behind me and ten feet above me. He was frozen in the water staring at the feeding frenzy. I could see his razor sharp teeth.

Christina snuck up behind me and pulled some hair out of my thigh, scaring the hell out of me. I thought something had bit me. She took off, kicking her fins. I gave chase. She was fast. I followed her through tunnels and archways. I finally caught her by the fin and pulled her into my arms. She shook her head "no," and gently took my arms off her. She wagged her index finger back and forth. Mr. Happy was disappointed. She was all show and no go. I was relieved, married women are not cool.

After checking her air and my air, she put her bikini back on. We slowly ascended. When we surfaced, an attendant was waiting for us. He helped us out of the water and took our dive gear. Christina didn't mention what happened and neither did I. I ate my lunch in my room and did some yoga.

Arturo showed up in the afternoon. Arturo had gotten the Don hooked up on a marlin. The Don was not strong enough to land it himself and had the Captain reel it in. It had been a lifetime goal for the Don. He was very happy. He had the marlin in ice and was going to have it stuffed. As a reward, he gave Arturo the back up outboard from the boat they had fished on. It was a generous gift. We would be leaving in the morning.

Everyone was tired, so it was a pretty quiet dinner. The meal was out of this world, lobster tails and a pasta that was insane. Arturo and I would be leaving early in the morning, so we said our good-byes and thanked everyone again. The Don was still beaming from his fish. Christina was quiet and distant, which was fine with me. She had tortured Mr. Happy.

When we got up the next morning, a note had been pushed under the door. Arturo found it. It was folded and had my name on it. Arturo had no comment. He handed it to me. The note had an address in Puerta Vallarta and a date, that's all. The note smelled of Christina's perfume. I crumbled it up and threw it in the wastebasket, but Mr. Happy made me get it out and put it in my pocket. The trip back was uneventful. We went back and loaded up on fish before returning home.

Cecelia and Isabella cried with joy when we got back. Isabella even hugged me. They made us tell the story three times. We had to model our new clothes. If I wasn't mistaken, Isabella looked like she was physically attracted to Arturo in his new clothes. Cecelia made me draw the hairdo, the jewelry and the clothes that Christina wore. Arturo requested we all kneel and give thanks. We did.

Mr. Happy made me take the note and put it by my bed with a calendar. He made me put a big "X" through the days. The date Christina had written was two and a half months away.

I was satisfied with my life with the Cruzes. Isabella liked me after our rescue. Cecelia was teaching me Spanish. I would help her with her math homework. I tried to be a friend to her and listen.

It was lonely for her. Arturo and I, when we weren't fishing, were digging a hole for a septic tank. It was one of Isabella's dreams to have toilets.

The house at this stage had plumbing to the sinks and showers. The water from the sinks and showers drained outside into tank. Arturo used this water for his garden. The outhouse was moved every three days over a new hole, but it was still rough especially at night when you would have to take a lantern.

I was doing yoga and meditation with Arturo. The health benefits were obvious and I was starting to enjoy some inner peace. I was in the best shape of my life. My diet was all natural except for the sweets that Isabella would bake. The nightmares had stopped. I was becoming concerned, things were going too good.

The day to go to Puerta Vallarta had arrived. Isabella packed me a lunch and I walked the trail to the road. I had to wait for a family of skunks to cross the trail. Skunks are not concerned with other animals messing with them. They know they are holding the chemical arsenal. A week ago Chupa came back to the house reeking of skunk. Arturo wouldn't let him go in the boat with us because he stunk so bad. In fact, he still had a trace of the scent on him after numerous tomato baths.

Puerta Vallarta was a five-hour bus ride. The bus drivers are like frustrated race car drivers. They pass on blind curves and drive like maniacs. The Mexican people are very courteous. They will always acknowledge a "hello," or a nod. Most sit quietly in their seats waiting for their destination. I tried to take a siesta, but there were to many bumps in the road. Every town has one tope, a speed bump, and some towns have many.

I arrived in Puerta Vallarta in the afternoon. Vallarta is a tourist town located in the Bay of Banderas, the eighth largest bay in the world. The bay is an amazing fifteen hundred feet deep in places. In the winter, they have humpback whales come into the bay. Puerta Vallarta has grown considerably in the last twenty years.

Once they built a decent road and an airport, the gringos came in mass. The city is spread along a beautiful beach with lush jungles climbing the surrounding hills. There are some major hotels right on the beach packed with the rich tourists.

I walked down the Malacon, the main street in Vallarta. I had no idea where I was going and had to ask directions at least five times before I found Christina's condominium. The guard at the front gate handed me a pass. "She is expecting you Senor." He smiled.

The rich in Mexico like security since there is a real problem with kidnapping and the police are incompetent. The condo complex was luxurious with a giant fountain in the middle of a swimming pool. Christina's condo was on the third floor facing the ocean. I knocked on the door with the feeling this was either going to be a great thing or a disaster. Christina opened the door in shirt and shorts. "Will, please come in. I'm glad you came. Let me get you a cold drink."

I sat in a chair looking out the sliding glass door to the ocean. Christina brought back a drink made from hibiscus called "Jamaica." It was different and good. "Let's sit on the deck."

We went outside and watched the activity on the bay. There were numerous boats scattered across the water. We could see people swimming and laying on the beach in front of the condo. Christina and I made small talk. She really was a good conversationalist. I felt comfortable with her.

"Will, this is my treat. Please don't argue with me, I am paying for everything the next few days." I listened. "I have more money than I could spend in five life times. This is one of the benefits of being married to a mature man who is wealthy."

"I don't know how to respond."

"Just enjoy yourself."

I cleaned up while Christina got dressed. We took a taxi to a very expensive restaurant on the south side of town. The restaurant was terraced into the hillside and had a view of a waterfall and the ocean. We ate, drank and watched the sunset.

We took the taxi back to Main Street. We walked and window shopped.

Christina gave me some of the history of Puerta Vallarta. There was a shipyard in the sixteenth century when it was known as Humpback Bay because of all the whales. The bay has had silver mining, farming and ranching in its past. Tourism has replaced them all as the most lucrative.

It was a beautiful night. We walked back to her condo. Christina poured us both a brandy.

"Will, we need to talk." I looked at her, she was a goddess. "My husband and I have an agreement. When we discussed marriage, he realized he could never keep up with me physically. He is a very proud man, so it is crucial I am discreet. He loves to show me off at his social functions.

We do have sex, but not very often. The sex is not very good because he has a few limitations related to his health and the medications he has to take. I love him as a person and I would never do anything to hurt him, but he knows that occasionally I need to cut loose."

She came and sat next to me on the couch.

"I believe sex should be fun. How do you feel about it?" I was tongue tied, so I nodded my head. "Good! I have set some clothes out for you in that bedroom and some instructions. Meet me in the dining room in fifteen minutes."

I went into the bedroom. There was a butler's outfit laid out on the
bed.

On top of it was a note that read, 'Your name is James. You are the family butler. You must obey at all times.' I put the suit on. It looked ridiculous and I felt like leaving. I looked in the closet, there were uniforms of all types from policeman to construction worker.

I self-consciously walked out to the dining room. Christina had on a halter top with no bra and a mini skirt.

"James, I seemed to have lost an earring under the table. Would you be a dear and look for it."

"Yes, ma'am."

I crawled under the table. There was no earring, there also was no underwear under the mini skirt.

"I can't find it, ma'am."

"Okay, James. Come on out of there."

I crawled out from under the table. Christina got up and walked in front of me. She bent over and started looking into the rug. Her skirt was so short that I had quite a view.

"It might be over here, James. What do you think?"

"Anything's possible, ma'am."

I followed her around the room. Every ten feet she would bend over and do a thorough search.

"You know, James I can't find it. I'm going to give up. I do need you to do some dusting in the bedroom."

"Is that in my contract, ma'am?"

"James, you know it is. Now get on your dusting apron that's under the sink and go into the bedroom. James, you can be replaced."

"Yes, ma'am. Sorry ma'am."

I came back with an apron and a duster.

"James, before you start dusting, I think I may have been bit by a mosquito. Will you come and look."

"Where, ma'am?"

She lifted up her skirt and pointed to her inner thigh. I put my hands behind my back and bent over for a close examination.

"No, ma'am. No bite."

"How about here?" She pulled down her halter top, arched her back and pointed to her left breast.

I looked. "No, ma'am."

"You need to look closer, James."

I got an inch from her breast. "Still can't see anything, ma'am."

"I'm sure its there. Feel for the bump."

I felt. "No, ma'am. No bite."

"Okay, James. I'm going to take a little nap while you dust."

"Yes, ma'am."

I started dusting around the room.

"James it's very hot in here."

She removed her clothes and lay on the bed naked. I continued dusting.

"It is so hot I can't sleep."

She had her eyes closed and was tossing and turning on the bed. I stripped out of the uniform. I stood by the bed.

"Ma'am, I quit."

She opened her eyes, smiled and beckoned to me with her index finger. We had wild, passionate sex into the wee hours of the morning.

I really do not want to divulge all the games we played as some were downright embarrassing. Mr. Happy was in heaven.

After three days, it was time for me to head back. Christina walked me back to the bus station. "Thanks, Will. I had a wonderful time." "Christina, I want to thank you. I'll never forget these last three days."

She kissed me on the cheek, then turned and left. Mr. Happy went back into hibernation.

# CHAPTER 13

# EL MONSTRUO

Capitan Lorenzo was sitting on the hood of his squad car waiting for his daughters to get out of school. He was angry with his wife, which was not really unusual. He was always upset with her. She had demanded that he pick them up from school instead of riding the bus. 'She treats me like a taxi driver,' he thought.

The girls and their mother were going to their Aunt Yolanda's house. He hated Yolanda, in fact he hated all of his wife's family. He had contemplated divorce, but it was impossible. Her father was a very powerful attorney and If he tried to divorce her, he would end up penniless and possibly in jail.

Lorenzo had married his wife, Griselda, with the intention of inheriting some of her father's wealth. To Lorenzo's dismay, her father presented him with a document to sign while they were in the sacristy of the church minutes before the ceremony. The document stated that he was waiving all rights to his wife's family fortune. Lorenzo was so mad he didn't have sex with Griselda on their wedding night.

She was a very plain looking woman, but with make up and the right clothes she was attractive enough. After each child Griselda had put on twenty pounds. Now, Lorenzo was lucky if she had sex with him twice a month. He never considered that his love making techniques might be at the root of the problem. He was a crude and selfish lover who became most amorous when he was under the influence.

Two of Lorenzo's daughters walked out of school with the rest of the children. He waved his arms to get their attention. They got in the backseat and talked about their school day. Lorenzo had to wait another five minutes for the high school grades to get out. His other two daughters came out of the school walking with Cecelia.

The Capitan was overwhelmed with Cecelia's beauty. He watched her every movement like a predatory animal. He scrutinized her from her legs to her flat waist to her small breasts. His heart was pounding with lust.

"Who is the girl you were walking with, Pilar?" he asked his oldest daughter.

"That is Cecelia."

"Where does she live?"

He looked at Cecelia's bottom in the rear view mirror.

"She lives in the jungle past Chakala."

"What is her father's name?"

"Arturo Cruz."

"The fisherman?"

"Yes. Why are you so curious father?"

"No particular reason. I have not seen her in town before."

The girls chattered while Lorenzo tried to picture Cecelia naked.

Lorenzo was home alone, the family was still at Yolanda's. He had a mirror in front of him with a pile of cocaine. On the table was a bottle of tequila, a bowl of limes, and his cigars. He was watching graphic pornography from his numerous video collections. Lorenzo was not getting aroused.

Usually this particular tape with its sadistic theme and bondage scenes would be stimulating enough for him to masturbate, but now he could only think of Cecelia. 'How could I possibly get permission to date her?' he thought. 'They are poor, so there has to be something they need.'

He remembered that he had an outboard motor that one of his men had stolen from some gringo. He shut off the television and went out to the garage. He lifted the tarp off the motor, it was practically brand new. 'Perfect!' he thought. Lorenzo was so happy he decided to go into town and see Lucinda.

The next day, when Cecelia was in school, Capitan Baca drove his truck out to Arturo's. Arturo came walking up from the beach with his catch of fish, surprised to see the Capitan at his house. 'How unfortunate,' Arturo thought, 'if I had known he was coming, I could have hid my best fish.'

"Buenos Dias, Capitan."

The Capitan smiled and vigorously shook Arturo's hand. This made Arturo very suspicious.

"I have something to show you, Arturo."

The Capitan pulled the tarp off the shiny outboard motor.

"It is beautiful, but why show me? I could never afford such a nice motor. It is worth almost a year's pay."

Isabella came out of the house drying her hands on her apron.

"This fine motor could be yours at no cost for a small favor."

The Capitan was happy that he had brought a very valuable gift.

Isabella stood behind Arturo, looking at the motor. Chupa sniffed the Capitan's tires and relieved himself on one. Arturo waited for the Capitan to speak.

"I would like permission to take Cecelia to dinner."

Before Arturo could speak, Isabella exploded, "Are you loco?! Never ever will you go near Cecelia, you fat, stupid, ugly, drunkard! You are a disgrace and a thief. You are married, you burro! What about your wife? Have you no honor? You have children Cecelia's age! You disgust me! Leave our property!"

Chupa started to growl at the Capitan. The Capitan held up his hand in silence. He felt like slapping the old woman.

"Please! Stop your insults. I am talking to the man of the house. Arturo talk to me."

Arturo looked pained as he slowly shook his head. "Capitan, we are poor, but we do not sell our children. I am ashamed for you. You, as a father, must know how I feel. Cecelia, when she is ready, will choose a man, hopefully out of love. It will be her choice. I am sorry, but it would be best for you to leave."

"I am sorry you feel that way, I hope you don't regret your decision later."

Isabella wagged her finger at the Capitan. "Don't come back you swine!" she hissed.

"Woman, you had best learn to keep your wicked tongue in your mouth." he growled at Isabella. With a quick kick aimed at Chupa, which missed, he got in his truck and left seething.

'Those peons need to learn some respect,' he thought. He then imagined making love to Cecelia, passionate love. She was receptive and loved everything about him. Maybe he would divorce Griselda, she was worthless and a horrible lover. He would have to get a job somewhere else, but it would be worth it. He could imagine coming home to Cecelia and she would be waiting for him naked. He fantasized all the way back to town.

Cecelia got off the bus at the trail to the house and was surprised to see the Capitan parked and waiting for her.

"Cecelia?"

"Yes? Is something the matter?"

"There's been an accident. Your grandfather has been injured. I am here to take you to the hospital."

"Oh, my God! Please, tell me. How bad is it?"

"Do not worry. It is a minor injury. He will be alright."

"Where is my grandmother?"

"She is already at the hospital, waiting for you."

The Capitan put on the blinking lights and the siren and sped off.

Cecelia tightly gripped her knapsack. The Capitan was pleased, he knew the lights and siren would impress her. After a few kilometers, he turned them off and made a right turn down a dirt road.

"Where are we going, Capitan?"

"This is a shortcut." he lied.

After ten minutes he stopped the car.

"What is happening?" Cecelia asked. She was becoming very scared.

"I need to get something out of the trunk of my car. Don't worry. I will explain."

The Capitan opened his trunk, leaned in, then put a straw into a bag of cocaine and inhaled mightily. He was extremely nervous and felt like a teenager on his first date. He then took a long swig from his bottle of tequila. He rinsed his mouth with mouthwash. He pulled out a bottle of wine with two glasses.

When he sat back in the car, Cecelia was looking very frightened.

"Capitan, please. I don't understand."

"Cecelia, you have nothing to be afraid of. Please, let me explain. Your grandfather is fine. I needed to get you alone so we could talk."

Cecelia looked relieved that her grandfather was all right.

"What do you want to talk about?"

"Cecelia, I think I am in love with you. I know this sounds unusual, but sometimes it happens quickly. I would like you to get to know me and then maybe you would love me too. I brought you some very expensive wine."

Cecelia felt light headed like she was in a dream.

"Capitan, you are Pillar's father. I could never love you. I would like to go home. Please."

The Capitan drank his wine and offered Cecelia a glass, she pushed it- back shaking her head no.

"Alright. I will take you home on two conditions. One, you consider what I said and two, you give me a little kiss."

Cecelia decided to go along with this so she could go home.

"Alright." The Capitan grabbed her shoulders and made her face him. He kissed her hard on the lips, forcing his tongue down her throat while grabbing her small breast. Cecelia had never been kissed like this and it repulsed her. The Capitan was hurting her breast, so without thinking she slapped the Capitan hard across the face. The Capitan pulled back and looked at her with a wild look. "So, you are spirited, like your grandmother!"

He slapped her back, hard. She screamed, got out of the car and started running into the jungle. She could hear him running after her. She was terrified and she could hear herself squealing like a wild animal. She was much faster then the Capitan and soon put some distance on him. Just as she was feeling some hope, she ran into a thicket of kiawve, which with its long thorns was impenetrable.

Desperately, she ran to one side, but it turned into a right angle. She was trapped. She turned to run back, but he was there with his gun drawn. "Cecelia, be a good girl and come here," he said softly.

His eyes looked satanic. She came forward slowly and when she was right up to him, she darted quickly around him. He caught her arm and threw her to the ground. She screamed. He slapped her, causing her head to bounce off the ground. She was dizzy. She felt thankful for the dizziness as the Capitan removed her skirt and panties.

"You will enjoy this," he whispered.

He could not penetrate her unbroken hymen and crudely stuck his finger into her, tearing her. She whimpered in pain. He slowly inserted himself, mistaking the blood for lubrication.

"See? I told you you would like this."

Cecelia put her mind in her grandfather's boat. They were fishing together and it was a beautiful day. She felt completely detached from her body. The Capitan was rough with her. She was able to block out everything but his loudest grunts.

Thankfully, it did not last long. She pulled on her panties and skirt. She could feel moisture between her legs. They walked slowly back to the car. He held her hand. The Capitan stopped his car where he had picked her up.

"Cecelia, Cecelia look at me. Do not say anything. If you do, I will have to hurt your grandparents, understand?" He squeezed her arm. She slowly nodded her head.

Walking back on the trail, Cecelia could feel blood and semen drip down her legs. She didn't feel like Cecelia, she felt like someone else. When Cecelia walked through the door, Isabella knew immediately something had happened.

"Cecelia my child, what is it?"

"I've been violated, grandmother." she said without emotion. "I've been violated."

"Oh, my darling. Let's get you cleaned up." Isabella tried not to cry, but she couldn't help herself. The tears ran down her cheeks as she washed the blood from Cecelia's legs. Cecelia was in a trance and remained expressionless. Isabella put her in her nightshirt and lay with her in bed, cradling her head and stroking her hair. Isabella continuously whispered, "It will be okay." even though she doubted it.

"Cecelia, we will need to report this to the policia."

Cecelia shook her head. "Grandmother, it was the Capitan who did it."

"Oh, you poor child." Isabella started crying again.

Arturo could not see any lights in the kitchen window as he tied the rope from the tree on to the front of his panga. He had gone back out fishing in the afternoon because the morning catch had been poor. He had done a little better, but not much.

"Why is she not fixing our supper?" Arturo asked Chupa.

Chupa looked at Arturo and wagged his stub of a tail. Arturo reached down and massaged Chupa's neck, which caused Chupa's eyes to close. Chupa loved Arturo to pet him.

"Let's go see what is happening, Chupa." Chupa bounded toward the house stopping every ten feet to make sure Arturo was coming.

Arturo walked in the door and saw Isabella sitting in the semi darkness.

"What is the matter?" he quietly asked, expecting to get another one of Isabella's moods. Isabella motioned for Arturo to come to her. When he did, she whispered what had happened to Cecelia in his ear. Arturo went to Cecelia's room with a lamp.

She was lying on her bed staring up without really focusing.

"Cecelia, I must talk to you." He gently helped her into a sitting position, she remained expressionless. "Cecelia, this is very important. Please, listen to me." He held one of her limp hands.

"Listen, you have been hurt physically, but more importantly you have been hurt mentally. It is a deep and terrible wound that could affect the rest of your life. It has to be cleaned out, or it will fester and never heal properly. We all come to crossroads in our lives and this is one of yours. If you love yourself, you will do what is right. The old Cecelia is dead. She will never come back, never. If you try and hang on to her, your life will be miserable. You must mourn for her, you must feel her pain, you must say good bye to her."

Arturo squeezed her hand hard. "Cecelia won't you help me say goodbye to the old Cecelia?" He squeezed her hand again. "Won't you? She was such a nice girl, we loved her didn't we?"

Arturo saw a flicker in Cecelia's eyes. "Help me, Cecelia." Tears slowly welled up in her eyes. She squeezed Arturo's hand.

"Oh, grandfather. I was so scared." Tears spilt out of her eyes.

"Grandfather he hurt me." She reached out and put her arms around Arturo's neck. "He said he would hurt you and grandmother." Cecelia started sobbing.

"He will not hurt us and he will never hurt you again my child."

Cecelia's tears saturated Arturo's shirt and ran down his chest. Arturo's tears fell into Cecelia's hair. Isabella, who was standing in the doorway, wiped away her tears in her apron. Cecelia slept between Arturo and Isabella that night.

The next day, Arturo and Cecelia walked on the beach with Chupa. "Grandfather, if the old Cecelia is dead, who am I?"

"Do you remember when you were an infant?"

"Yes."

"Well, you can never go back to being an infant, right?"

"Right."

"In the same way, you can never bring back the innocence you had. How you choose to live your life from now on is up to you. You can hate and be consumed with it, or you can choose to live a healthy life."

They sat on a log and threw stones into the waves. Cecelia felt a wave of sadness come over and she started to weep. Arturo held her.

"Good girl. Clean it out."

When she stopped crying, she asked. "Why would God let this happen to me? I am not a bad person."

"If God told you what to do every day, would you feel in control of your life?"

"No."

"That is what makes God so great. He gave us free will so we can choose."

"I did not choose this Grandfather."

"No, but you can choose how you will deal with it. Every person has adversity, every person. Some live their whole lives hating. Who does it really hurt? Only themselves."

"It still hurts, Grandfather."

He hugged her. "Do you know that Christ knew what was going to happen to him and prayed for strength. He knew how terrible it would be, but still did it. He is our inspiration and there have been others as inspirational. Think how much compassion you will feel for someone else's pain."

They walked back to the house.

"I love you, Grandfather."

"Cecelia, it is going to take time to heal. Be patient with yourself. Someday, you will need to forgive."

"I am not ready, grandfather, but I will consider it."

Arturo fished just enough to put food on the table. He would spend the rest of the time with Cecelia, walking, talking, sometimes crying, gardening, fishing from the shore. Slowly, as the days passed, Cecelia got better.

One night when Cecelia was sleeping, Isabella told Arturo she needed to oil his hands. Arturo sleepily sat down at the table. Isabella affectionately rubbed Arturo's hands. Arturo noticed a difference and looked up at Isabella. She had her hair combed out and she squeezed his hand.

"What is happening, Isabella?" "I am so proud of you Arturo. You have given Cecelia a chance at living. Your love has been stronger than Lorenzo's evil."

Arturo smiled and she smiled back. "Everything you have told Cecelia has meaning for me. I hated life for being so cruel and taking Estaban. You have helped me to start to heal also. Now, come and sleep with me like a good husband."

She led him into their bedroom and closed the door. They lay together naked for a long time. Arturo remembered, besides the sex, he liked the touching and the closeness. Isabella was a wonderful lover and they made slow passionate love. Arturo fell into a dreamless sleep. Isabella looked at his face and realized how much she missed loving him. Eventually, she drifted off to sleep holding his hand.

# CHAPTER 14

# JUDGMENT DAY

Something was terribly wrong at the house. I could feel it the minute I walked through he door. Arturo got up, took me by the arm and walked me out to the porch. We sat down and he told me about Cecelia. I was so enraged, I felt like I was going to explode.

"Arturo, I am going to do something about this."

"Will, he is the Capitan. He can do what he wants."

"That's bullshit. He must answer to some one."

"This is not the United States. This is Mexico. Our courts are corrupt, the poor have no say."

I held up a fist.

"Maybe he will listen to this."

Arturo put his hand over my fist.

"Will, that just creates a never ending cycle of violence."

"What about Cecelia? She deserves justice."

"Cecelia will be okay. With love she will grow stronger with hate she will kill her spirit."

"Arturo, I have to go to town."

"Will, I beg of you. Do not create more violence."

I went in and found Cecelia in her room. I hugged her and she hugged me back, tight. I couldn't help it. I started crying. She pulled away from me and wiped away my tears.

"Thank you, Will. You are like a brother to me."

I was speechless.

"I will be okay. Grandfather has been helping me. I am not all the way better, but it will take some time."

She smiled at me. I gave her a quick hug and left.

I walked to the highway and caught a bus into town. Everyone knew where the Capitan was, in the cantina. I sat across the street until it got dark. I cut two holes in a bandana. After dark, I positioned myself by the Capitan's new pickup truck, which was parked behind the cantina under a big tree. Like a child, I put a few scratches in his paint job and punctured one of his tires while I was waiting.

Around eleven o'clock, he came stumbling out. I put the bandana over my face. He opened the driver side door, unzipped his pants and started to urinate. He farted and let out a little sigh.

"Capitan, I've been waiting for you," I said in Spanish.

"Who is it? Juan, is that you?" His speech was slurred. He zipped up his pants, then turned around and came to the back of the truck.

"Who are you and why do you have that stupid bandana over your face?"

"So, you are the mighty Capitan Lorenzo? You look like a drunken pig."

"Stranger, if you are going to insult me, I will arrest you."

"No, you won't."

"And why not?"

"Because you are too slow."

He fumbled for his gun. I plucked it out of his hand.

"Hey! Now you are in real trouble Senor! Give that back!"

I stuck it in my waistband.

"Take it back."

He charged me. I stopped him in his tracks with a hard left jab.

"Why are you doing this?!" he bellowed.

"You raped my sister, you pig. You deserve to die, but instead I will give you a beating."

He took a drunken swing at me that missed by a foot. I peppered him with combinations. Before I could even get going, he passed out. I don't know if it was from the booze or the punches.

I was not satisfied. I pulled my knife out and cut off his belt. I then cut his pants and his underwear off. I thought about cutting off his penis, but instead I drew a line with my knife the length of it. I took off the bandana, threw it on top of him and started walking home. I hid the Capitan's gun in the shed.

Two weeks passed before the Capitan showed up at the house. Isabella was hysterical and was swearing epitaphs at him. Cecelia did not come out of the house.

"Keep the woman quiet, fisherman, or I will arrest her." Arturo made Isabella go in the house.

"You are not welcome here, Lorenzo," Arturo said.

"I will not be long. I've come for the gringo." He pointed to me sitting on the porch. "Bring him over here, fisherman."

Arturo waved for me to come over. The Capitan pulled his gun on me.

"No tricks, gringo."

"I don't know what you are talking about, Capitan."

"Oh, I think you do. Put your hands on the hood of my car."

He frisked me and pulled out my pocketknife then studied the scar tissue on my knuckles.

"You are under arrest.

Arturo asked, "What for?'

"Assault."

"On who?" said Arturo.

"The gringo knows."

He threw Arturo his handcuffs. "Put them on him while I keep my gun on him." The Capitan said to me," If you try anything funny, I will shoot the fisherman."

He then made Arturo put leg shackles on me before loading me in the back of the car. I looked back at the house as we drove down the road. Cecelia, Isabella and Arturo were all standing together watching me.

"She isn't even your sister, gringo."

"I don't know what you're talking about."

"Did you know I had to get six stitches where you cut me? The doctor says there may be nerve damage. Gringo, you better pray there is no nerve damage."

"I don't know what you're talking about."

Halfway down the road, he stopped the car. He pulled me out of the back of the car. I landed on my side. He started kicking me with his cowboy boots. He kicked me in the stomach, ribs and back until he was breathing hard and had worked up a sweat. "You know, I should just kill you, gringo! Who the hell do you think you are to attack a Capitan of police?"

"I don't know what you're talking about."

He went back to kicking me until he finally got tired. I hoped I didn't have internal bleeding. He loaded me back into the car. "You are going to wish you were dead by the time I finish with you, pinche gringo."

At the station, he had some of his men take me into a back room where they pulled down my pants and underwear and tied me to a chair. They brought in a car battery with wires attached to it. The Capitan came into the room and waved for his men to leave. The Capitan sat in a chair in front of me.

"Do you know what we use this battery for?"

"I can imagine."

"We use it to make prisoners talk, to confess their crimes."

"I'll talk."

The Capitan smiled.

"Who said I wanted you to talk?"

He stuck the wires on my testicles. I screamed. He stuck the wires on my testicles again. I screamed. I was covered with sweat. I smelled burnt flesh. The back door opened. An elderly man in a suit stood beside the Capitan.

"What is going on here?"

"Just a little questioning, your honor. I am almost done, Judge Rentaria."

"Cease immediately. I can hear screams in the street. No more. I am serious, Lorenzo."

"Alright, but this man must be sent to the penitentiary. He is dangerous."

"So be it. No more torture. Put him in a cell. Now!"

"Yes, your honor."

After the judge left, the Capitan gagged me and gave me a long jolt until I finally passed out.

I woke up face down in a cell. I was in extreme pain. One of the men in the cell helped me get my pants back on. I sat with my back against a wall and looked around. There were six cells, three meters wide by three meters long. There were two other prisoners in my cell. The cell had no bunks, just a concrete floor and a toilet that was stopped up. There were no windows. A broken fan was on the ceiling. The jail was filthy ·and had a stench to it.

One of the men spoke to me in Spanish. "You must have made the Capitan very angry."

I nodded my head.

"Beto over there has also felt the burn of the battery. Right, Beto?"

Beto was a thin man with crude tattoos on his arms. "Yes, I have felt the burn. The pain takes a long time to go away."

"Show him your scars, Beto."

Beto unzipped his pants and pulled out his testicles, which had scar tissue on them.

"I still am fertile. I have had five sons, even after the burning." he said proudly.

"Why did he shock you?"

"My friend and I robbed a bank, it was the Capitan's bank. We didn't know. He caught us and tortured us, even after we confessed."

"What is going to happen to me?" I asked Beto.

"You are going to the penitentiary in Lazaro Cardenas."

"Have you been there?"

"No, but I heard it was not bad if you had lots of money. Are you a drug dealer?"

"No, and I have no money."

"Well, it is still better than here. This place smells and there are no beds."

"How long have you been here?"

"This is my third and last day. My girlfriend gets paid today and will pay my fine."

"Did you know the Capitan does not supply food or drink here?" the other prisoner asked me.

"Is that legal?"

"The Capitan makes the laws. Your family needs to bring you food. If you have no family, the ladies from the church will bring you something."

I lay on my back and tried to distract myself from the pain.

In the late afternoon, a policeman came and got me. He handcuffed me and shackled my legs. We walked out the back door. There was a prison bus waiting, it had bars on all the windows and a cage to protect the driver. The policeman pointed to a seat on the bus. He then ran a chain through my leg shackles and put a lock on it.

The bus was half-filled with prisoners, most of whom were sleeping.

The bus stopped in all the towns that had holding jails, so by the time we got to Lazaro Cardenas, it was already dark.

The prison had two fences, both about twenty feet high with razor wire on top. The building that held the cells looked like a big dormitory. We were all strip-searched, then sprayed for bugs. I was put in a cell with four other men. There were two bunks, both of which were occupied. I sat in a corner. Two of the men were reading, one was sleeping and the fourth one came over and sat real close to me and stared.

"Buenas noches," I said.

"Buenas noches." he answered.

"Why are you staring at me?"

"Why are you staring at me?" he said.

"I am not staring at you. You are staring at me."

"I am not staring at you. You are staring at me." he said.

"Why are you repeating everything I say?"

"Why are you repeating everything I say?"

The other prisoners laughed.

One of them said, "He is loco. He repeats everything. We call him the Papagayo for he is just like a parrot."

"Why is he repeating what I say and no one else?"

"Why is he repeating what I say and no one else?"

"No one knows. He always picks out one person. He never says anything for himself. He only repeats."

"What happened to him?"

"What happened to him?"

"Some say he was born this way, some think it might have been drugs. He can't tell us."

I looked at him. He must have been about twenty-five. His hair looked like it had never been combed and his teeth were rotten. He wouldn't have been bad looking if it weren't for his hygiene. I touched my nose and so did he. I stuck my finger in my ear and so did he.

"I am a moron," I said.

"I am a moron."

I couldn't resist and started singing 'Row Your Boat' and dancing a jig. Papagayo did the same. The other prisoners were laughing. I started laughing. Papagayo laughed, too. For a few minutes he had taken my mind off my pain. One of the men told me they rotated on the beds and that I would get a bed in two days. That night I barely slept. The nightmares returned. Papagayo slept next to me.

In the morning, they opened the cells. Everyone went outside. There were armed guards patrolling the fences and in the towers. There was a room downstairs where they served food. Only the poorest prisoners ate there. If you had money, you would buy food from the vendors that set up by the main gate. The vendors paid the director of the prison for permits to sell their food and goods.

Anything could be bought at the prison, including drugs. I had no money so I ate with the poor. They gave me some tortillas and a mixture of rice, beans and I think it was chicken. It was some type of meat, but mostly gristle. It had no flavor and smelled bad, but I hadn't eaten in two days, so I gagged it down. Another gringo approached me.

"Hello. My name is Greg."

"I'm Will."

"I'm Will." Papagayo repeated.

"Who's this?" He pointed at Papagayo.

"He's my shadow."

"He's my shadow." Papagayo repeated.

"Why does he repeat everything you say?"

"He's loco. Watch this."

"He's loco. Watch this."

I started doing jumping jacks and so did Papagayo.

Greg laughed.

"That's weird. Pretty funny. "

"After a while, its not so funny. "

"After a while, its not so funny."

We all sat on a bench.

"What did you do?"

"I beat up a police capitan."

"I beat up a police capitan."

"Are you kidding? Wow! That's great. I'd like to do that. The police here are assholes."

"What are you here for?"

"What are you here for?"

"Selling drugs. I'm waiting for my partner to bring down some money so I can rent one of the apartments."

"What apartments?"

"What apartments?"

"There are apartments down stairs in the basement. You can buy anything you want down there. You can get women to live with you, or your family can stay with you. You can have satellite T.V., stereo, booze, drugs, anything you want. You can party all night."

"Why don't you buy your way out?"

"Why don't you buy you way out?"

"This is my second offense. I was supposed to get ten years, but my partner bought it down to sixteen months. It's not bad here if you have an apartment. I just smoke weed all day and watch T.V. Let me give you some money for the vendors. You can't eat the prison food. It will give you the shits."

He handed me five hundred pesos, the equivalent of fifty dollars. "That will buy you a month's worth of food."

"Thank you."

"Thank you."

"I'll see you later. Your echo is getting on my nerves. If you need any help, look me up."

"Thanks again."

"Thanks again."

I fell into a routine: exercise in the morning, eat fruit for breakfast, an hour of yoga. an hour of meditation, exercise, siesta, eat dinner, another hour of meditation, exercise, eat supper, then lock up. Papagayo would mimic my every move. It was like doing yoga in a mirror. When I would meditate, he would keep one eye slightly open so he could see. I have to admit he cracked me up.

My life was very simple with simple pleasures. I looked forward to the nights I got to sleep in the bunks. I savored my meals, which were quite good. One of the female vendors was an excellent cook with very tasty salsas. I took time to eat my fruit. I was becoming very peaceful, it felt good. Days, weeks, months passed.

Some of the prisoners played soccer, while others played cards. Most sat in the shade and talked. I was meditating when one of the guards tapped me on the shoulder.

"Will Callahan?"

"Yes?"

"Yes?"

"The director wants to see you."

I followed him into the prison. The guard pushed Papagayo back and closed the door on him so he couldn't follow us into an office.

The director was a small fat man wearing a suit. He was bald with his hair grown long on one side and combed over. It must have taken him a long time to get it just right.

"Please, sit down."

I sat in one of the chairs in front of his desk.

"I have not got any complaints about your behavior. Do you know anything about Mexican law?

"No, sir."

It was weird not to hear myself repeated.

"We have what is called Napoleonic law. You are guilty until proven innocent. We can hold you here for seven years without a trial, but there is a way to get an early release."

"How?"

"A discreet donation of ten thousand U.S. dollars in cash to me."

"I don't have it."

"What about family? You can call them on my phone."

"None of my family has money like that."

"Can't they mortgage their houses?"

"They don't have houses."

"This is very unfortunate."

I wasn't too happy about it either.

"I have been getting calls from a Capitan Lorenzo Baca. Are you familiar with him?"

"Yes."

"It has taken him this long to locate you. He has been calling all the prisons looking for you. Apparently, someone misspelled your name when you were admitted. He wants your stay here to be as miserable as possible. He wants me to lock you in solitary for a month. The human rights advocates have limited the time in solitary to a week. Even though you have not been a problem, I must comply with the Capitan's request. I am sorry."

The guard led me down some stairs into what looked like a dungeon. A single light bulb on the ceiling lit the room. The place smelled of feces. A pathetic face looked at me from a small slot in a metal door. There were eight metal doors, the guard opened one at the end. It was four feet by four feet and six foot tall. It was like a closet. There was no way you could lie down comfortably. There was a bucket in the corner for going to the bathroom. It had maggots crawling on the rim.

The guard closed the metal door and shut off the light. It was pitch black. I stood because I didn't want to get near the maggots. I heard a voice whisper in the darkness.

"Senor, can you hear me?"

"Yes."

"I think I am going loco in here. What should I do?"

Personally, I was going through an anxiety attack myself. I felt claustrophobic and I was positive the maggots were crawling up my leg. "What can I do for you?"

"Anything. I feel like I am losing my mind."

"Do you believe in God?"

"I have been a bad person. I try not to think of God. I am afraid He is mad at me."

"What if I told you that God loves you?"

There was a silence. "Did you hear me?"

"It doesn't seem possible. I have hurt some people."

"God loves everybody the same, unconditionally. He loves the saint as much as the sinner."

Again there was silence.

"I have killed some people."

"God still loves you."

"Why should he?"

"We are his children. He loves and cares about all of his children."

"Why did he make me to be such a bad person?"

"He didn't make you anything. You did it. He gave you free choice. You chose this just like you can choose to ask forgiveness. You can ask him to help guide you in your time of need."

"Are you a priest?"

"No. Far from it."

"You seem so sure of this."

"I know a holy man."

"I will ask for forgiveness. Do you know any prayers?"

"The best prayers are not rehearsed. Talk to God from your heart, be sincere. Make this the moment that you change forever. God will listen."

"Thank you, stranger."

I sat on the floor and meditated. I had no idea for how long. I started singing one of Arturo's chants..."They have heard Thy

Name. The blind, halt and lame, they have come to Thy door, Lord. They have come to Thy door. Give them an audience, Lord. They have heard Thy Name. The blind halt and lame. Those who are in despair, wipe Thou their tears. They have come to Thy door, Lord. They have come to Thy door. Give them an audience, Lord. Those who are drowned in sin, to whom will they go? They have no one, Lord. They have no one. Do not turn them away. They have heard Thy Name. The blind halt and lame..."

After three times, the man joined in with me. We chanted for hours. I felt better and drifted in and out of sleep. Suddenly the light went on and I heard a guard open the other man's door. After a while, he came and opened my door. He removed my toilet bucket and handed me an empty one. He gave me some water, some tortillas and two limes. He closed the door. The light went off. I ate and drank slowly trying to pass time.

"Hey stranger, I feel better today. I have been praying. Could you sing another song?" I chanted, "I am Aum, I am Aum, Aum, Aum, I am Aum."

We sang for hours. I then went into a deep meditation. Afterwards, I did some deep knee bends for exercise. That night, I had a dream that I was fishing with Arturo. I told him I loved him. The days passed excruciatingly slowly. On the fourth day, the other man was released from solitary. He came down to my cell.

"Thank you, stranger. I never would have made it."

"Peace be with you."

Finally, my seventh day came. The guard came and got me. I was weak and my legs were shaky. I was blinded by the sun and had to cover my eyes. The sun was giving me a headache. I sat and smelled fresh air, it was so sweet.

I quickly got into my old routine. I saw that Papagayo had latched on to someone else. My strength returned. The days, weeks and months started to pass. I thought of the Cruzes and how I missed them. I thought of Danni and how I missed her too.

One day, I was sitting in the shade when a guard came up to me.

"The director wants to see you."

I sat in the same chair in front of the director.

"Capitan Lorenzo called?"

"Oh, no. I have good news. You are free to go."

"How is that possible?"

"A lady made a very generous donation in your name. Here. She left a note for you."

The note said, "Will, sorry it took so long to get you out. I couldn't find you because they misspelled your name. Don Justo is gravely ill right now. I cannot leave until he is out of danger. Otherwise, I would have come and delivered this myself. Hope all is well, Christina."

"She also sent a bus ticket and two thousand pesos."

I could not believe it and sat dumbfounded.

"You mean I can get up and walk out the door?"

"By all means. Here is your paperwork."

I went straight to the bus station. Within an hour, I was sitting in a bus headed back.

# CHAPTER 15
# BURNING CANDLES

The Capitan's wife was packing her car for a trip to visit her parents, an extended trip. She was fed up with Lorenzo's drinking. Lorenzo came out of the house in his underwear and T-shirt just as she was loading the last of the children in the car. "Where are you going?"

Griselda waved her finger in the Capitan's face. "I am through with you and your drinking!" The Capitan had a headache and Griselda's screeching didn't help. "I am going to my parents, and if you are not sober permanently in a week, my father will file for divorce."

"What is the problem?" the Capitan asked.

"What is the problem? Are you an imbecile? You drink to all hours of the night! You are too hung over to pay any attention to the children! I wouldn't doubt if you see other women! I am tired of it! You will change, or you will be washing toilets after my father gets through with you!"

"I will change tonight."

"No! That is what you always say. I will be back in a week and I will be able to tell if you have been drinking. I also have my spies who will report to me. I am not kidding with you, Lorenzo. This is your final chance!"

With that, she turned, got in the car and slammed the door. Lorenzo watched them drive off.

'I need a drink,' he thought. He went into the garage and got a bottle of Vodka he had hidden. Lorenzo sat in front of the television watching CNN in Spanish, drinking vodka and orange juice. 'I need to kill my wife and her sister,' he thought, 'but how can I make it look like an accident? I will need to plan this thoroughly. Luckily, I don't need to solve this today. I have a week.' Lorenzo was terrified of his father in law, who was a very powerful man.

The vodka and orange juice made Lorenzo feel better. He got dressed and headed for the police station. Lorenzo had to hide his cocaine in his office since he was afraid that Griselda would find it. Lorenzo got his bag of coke out of his file cabinet. One of his officers was at the front desk.

"Jose, only call me if it is an emergencia, understand?"

Jose thought to himself, 'The Capitan never works. I hope to be Capitan someday.'

Lorenzo drove home, then parked himself in his big chair in front of the television with his cocaine, cigarettes and beer. He did not move for eight hours, except to go the bathroom and go to the refrigerator. In the afternoon, he switched from beer to scotch. A couple of times, he thought he should eat, but the cocaine suppressed his appetite. He had gotten very horny but none of the other whores worked for him. Lucinda had left town.

Lorenzo started fantasizing about Cecelia. He was delusional. He felt that deep down she cared for him. In his intoxicated state he decided to go see her. He was now drinking straight tequila. His driving was so impaired that he almost went off the road a couple of times.

Arturo and Isabella heard a truck drive up. They had just gone to bed. The Capitan pounded on the door, causing Chupa to bark. When Arturo answered the door, the Capitan pushed past him.

"Where is Cecelia?" he slurred. He was swaying. Cecelia sat up in her bed.

Isabella stood in front of the Capitan.

"You are an ignorant, drunken donkey! Satan possesses you! Get out of here before I hit you over the head with my cooking pan!"

"I am tired of you old woman, stand aside"

Isabella tried to push the Capitan back through the door. The Capitan backhanded Isabella across the face, causing her to fall backwards. Arturo rushed to Isabella. Chupa charged the Capitan and bit him on the calf. The Capitan drew his pistol and shot Chupa in the base of his spine, shattering it. Chupa flipped backwards with a horrible howl and started convulsing in pain. Arturo sprung from Isabella and grabbed the Capitan in a bear hug, pinning his arms to his sides. "Run Isabella get Cecelia and run into the jungle! Run"

Cecelia was standing in the hall when Arturo yelled. She helped Isabella to her feet and they went out the door. The moon was bright. As they ran down the trail, Isabella was crying.

The Capitan could not believe how strong the old fisherman was. He could not break his hold. The Capitan spun in circles with Arturo hanging on. They fell over the table and crashed to the floor with the table rolling on top of them. The Capitan rolled back and forth, trying to break Arturo's grip. Arturo was talking to the Capitan. "You must leave. You must never come back. You must not bother my family."

The Capitan was getting desperate. His hand felt some glass that had broken when the table tipped over. The Capitan gripped the glass and rammed it into Arturo's thigh. Arturo cried out in pain as he grabbed for the glass and pulled it out. The Capitan used the distraction to break Arturo's grip.

The Capitan jumped to his feet and pummeled Arturo with the barrel of his pistol, whipping him again and again across the head.

Arturo had gotten to his knees. The end of the barrel was ripping Arturo's scalp. Blood rolled down his face. Arturo tried to cover up with his arms, but he could not stop the blows. Arturo reached blindly up and caught the Capitan's wrist that held the pistol. The Capitan pounded Arturo with his free fist. Arturo slowly pulled himself to his feet, trying to absorb the blows with his free arm. When Arturo got to his feet something in him snapped and he grabbed the Capitan's throat.

Arturo was wild with rage! He could hear Chupa dying and tightened his grip. The capitan continued to beat Arturo with his free hand. Arturo lowered his head and gripped tighter, wanting to kill the Capitan. He squeezed the Capitan with all of his power and his fingers sunk into the Capitan's windpipe. The Capitan started to gag and turn red in the face.

Arturo had never been this angry. He could barely feel the Capitan hitting him. The Capitan was starting to lose consciousness, his punches becoming weaker and weaker until they eventually stopped. Arturo kept his head down and squeezed. He heard the gun drop out of the Capitan's hand.

Arturo slowly realized he was going to murder a man. The realization stunned him. He released his grip. The Capitan crumbled to the floor, gasping for air. Arturo was ashamed. Arturo whispered, "I am sorry. Forgive me."

The Capitan was surprised, but he was not going to miss his opportunity. He picked up his gun and shot Arturo in the chest. Arturo felt the slap on his chest and he looked down to see that there was a hole in his shirt. The bullet had punctured his heart. Arturo slumped to his knees, aware his life was about to end. He wanted to tell the Capitan that he forgave him just like the gurus would have done but he couldn't get the words out. He fell backwards, right next to Chupa. The capitan was catching his breath. The dog's whimpering was annoying him. He couldn't think, so he went to Chupa and put a bullet in his skull.

Isabella and Cecelia stopped running when they heard the first shot. "Oh, my God!" Isabella whispered. They stood still. That's when they heard the other shot.

"What should we do, grandmother?"

"If Arturo is alright, he will come for us. We must wait."

They walked a little ways off the trail and sat.

The capitan pulled a sheet off of the bed and wrapped Arturo in it. He then wrapped him in a plastic tarp, so the blood wouldn't get all over the back of his truck. After putting Arturo in the truck, he waited a while to see if Cecelia and Isabella returned. Finally, he tired of it and drove off.

Isabella and Cecelia heard the Capitan's truck start up. Isabella knew Arturo was dead and let out a pitiful moan.

"Grandmother, maybe he is still alive." Isabella followed Cecelia up the trail, but stopped at the door.

"Cecelia, I can't see him dead. Please go in." Cecelia went in and came right back out.

"He's not here. Chupa's dead."

Cecelia was still fearful of the captain. Isabella went into the house and saw all the blood on the floor as well as Chupa with his terrible wounds. Cecelia hugged her grandmother. Isabella whispered to Cecelia,

"What will we do? What will we do?" Cecelia had no answer.

All of the excitement had sobered up Lorenzo. He stopped halfway to the paved road, got out with his flashlight and searched the jungle. He found a dry stream bed. He went and got Arturo and hoisted him on to his shoulder.

When he was a couple of hundred feet into the arroyo, he dropped him and then dragged him for a while. Lorenzo then pulled him into the jungle a couple of meters. The Capitan went back for his shovel. He then dug a shallow grave, cursing the whole time. "You're making me sweat, old fisherman. You're getting my clothes all dirty. Why would you try and fight me when you could not win."

He pushed Arturo into the grave and covered him up. For the first time in a long time the Capitan did not feel like a drink. When his wife checked in on him, he was sober. His wife moved back in and he remained sober.

The bus dropped me off at the end of the trail. I had been gone for three months. I had a long talk with Danni, who said she still loved me. She said she loved me even more. How was that possible? Maybe she loves the idea of me and not the real me. Whatever. I am going to head back after I see Arturo, Isabella and Cecelia.

Something felt different as I walked the trail. I couldn't put my finger on it. It couldn't be a storm coming since there were no clouds. It felt ominous, also sad.

When I got close to the house, Chupa didn't bark.

I yelled, "Chupa! Chupa!" He must be on the boat with Arturo. It was unusual for Arturo to be fishing in the midday. There was a Cherokee Jeep parked in front of the house. When I went in, Isabella was sitting at the table with a young man. Isabella got up and hugged me and started to cry. "Isabella, what is the matter? Where is Arturo?"

She could not speak, she pointed to the man at the table. He rose and shook my hand. "I'm Cholly. Arturo and Isabella's son." I could see the resemblance to his mother.

"What is going on, Cholly?"

"We suspect my father is dead. We have not seen him for two weeks."

I fell into a chair. This was not possible. Cholly related the series of events. "Where is Cecelia?"

"She has already moved to Guadalajara, where she is with my wife, her aunt. I am waiting to take mother with me, but she cannot leave until she finds out about my father."

Isabella had been wiping tears off her cheeks the whole time. She reached out and held my hand, "Will, you must find out what happened.

Please. He may still be alive. We have called the prisons, but they say they do not have him. Lorenzo denies ever being here." I looked into her eyes.

She was begging me, "Will, if he is dead, then I will know that it is over. It will be done. I want to bury him next to Estaban. Will, I want to light a candle in the shrine and say a prayer for my beloved husband. I miss him so much. I don't want to live. But what if he is alive? Please Will, can you help?" She grabbed my hands with both of her hands and squeezed.

"Please!"

"I will find out, Isabella."

"Oh, thank you, thank you."

"Isabella, I love him too."

She nodded, "I know, Will. I know you do."

I went to the shed and got the Capitan's pistol that I had stolen a long time ago. I drove into town in Arturo's pick up truck and parked in front of the police station. I walked through the front door, past the reception desk, down the hall to the Capitan's office. With two kicks I busted it off the hinges, then walked up to the Capitan and put the gun barrel right between his eyes.

Four policemen ran into the office after me. One put a shotgun in the back of my neck. Another stuck one on my cheek. The others had their revolvers drawn and they were aimed at my head.

"Well, gringo. You are not a fast learner. Maybe you need some more time in solitary."

"Lorenzo, you are going to have your men lock themselves in one of the cells, then you are going to take a little ride with me."

"And if I don't?"

"You die."

"What if my men shoot you right now?"

"They won't do it without you telling them to and if you do, you die."

"But you will die also."

"My bag is packed. I'm ready to die."

The Capitan sat silent. "What is it going to be, Lorenzo?" Lorenzo ordered his men into a cell.

"Tell them to throw all weapons outside of the cell."

I took the keys for the cell and put them in my pocket. I took Lorenzo's handgun out of his holster, threw it in the pile. I marched Lorenzo into the back room. "Drop your pants."

"What are you doing, gringo?"

"A little interrogation. You remember how it works, right?"

"I will tell you anything you want to know."

"Where is he?"

"Who?"

"Drop your pants!"

"He's dead."

The gun began to shake in my hand.

"Where?"

"In the jungle."

"Let's go. You are going to show me."

I made the capitan drive while I had the gun stuck in his ribs. I wouldn't allow myself to think about Arturo being dead. We stopped by an arroyo.

"Show me."

"You know, gringo, they are probably looking for you right now. You are going to jail for the rest of your life."

"Just show me!"

The Capitan took me to the grave. I threw him the shovel.

"Dig him up, you son of a bitch!"

The Capitan dug. I was enraged.

"How could a worthless piece of shit like you kill a beautiful human being like Arturo?"

"I never said I killed him. I just know where he is."

"Whatever. Keep digging."

The grave was shallow, so the capitan soon unearthed Arturo's body wrapped in plastic. We carried it back to the truck.

"Now what gringo?"

"I want to put a bullet in your head. I want to kill you so bad I can taste it. The irony is the man you killed didn't believe in an eye for an eye. He believed in turning the other cheek. He was my best friend, so in his honor I will not kill you but I would love to. "

"So then, what?"

"I am going to bring you in for murder."

The Capitan laughed.

"You gringos aren't too smart, are you? They will never put me in jail. In fact, when you take me in, they will arrest you for kidnapping. You will spend the rest of your life in solitary. You will wish you were dead."

The Capitan tilted back his head and laughed.

"You stupid pinche gringo. Now what are you going to do?"

I stood looking at Arturo's wrapped body, listening to the Capitan laugh.

"Does your wife know about the rape?" The capitan stopped laughing.

"How would she feel to know you raped one of your daughter's classmates?"

The Capitan swung the shovel and before I could react knocked the gun out of my hand. The gun flew over the truck. The Capitan ran for the gun. So did I. He beat me to it, but not by much. We both had our hands on it, my hands were on top of his. He had a finger on the trigger. We rolled over and over. The gun went off. A bullet went by my cheek. He kneed me in the groin. I pushed my elbow in his face. He rolled me on my back. I took one hand off the gun and punched him in the face. With both hands he forced the gun barrel into my chest.

"Adios, gringo," he smiled.

I chopped on the gun barrel with my free hand just as it went off. The gun was pointed down between us. The capitan let go of the gun. He looked down. I rolled him off me and saw that he was wounded in the groin. He reached down and felt himself.

"You shot off one of my balls!" He was in shock. The bullet must have also hit an artery as he was bleeding profusely. Blood was saturating his pants in an ever growing circle. He sat looking between his legs.

"You pinche bandejo, you shot me."

"You shot yourself."

"Take me to the hospital!"

"We'll never make it in time. You're losing too much blood."

He grabbed his crotch with his hands, blood seeping through his fingers.

"Help me, please! Have mercy! " he whimpered. "I don't want to die! Help me! " His face was draining of color. He was pathetic. He became incoherent and was mumbling something I could not understand as he fell onto his side. I could see a pool of blood forming in the dirt. His breathing was labored. I got in the truck and headed for the house.

I dreaded telling Isabella. She was waiting for me at the door. I shook my head slowly indicating no. She hugged me.

"Will, thank you. Now, I can complete my grief. Where is he?"

"In the back of the truck."

"What about the Capitan?"

"He is dead."

We went to the truck with Cholly. They stood and looked at Arturo's wrapped up body. Cholly started to cry. Isabella put her arm around him. "My dear husband, thank you for such a wonderful life. I adored you."

Isabella turned to me. "We will have time to mourn and pray later. We must get you out of the country. Follow me." We went into the house. "Sit down. We need to change your appearance."

She started cutting off my hair. I watched long blond bunches of hair hit the floor. Isabella cut my hair down until it was about two inches long. She then dyed it black. While the dye was on, she cut off my beard. I used Arturo's razor to shave myself clean. Even I was amazed at the transformation. Isabella took a pair of Arturo's glasses and knocked the lens out. The look was complete. I needed to get some sun on my face because where my beard had been was pale.

"Perfect." Isabella said. "You must go. They will come here first."

I hugged Isabella for the last time. "I never got to tell him I loved him." I said.

We cried. "He knew. He knew, Will."

"I have a motorcycle in town. Could you sell it and put the money towards Arturo's casket?"

"Yes."

"Give my love to Cecelia."

"Yes, now go. Cholly will give you a ride to the road."

"I love you, Isabella."

She kissed me on the cheek.

"Good bye, Will."

Cholly and I stopped, dragged the Capitan back to Arturo's grave and rolled him in. Cholly spit on him.

"Rot in hell, Lorenzo." We walked back to the car. "Thank you for your help in finding my father, Will. I will cover the Capitan up on my way back."

He waited with me until a bus came. We shook hands goodbye. I headed south on the bus. Near town, police cars zoomed with their sirens going. I got on another bus and headed farther south, figuring they would not look for me going south. I got into Acapulco late at night. I ate and then caught a bus to Mexico City where I got a ticket to Nogales, which was where my truck was. I slept and read.

At Zacatecas there was a roadblock. The police were looking in every car and sometimes making them open the trunk. A policeman boarded our bus holding a sketch of my face. In the sketch I had long hair and my beard. I put on my fake glasses. As he looked at everyone in each seat, my heart pounded. When he came to me, I asked, "What is it, officer?" He ignored me and kept going down the aisle, not even looking at me on the way back.

At Nogales, I bought two baskets and went to the customs crossing.

"Citizenship?"

"United States."

"How long have you been in Mexico?"

I could see the sketch of my face on the back wall. "Two hours."

"Purpose of your visit?"

"To get these baskets."

"Thank you, Have a nice day."

"Thank you."

I threw the baskets in the trash. My truck was were I left it, but it wouldn't start. I got a guy to jump it for me. The truck brought back memories of a different life, a life that I lived so long ago. In honor of Arturo, I sang one of his chants and prayed for guidance. I got on the freeway and headed back to where I had started.

All of the children, grandchildren and close friends attended Arturo's funeral. At the burial site next to Estaban, they all sang one of his chants and meditated in his honor. Isabella and the children decided they would keep the house in his memory and use it for family reunions. They put a picture of Arturo, Estaban and Herminia in the shrine.

I called Danni from Tucson. "Are you sure you want to see me? It's been a long time."

"Will, I cannot tell you how happy I am to hear from you. I have been miserable ever since you left. I miss you. Have you got past my mistake? Have you forgiven me?"

"Yes."

"What are you going to do about your warrants?"

"There's more than one?"

"Yes. They weren't happy about you leaving."

"I'm going to deal with it. I'll tell them the truth. I'm not afraid anymore."

"When will you be here?"

"Ten tonight."

I made it to Danni's an hour early, it was dark. I parked across the street and sat in my truck, looking through her front window. I could see her walking back and forth, straightening up the house. She looked great. She had on a tank top and some really short cut off jeans. Mr. Happy made a comment, but I told him to shut up. Danni lit a candle by the window. We used to make love in the candlelight. I got out of my truck. I had bought her a single red rose and a bottle of champagne. I made it as far as the driveway.

I stood there. Inside, I knew I would find comfort, but at what cost? I didn't know whether I loved Danni anymore. I left the bottle of champagne and the rose on her doorstep. I just wasn't ready yet. I would like to have told her in person, but I know I would have been talked into staying. I was different now. I slowly walked back to my truck. I didn't know where I was going to go, maybe Van's, maybe Walter's. I didn't know. All I knew was I wasn't staying here. For the first time in my life I had faith things were going to work out.

In Mexico, three candles were lit in the shrine. The flames flickered in the wind. One by one the wax from the different colored candles overflowed. The hot wax formed in a pool until the pool became so large it flowed over the side in one single stream of one color.

# ABOUT THE AUTHOR

 Pat Steele was married at a young age and had children shortly thereafter. He provided for his family by working in the roofing industry, and he owned and ran his own roofing company for forty-seven years. Steele was inspired to write a book while he was house-sitting in Mexico.

Made in the USA
Columbia, SC
31 December 2017